# GOOD HALF GONE

## TARRYN
## FISHER

THE *SUNDAY TIMES* BESTSELLING AUTHOR

ONE PLACE. MANY STORIES

HQ
An imprint of HarperCollins*Publishers* Ltd
1 London Bridge Street
London SE1 9GF

www.harpercollins.co.uk

HarperCollins*Publishers*
Macken House, 39/40 Mayor Street Upper,
Dublin 1, D01 C9W8, Ireland

This edition 2024

1

First published in Great Britain by
HQ, an imprint of HarperCollins*Publishers* Ltd 2024

Copyright © Tarryn Fisher 2024

Tarryn Fisher asserts the moral right to be
identified as the author of this work.
A catalogue record for this book is
available from the British Library.

ISBN PB: 9780008665265
ISBN TPB: 9780008665272

MIX
Paper | Supporting
responsible forestry
FSC
www.fsc.org
FSC™ C007454

This book contains FSC™ certified paper and other controlled
sources to ensure responsible forest management.

For more information visit: www.harpercollins.co.uk/green

Printed and Bound in the UK using 100% Renewable Electricity at
CPI Group (UK) Ltd, Croydon, CR0 4YY

For my sister
Cait

# 1

*"911, WHAT IS your emergency?"*

*"Hello? Help me, please! They took my sister! Please hurry, I don't know where they are. I can't find them."* ⋆rustling noise⋆ ⋆yells something⋆ *"Oh my god—oh my god. Piper!"*

*"Ma'am, I need you to calm down so that I can understand you."*

*"Okay…"* ⋆crying⋆

*"Who took your sister?"*

*"I don't know! I don't know them. Two guys. Dupont knows them, I—"*

*"Miss, what is the address? Where are you?"*

*"The theater on Pike, the Five Dollar…"* ⋆crying⋆ *"They took my phone, I'm calling from inside the theater."*

*"Wait right where you are, someone is going to be there to help shortly. Can you tell me what your name is?"*

⋆crying⋆

*"What is your name? Hello…?"*

⋆crying, indecipherable noises⋆

*"Can you tell me your name?"*

*"Iris…"*

*"What is your sister's name, Iris? And how old is she?"*

"Piper. She's fifteen."

"Is she your older sister or younger sister… Iris, can you hear me?"

"We're twins. They just put her in a car and drove away. Please hurry."

"Can you tell me what kind of vehicle they were driving?"

"I don't know…"

"—a van, or a sedan—?"

"It was blue and long. I can't remember."

"Did it have four doors or two… Iris?"

"Four."

"And how many men were there?"

"Three."

"I'm going to stay on the line with you until the officers get there."

He leans forward, rouses the mouse, and turns off the audio on his computer. *Click click clack.* I was referred to Dr. Stanford a year ago when my long-term therapist retired. I had the option of finding a new therapist on my own or being assigned someone in the practice. Of course I considered breaking up with therapy all together, but after eight years it felt unnatural not to go. But I was a drinker of therapy sauce: a true believer in the art of feelings. I imagined people felt that way about church. At the end of the day, I told myself that a weird therapist was better than no therapist.

I disliked Allen Stanford on sight. Grubby. He is the grown-up version of the kindergarten booger eater. A mouth breather with a slow, stiff smile. I was hoping he'd grow on me.

Dr. Stanford clears his throat.

"That's hard to listen to for me, so I can only imagine how you must feel."

Every year, on the anniversary of Piper's kidnapping, I listen to the recording of the 911 call I made from the lobby of the Five Dollar. When I close my eyes, I can still see the blue diamond carpet and the blinking neon popcorn sign.

"Do you want to take a break?"

"A break from what?"

"It must be hard for you to hear that even now…"

That is true, reliving the worst day of my life never gets easier. The smell of popcorn is attached to the memory, and I feel nauseated. A cold chill sweeps over me. Swallowing the lump in my throat, I nod once.

"What happened after you hung up the phone?"

"I waited…what else could I do? I was afraid they were outside waiting to take me too. My brain hadn't fully caught up to what was happening. I felt like I was dreaming."

My voice is weighed down with shame; in the moments after my twin was taken, I was thinking of my own safety, worried that her kidnappers would come back. Why hadn't I chased the car down the street, or at least paid attention to the license plate so I could give it to the cops? Hindsight was a sore throat.

"I wanted to call Gran." I shake my head. "I thought I was crazy because I'd dialed her number hundreds of times and I just… I forgot. I had to wait for the cops."

My lungs feel like they're compressing. I force a deep breath.

"I guess it took five minutes for the cops to get there, but if you asked me that day, I would have said it took an hour."

When I close my eyes, I can still see the city block in detail—smell the fry oil drifting across the street from the McDonald's.

"The cops parked their cruiser on the street in front of the theater," I continue. "I was afraid of them. My mother was an addict—she hated cops. To certain people, cops only show up to take things away, you know?"

He nods like he knows, and maybe he does, maybe he had a mom like mine, but for the last twenty years, he's been going to Disney World—according to the photos on his desk—and that somehow disqualifies him in my mind as a person who's had things taken away from him.

I take another sip of water, the memories rushing back. I

close my eyes, wanting to remember, but not wanting to feel—
a fine line.

I was shaking when I stumbled out of the theater and ran toward the cop car, drunk with shock, the syrupy soda pooling
in my belly. My toe hit a crack in the asphalt and I rolled my
ankle, scraping it along the side of the curb. I made it to them,
staggering and crying, scared out of my mind—and that's when
things had gone from bad to worse.

"Tell me about your exchange with the police," he prompts.
"What, if anything, did they do to help you in that moment?"

The antiquated anger begins festering now, my hands fisting
into rocks. "Nothing. They arrived already not believing me.
The first thing they asked was if I had taken any drugs. Then
they wanted to know if Piper did drugs."

The one with the watery eyes—I remember him having a
lot of hair. It poked out the top of his shirt, tufted out of his
ears. The guy whose glasses I could see my face in—he had
no hair. But what they had both worn that day was the same
bored, cynical expression. I sigh. "To them, teenagers who
looked like me did drugs. They saw a tweaker, not a panicked,
traumatized, teenage girl."

"What was your response?"

"I denied it—said no way. For the last six months, my sister
had been hanging with a church crowd. She spent weekends
going to youth group and Bible study. If anyone was going to
do drugs at that point, it would have been me."

He writes something down on his notepad. Later I'll try to
imagine what it was, but for now I am focused.

"They thought I was lying—I don't even know about what,
just lying. The manager of the theater came outside to see what
was going on, and he brought one of his employees out to confirm to the police that I had indeed come in with a girl who
looked just like me, and three men. I asked if I could call my
gran, who had custody of us."

"Did they let you?"

"Not at first. They ignored me and just kept asking questions. The bald one asked if I lived with her, but before I could answer his question, the other one was asking me which way the car went. It was like being shot at from two different directions." I lean forward in my seat to stretch my back. I'm so emotionally spiked, both of my legs are bouncing. I can't make eye contact with him; I'm trapped in my own story—helpless and fifteen.

"The men who took my sister—they took my phone. The cops wanted to know how I called 911. I told them the manager let me use the phone inside the theater. They were stuck on the phone thing. They wanted to know why the men would take my phone. I screamed, 'I have no idea. Why would they take my sister?'"

"They weren't hearing you," he interjects.

I stare at him. I want to say *No shit, Sherlock*, but I don't. Shrinks are here to edit your emotions with adjectives in order to create a *TV Guide* synopsis of your issues. *Today on an episode of* Iris in Therapy, *we discover she has never felt heard!*

"I was hysterical by the time they put me in the cruiser to take me to the station. Being in the back of that car after just seeing Piper get kidnapped—it was like I could feel her panic. Her need to get away. They drove me to the station…" I pause to remember the order of how things happened.

"They let me call my grandmother, and then they put me in a room alone to wait. It was horrible—all the waiting. Every minute of that day felt like ten hours."

"Trauma often feels that way."

"It certainly does," I say. "Have you ever been in a situation that makes you feel that way—like every minute is an hour?" I lean forward, wanting a real answer. Seconds tick by as he considers me from behind his desk. Therapists don't like to answer questions. I find it hypocritical. I try to ask as many as I can just to make it fair.

He leans his chin on a hairy fist and assures me again that most people feel similar in situations such as mine.

I yawn and check the time on my phone.

I was still in a state of shock when the detectives came in to take my statement that day. The man introduced himself as Detective Audrain without looking at me. The woman—in her early twenties and named Poley—was the object of his attention. I'd caught them on the end of a story or joke they were still recovering from before they walked in the room. They spent the first ten minutes of the interview half laughing, half listening. I hadn't understood the dynamic when I was a fifteen-year-old girl. The story of their affair only came out three years later; the scandal forced Audrain into early retirement.

My ankle looked like rotted fruit—bloated purple and oozing blood beneath the cuff of my jeans. I was surprised that it didn't hurt—it didn't feel like anything. The hurt was in my chest, crushing my lungs.

"They didn't believe me. Kind of blew me off and insinuated Piper went with those guys of her own volition. Just like the other two cops."

A knot forms behind my breastbone and floats up to my throat, lodging. I swallow but can't get it down. There were so many things that went wrong that day.

Audrain would give Poley a look like, *You're up!* and she'd smile at him and bat me another question. If she asked me a question he was impressed by, he'd nod in appreciation.

"I told them over and over that she didn't get into the car; she was forced into the car. They'd wanted to know how we knew the men. What they looked like. What Piper was wearing. I was trying to answer their questions, but I felt weird, like my thoughts were thick. Eventually they came to the unanimous decision that I was in shock."

I remember Poley leaving the room and coming back with a doughnut, four chocolate Kisses, and a bottle of Dr. Pepper.

She lined them up in front of me one after the other—*plunk, plunk, plunk*. I wanted to throw up when I saw the scrounged picnic, but my hand mindlessly began unwrapping the Kisses.

Poley eyed my green face and said to Audrain, "Hey, screw off that cap for her, won't you?"

I'd taken a sip of soda to wash away the chocolate sticking to the roof of my mouth, and that's when I remembered. "It was the soda!" I'd cried out.

And then Gran walked in and I'd dissolved against her, crying so hard my words wouldn't come out. She cradled me in her arms, and I folded up in shame against her pink sweater. I'd lost my sister. Gran told me to take care of her, and now she was gone.

He's listening hard. I have his attention. The novelty of being an adult is that you can pay for what you didn't get as a child. I get high on therapy, the nurture drug.

"Time's up."

He startles. "What?"

I point to the clock—his clock. "Our session is over."

He looks momentarily lost, and then he sits up straighter in his chair. I'm a pretty good storyteller after all these years.

Setting down his pen, he frowns. "It's my job to say when time is up."

I nod. *Of course, of course.* Men like to feel that they are in control. I wonder who has more issues: me or him.

I gather up my things. "See you next week," I call over my shoulder. I don't wait for him to respond.

I navigate my beater out of the almost empty strip mall and head south on 405. It's a pretty okay day; the October sky is still bright and blue, but that will be short-lived. In two weeks, the cloud cover will blanket the sky in dismal shades of gray. *Gray, gray, every day,* my sister used to sing. *It's not that I don't like gray, it's just not my best color…*

Memories of Piper should make me smile but they hurt instead. Once I start thinking about her, I can't stop. Piper's case is so cold it has freezer burn. I turn up the volume on the radio to drown out my thoughts; Lana Del Rey reminds me that I'm born to die.

I pull into my grandmother's driveway around six. The garage door is in front of me, plump azalea bushes springing from either side. I need to trim those back soon.

The house is cute as a button: white with black trim and a black front door. I grab my bag from the backseat as the engine putters out. I don't know who's more broke, me or my car.

Three years after Piper went missing, Gran's aunt, a widow with no children, died and left her house to Gran—a nice surprise after all the sadness. The house, which is located in an upscale neighborhood in Seattle, is just a short drive to where she works at the Seattle Public Library. Cal and I have lived with her on and off over the years. I tried to live on my own twice and failed miserably when I couldn't keep up with Seattle's rent crisis. Gran was gracious enough to offer her spare bedrooms for free until I completed my work-study, so Cal and I packed up our little apartment and moved in with her three months back.

Walking the path around the side of the house and to the front door, I feel the peace of being in a safe place. Everything is quaint and pretty, not like the apartment we lived in when it happened nine years ago.

As soon as the front door closes behind me, Cal flings himself across the living room and into my arms. He's small for eight, sweet and softhearted. Everyone says he looks like me, and that's mostly true. He has my blue eyes and rosebud mouth, but his hair is dark and wavy. My shaggy, smart boy. I wrap my arms around him, glad to be home. It's the same greeting I get every night—pure joy.

"You got a letter," he says. "It's on the table in the kitchen. Gran keeps picking it up and looking at it."

"Uh-oh," I say, glancing into the kitchen. Gran is at the sink, washing the dinner dishes by hand even though we have a dishwasher. I eye her tense little shoulders and feel a surge of hope. Could it be? I applied for four internships at the prompting of my professor, but there was only one I was interested in taking. It was the internship Gran had begged me not to apply for.

"Is she upset?" I whisper.

Cal nods, he's wearing his most serious expression. "She called off work tomorrow." His voice is low. "She wants you to take her to see the island where you're going to work."

The island? Did I hear that right? My heart speeds up. I'm shaking as I reach out to ruffle his hair. I lean down to give him a kiss.

"Thanks, little informant." He darts off—probably back to his iPad. I hang my things on the hook by the door and slip into the bathroom Cal and I share to wash my hands. By the time I step into the kitchen a few minutes later, Gran has my dinner on the table and she looks ready to argue. Propped against my water glass is a business-size envelope, crisp and official. The return address: Shoal Island.

"Oh my god."

Gran leans against the counter, pale and staring. I rip it open, too afraid to blink.

"I'm in…" I say. "Gran…"

When I look up, she has her eyes closed like she's on a ride she wants to get off.

"Don't do that, Gran, this has always been the plan."

"Your plan," she snaps.

"The only plan…" I shoot back.

"I don't want this for you. You are living her life, not your own."

We glare at each other with identical pond-scum eyes, refusing to blink. I will never have to wonder what I'll look like when I'm older; I look just like Gran. We have the same heart-shaped face and heavy bottom lip. She knows I'm right. That's the only reason she's not arguing back.

"Everything is going to be okay," I tell her. "I have things under control…" It is a bold statement but I believe it. Gran nods at the floor, turning back to the dishes. When she lets it go, I sigh in relief. My body relaxes back into the chair and I pick up my fork.

The truth is, I don't want Gran getting close to that place. Not because it is evil. I don't believe places can be evil. He is evil, and he is there, tucked away like a rotting tooth. It took me a long time to find him. The nights when Gran wanted to know why I wasn't on a date or out with friends, I was stationed in front of my laptop, looking for him. Searching, always searching. And then I had found him. He was in a private facility, a hospital for the mentally ill.

Living out his days on an island didn't sit well with me. I needed to lay eyes on him—hear him speak, feel his vibe. Did he care? Did he think about what he'd done?

I liked to imagine another version of myself: wholesome and hopeful. A woman who had a sister. I imagine she'd have outgrown her annoyance with me by now. Maybe we'd go to concerts together, or the movies—we never had time to find common ground. And now I'd never know.

I wash my dishes in the sink this time with Gran watching me from the table. Cal's TV shows are playing in the living room; he's pretending to listen, but I know it's our conversation he's after. I can feel Gran's eyes on my back.

"Thanks for the dinner."

"Iris," she says as I'm walking out. "Cal needs his mother."

I pause.

"He'll get her. I'm almost finished with this."

# 2

PAST

**"YO, PIPES, MY** cousin's friend thinks you're hot."

Piper glanced up from her phone, her eyes glazed over. She was texting, but when Dupont didn't go away, she slid her phone into the back pocket of her jeans and sighed. "What now?" Her eyes bounced off of him and to the crowd of students making their way out the front doors. The burden of having a popular sister...

Dupont stepped in front of her, blocking her view so he could have her full attention.

"My cousin's friend. He wants to know if you want to hang out at the mall sometime."

I finished loading my books into my backpack and slammed my locker, making them both jump. I gave Piper a look, and we started walking. It was three o'clock on a Friday, the bell had rung, and it wasn't raining. We could make it home dry if we hurried.

"Why would I want to hang out with your cousin's friend?"

Dupont shrugged like he didn't really care, but I could tell that wasn't the case. He was stuck to Piper's side, hedging her like I'd seen him do on the basketball court.

"Shouldn't you be at practice?" I asked. He ignored me.

Chris Dupont was a hustler in a beanie. Piper felt comfortable giving him an attitude because she was higher on the food chain; if she didn't laugh at his jokes, no one would. I, on the other hand, was afraid of him. He had a way of knowing your weakness and using it against you.

"Stop acting like you're too good for people, Piper, damn! You want to hang out with him, trust me. He's a senior. Not at this school…"

I rolled my eyes, anticipating how long this would take. I'd skipped lunch to finish my algebra homework, and I was hungry.

"Pipe, let's go," I nagged, tugging on her arm. Her phone buzzed in her back pocket. She took it out, frowning at the screen. For a moment, her face looked so distraught, I wanted to ask her what was wrong. My hand was still on her arm, and she shrugged it off, annoyed. I felt stupid. She'd been like this with me lately—vague…distant.

"Who's your cousin's friend?" My sister looked pointedly at Dupont. "And how exactly does this creeper know me?"

She started walking, long rose-gold waves bouncing against her back. I kept mine short and used gel to mat it down—which made my hair look darker than hers. We launched after her like minnows, darting through bodies to keep up. I looked over at Dupont resentfully, but he didn't seem to notice.

"Come on, Piper, everyone knows you. At all the schools. Before you danced for Jesus, you danced for us!"

That earned him a scalding look. Piper quickened her pace, but he slid into step beside her, knocking me out of the way. I harrumphed but hung back while he finished his appeal.

"I didn't know you were matchmaking now," she smarted without looking at him. I was endlessly impressed by how cool she was without even trying. How did we share a womb?

We were fifteen feet away from the door and freedom. I could practically taste my sandwich...

"He's on the Wildcats football team, but that is all I'm saying."

That's all he had to say. Piper was interested. I stepped over someone's lunch, bologna and mayo ground into the concrete. She was barely fifteen, but she had a definite type. Lately, my formerly boy-crazy sister's type had been Jesus.

The school was behind us now; we walked with the flow of traffic, me holding the straps of my backpack as I trailed them.

"Why can't he ask me himself?" Her voice was different— Dupont owned her in that moment. He seemed to know it too because he danced around, giving her the finger until she pinched him playfully on the arm. He had her full attention.

"Ouch! Okay! I'll tell you!" he said, laughing. "His parents took his phone away, that's all I know. He saw you at the game and asked about you."

"What game?" I heard her ask, though she knew exactly which one. Piper liked that the chase was her game.

"His last name is Crimball."

Dupont had just dropped her crush's name, and she looked bored. Piper had no reaction. I had to give it to her, girl was hard-core.

"Why would I want to meet him?"

Dupont started laughing. He bent over like one of those dancing sock puppets and slapped his knee twice before straightening up. "Because every bitch in that school would spread for Crimball." Lifting his arms straight up, he twisted his torso left, then right, then left again. His back cracked, and I frowned. He was right, but Piper was a sophomore and Matt was a senior. My sister was beautiful but so were plenty of juniors and seniors.

"I have to give him an answer," Dupont said. "Don't shoot the messenger... How about Saturday?"

We stopped at a red light as Piper considered this. "Oh, all right then, I guess I can." She looked back at me like I was her personal assistant. "We were going to the mall anyway, remember? I guess we could say hey or whatever..."

I nodded dutifully. There were spicy pickles in the fridge, I could use the leftover roast beef from dinner and—

"Awesome," Dupont said. He smiled at Piper, shot an air gun at me, and shuffled off to go hustle someone else.

"We were going to see a movie," I said as the light turned green. I'd been waiting to see that movie for weeks, and Piper promised she'd go with me.

"Not anymore," Piper shot back. I recognized the look on her face and knew I was fucked.

"You take Sundays, now you want Saturdays as well?"

"It's not my fault we go to church, Iris. I just leaned into what Gran made us do." She was right but I didn't care. We both used to complain about church all the time. Then all of a sudden, I was the only one complaining. It felt like a betrayal, for her to start liking something we'd hated together.

Later that night, when I was helping Gran make dinner, she asked if I was excited to see the movie. We were moving around each other to get to things, the kitchen a mere sliver of space. I heard the hiss of something in the frying pan, the TV playing in the living room. The commercial was about yogurt, and everyone was dancing.

"We're going to the mall instead." I was dismissive as I stood over the sink, rinsing vegetables. Gran leaned over from the stove to stare at me. She was wearing a lavender sweater set underneath a lime-green apron.

"You were born six minutes apart. Not six years, you know... You don't have to go along with whatever she wants."

"It's fine, Gran." I could hear the exasperation in my own voice. I dumped lettuce into a bowl with a handful of cherry tomatoes, and grabbed the ranch from the fridge.

"Will there be boys?" She held up the spatula as she glared at me, meat popping in oil.

"You look like a neon demon," I told her.

"Don't let her out of your sight," Gran said firmly. "I mean it. I'm not raising her babies."

I couldn't voice the irony even if I wanted to—that Gran was referring to the twin who actually went to church. Regardless, if Gran told me not to let her out of my sight, that's exactly what I'd do.

"What about me, who watches me?"

She rolled her eyes. "You take care of yourself, it's my favorite thing about you…"

I was so shocked by her words that I froze. What a thing to say, I thought, hands cradling the wooden salad bowl. Gran flipped the patties, oblivious.

On Saturday, I pretended to read a novel on my bed while Piper sat on her knees in front of our mirrored closet doors. There was an array of things around her: brushes and tubes in toddler colors. She slapped at her face with her fingertips, brushed her eyebrows with a wand. The end result was me with a good filter. "Does the cult know you're not attending service tonight?"

I was eating a Slim Jim, trying to get under her skin for changing our plans and being pretty. It had become a habit of mine to catalog our differences. I was the dull-skinned twin, the late bloomer, the one with a snaggletooth. People's eyes skimmed over me and landed on Piper. She'd been unfairly favored in utero. Though we both had blue eyes that curved up at the corners and our coloring was blond on olive, I looked sloppily put together, like a genetic afterthought. Piper looked like a designer doll.

"I hate it when you stare like that." She cast a glance at my reflection in the mirror as she reached for a section of hair. The curling process had begun.

"That's why I do it." I was down to the last inch of my Slim Jim and sad about it.

"You're just like Dad," she said.

"You're just like Mom." Neither was a compliment, so we glared at each other until Piper burned her hair and yelled at me to get out.

Another one of our differences: Piper's was an explosive anger, and I was passive-aggressive. Aggravating her was my one true joy.

My preparation for the mall involved wrapping my hair into a knot at the nape of my neck and putting on a clean T-shirt. We met outside the front door of the apartment—me snapping gum, her taking a selfie. There was no one to tell that we were leaving; Gran wouldn't be home until seven.

"Ready?" She didn't wait for my answer as she flipped the hood of her rain jacket up and darted for the bus stop, her Converses tiptoeing around the puddles. I took my time zipping up my hoodie before I followed behind her, hoping the bus would come and leave me. Oops. I could go back inside with a clear conscience and read.

"Hurry up, Iris!" The bus was wheezing to a stop. I had a brief moment of defiance where I wanted to run back to the apartment and lock myself inside, but the bond I so rudely shared with my sister pulled me forward. Where she went, I went.

We got Slurpees from the 7-Eleven because Piper thought walking around the mall with Burger King cups was trashy. She always got whatever flavor was red and filled her cup so full it mushroomed out of the plastic hole like lava.

"If you get the blue, you're going to have blue mouth," she warned. Ignoring her, I filled my cup with razzle dazzle blue raspberry. She frowned, disappointed. Piper considered herself the worldly one. I found her naive, but to each their own. I made her pay for our Slurpees, and she grabbed my arm on the way out, her baby-blue fingernails squeezing apologetically.

"Are you mad at me?"

She knew I was.

"You'd only have lain in bed and read all day. Come on, Iris…"

"We had plans," I insisted.

She stared straight ahead without acknowledgment, typical Piper. If she didn't like it, she'd pretend it wasn't happening. How often did her plans supersede mine? If she wanted to do something, she sulked until she got her way.

"What does Crimball want with you anyway? You can't think this is real."

Her face turned a bright pink, and her hand was abruptly gone from my arm— Oh, I'd pissed her off now. She stared straight ahead, her lips squishing together. "You're such a jerk, I swear to god." She walked ahead of me, her hips at a sway.

That was the precarious moment our futures could have forked; the bad, bad thing wouldn't have happened, and my sister would still be with us. As Piper's swaying hips got farther and farther away, I saw Gran's face looming larger. *Do not let that girl get pregnant!* Gran was still holding on to last year's version of Piper, and I couldn't blame her. Piper had been expelled for inappropriate behavior on campus, which boiled down to making out with boys in empty classrooms. Gran didn't seem to be buying into her religious stint any more than I was. My only choice was to follow her. Picking up my feet, I marched after her with a deep sigh, the resentment hot in my chest.

Who did she think she was, anyway? She looked ridiculous with her too-tight clothes, like she was playing at being an adult. If Piper had a baby, I'd be the one taking care of it. That thought pinged an alarm in my brain, and I ran to catch up—almost running into a mother and daughter coming out of Claire's. I gave them a brief apologetic smile and hurried on, oblivious to the fact that there was something coming for us that was far darker, far harder to navigate than a teen pregnancy.

They saw us before we saw them. "Hey, Piper!"

We turned toward the voice. Standing against the wall between Victoria's Secret and Jamba Juice was not Matt Crimball, the high school football star, but Colby Crimball, his meager younger brother. I could barely keep a straight face as we approached their leaning spot—Piper had been had.

Two years younger and five inches shorter, Colby had weepy eyes and a snub nose. To be fair, no one else in the Crimball family was good-looking. Matt was so much the outlier that there were rumors his mom had an affair with the high school coach around the time he was conceived, though I figured he was just gene pool lucky like my sister.

Piper was going to shit a brick over this.

Colby elbowed one of the guys next to him when he saw us. I glanced at her face and saw confusion flash to disbelief flash to her usual stony expression. "Where's Matt?"

"Matt who?" Colby joked.

A few steps closer and I could see the bar piercing his eyebrow. Colby was flanked by two of his friends and Dupont in a yellow beanie, lurking off to the side looking pleased with himself. Knowing he misled Piper made me angry, angrier than I was at Piper. I glared at him.

"Whoa, you guys are twins? You don't have the same vibe… at all." Colby pushed off the wall and came toward us, his jaunty little stride pissing me off. He was wearing a purple hoodie, and a frizzy tuft of hair shot out from under his hood. He looked like the kind of guy who always had crusts in the corner of his eyes and was too lazy to wipe them out.

I was surprised when I heard Piper's voice—"What's that supposed to mean?" Her eyes turned their fury onto him, and he shriveled.

"Nothing. I was making a joke."

"Yeah? It has to be funny to be considered a joke."

"Take it easy, princess." He backed away, palms up, then glanced over his shoulder at the other guys. His face was red, but other than that you couldn't tell he was angry. I could tell. I felt it rising off his body like a dampness. I looked at my sister to see if she noticed, but she was focused on her own offense, probably planning her next words.

Dupont must've decided to smooth things over, because a moment later he was circling us, stopping between Piper and Colby, and he threw an arm around each of their shoulders. I took a step sideways to get out of his range. I didn't want him touching me.

"Come on, we're all here now…" He stank of cigarettes. I blinked hard, hating the smell. It reminded me of living with our mother. I saw a flash of her in my mind, passed out on the brown suede couch, a cigarette burning to ash in the green shell ashtray.

Dupont was still talking. "What do you say we have some fun? We'll take you to the movies. Our treat."

My ears perked up at the mention of a trip to my favorite place. I could practically smell the popcorn, but I did not want to go with them.

Piper glared at him, but instead of shaking her head, she shrugged. She was tugging on the ends of her hair—something she did when she was thinking.

"What the hell, Piper?" I said under my breath.

"I don't want to go home…and besides, it's free."

I turned my head away and stared at the entrance to Claire's, where a kid a few years older than us was getting his ear pierced. His girlfriend was holding his hand. They were cute, and I wished I was tagging along with them instead.

"Iris!"

"What?" I turned my attention back to them, realizing we'd

become a group of six. Dupont, Colby Crimball, and the other two who he introduced as RJ and Angel—who looked like seniors or older. I made eye contact with the one he called Angel, who was looking from Piper to me with curiosity. He had short dark hair and a well-manicured goatee. The other one, RJ, had an elbow for a chin. His hair was dyed white-blond, and I could see an inch of brown roots.

Piper nudged me, and I pulled my eyes away from RJ. "You cool with that movie?"

I hadn't heard them say the name of a movie, though I highly doubted we were headed to see the Victorian one I'd planned on watching today. But I supposed anything was better than hearing these losers talk.

It was my turn to shrug. "Yeah, whatever."

We fell into step with Colby and Piper leading the way. Angel, RJ, and I fell into a line with me in the middle.

"Where's Dupont?" I asked, looking around.

"He's seen this movie, so he's not coming," Colby said over his shoulder. His hoodie—bright even in the color panic of the mall—guided me forward.

Ahead was the escalator that led to the theater. Angel and RJ had drifted a bit behind me, which made me feel like I was being herded. But Dupont's sudden absence bothered me. He treated these guys like celebrities, so why would he bail at the last minute?

I glanced back at Angel, who was staring at me again—it was creepy. I cleared my throat. "Wasn't this his idea?"

"Dupont has a lot of ideas." Colby's laugh was as annoying as his face. My sister, who had seemed revolted by the idea of him three minutes ago, was showing more than her usual number of teeth, dimples blaring. You'd think they were old friends.

Piper and Colby stepped on the escalator together, and I had a moment of panic as I stepped forward to take the stair beneath them. Sandwiched between my sister and Colby's goons,

I closed my eyes until it was time to get off. Something wasn't right. This was all off.

The movie was a comedy that had been out for weeks and was getting terrible reviews, and the theater was empty aside from us. Colby led the way up the stairs to the back of the theater and into the last row.

"You said this movie looked stupid." I slid into the seat next to Piper, putting her to my right. RJ sat on my left, and Colby and Angel took the end nearest the stairs—Colby right next to Piper, of course.

"Will you just relax?" she said between her teeth. "You ruin everything if you can't get your way."

I looked at her in shock. Did she really just say that to me? Her—the one who—

"What's the problem, preppy? You need some snacks?" Colby leaned forward to look at me. I stared back without saying anything until he broke eye contact and looked at RJ. "You guys good?"

RJ nodded, then both he and Angel stood up. "Snacks coming up," he said to me. His eyes were comically large like he was talking to a dog.

God, Piper was going to hear it later! Was she really giving this idiot the time of day after he tricked her into coming? I glared at them, but they were oblivious. Colby was showing her something on his phone, and she was squealing in either horror or delight. It didn't even matter that he wasn't Matt; he was a Crimball, and that's all my sister cared about.

"I'm going to the bathroom." I stood up, waiting for her to say she was coming with me. But when she didn't look up from Colby's phone, I huffed off on my own. It was what Colby shouted to me as I reached the bottom of the stairs that made the hairs on the back of my neck stand up.

"We don't need you to come back if you don't want to. We have what we need!"

# 3

**SHOAL ISLAND HOSPITAL:** a private facility for the criminally insane. I'd been chosen to enter their internship program, it was like winning the grad school lottery. My advisor, along with two of my professors, wrote letters of recommendation. Two days after receiving the acceptance letter, an email pings into my inbox from a woman named Jordyn Whyte, who introduces herself as the hospital coordinator. The packet, as she called it, holds all the information I'll need for my first day: I would need to catch the ferry from Seattle to Anacortes, from Anacortes a water taxi would take us to Shoal Island. Jordyn included the ferry schedule and the name of the water taxi: The Sea Glass. I print the vague map of the island, an even vaguer map of the hospital, and the rule handbook. I will need a badge to board the water taxi, but I won't get it until my first day of work. She explains that she'll call ahead to let the captain know that a new hire would be boarding his vessel. I'd have to take a ferry to reach the dock where the water taxi would pick me up: a watery quiet bus route.

It all seems so quaint—the upside of taking a boat to work, is the down time. Being a mom is a noisy task. Quiet thoughts were a luxury, I was my kid's personal assistant. I was...am...a nurturing tour guide, and my little tourist asked a lot of questions: Why do we have to go? What is beach sand made of? What time are we leaving? Why do I have to eat that? Gran asked as many questions as Cal, but hers were about my personal life: Who are your friends? Why aren't you dating? Why have you stopped drinking milk?

"Of course, I want to see where you're working..." Her voice drops off, and I know what she's thinking.

On Friday morning, we float by Shoal Island on the 9:20 a.m. ferry. The place is unreal—like it's filtered. I snap a few photos from my phone, extending my arms over the side of the railing to get a better shot.

I'm studying the photos when Gran speaks close to my ear. "Manmade things can't capture that type of beauty. Look with your eyes..."

I almost drop my phone in the water. "Gran, why?" She was forever sneaking up on me with her librarian stealth.

She smiles. "So jumpy!"

I hold my smart-ass retort on the tip of my tongue before swallowing it down. I am twenty-four years old and still frightened of my teeny-weeny grandmother. But in my defense, before Gran was a librarian, she was a prison guard. And before that, she stripped at the Emerald City Gentleman's Club. Back then her stage name was Emele Dickinson, and she danced during the busiest hours of the night. Resourceful, tough, smart—and one hundred percent unapologetic. My hero.

Gran smirks at me and looks back at the water, smug. I tuck my phone away and look with my *eyes* at the oversaturated greenery of Shoal Island. One hundred thirteen acres of rock, beach, and forest, the island juts grandly from the Salish Sea like a wine cork. There is no public ferry service to Shoal. Access is by water taxi or private ferry only.

We lean over the railing, letting the wind hit our faces and breathing in the smell of the sound. In front of us, a sheer cliff-side gives way to a rocky beach; a hundred yards more, and the beach gives to a dock. A water taxi bobs in the water as people in green scrubs make their way off. From the dock, there is a pathway that leads up an incline, disappearing over the other side. The island is hilly, and for a minute I worry that we won't be able to see the hospital from the water. But as the ferry hustles north alongside the shoreline, the view opens up briefly, giving us a look at the rear of the building perched atop a rock cliff and staring toward the ocean. It is three stories high, and dozens of windows dot the brick, giving their occupants an endless view of the water.

"Those are the patients' rooms," I tell her. She stares tight-lipped as the rock cliff curves and dips down. We see trees tightly packed into a forest, and then through a clearing we're given our first glimpse of the front side of the building nestled between two forests on a huge expanse of green lawn.

In the center of all that green is the fog, thick as clouds and holding a hulking structure in her fist: Shoal Island Hospital for the criminally insane.

"That's the scariest place I've ever laid eyes on, and my eyes are *old*." Gran, aggressive about her disapproval, turns her back to me, her shoulders stiff. But it doesn't look scary to me; it looks like a building that has gone through dozens of renovations. A Victorian house in the front, a lodge house to the side, and to the rear is the hulking brick structure that sits on the cliff.

If I'm being honest, Gran has a right to be worried. She's already lost a granddaughter, and she is great-grandmother to a eight-year-old boy. If something were to happen to me, she is too old to take care of Cal by herself. She'd do it, of course, but what would happen when she—

I shake off the thought. If everything works out as planned, I'll have my answers soon. But then what? That's the next obvious question. Will I be free to move forward, or still be addicted to chasing the past—a trauma-drunk Indiana Jones? I've been raising a boy and going to school for the last nine years, but every second in between has been spent on my sister's case. I honor her with those minutes and hours and days—because the police never did.

"It's kookamatoo," Gran says—her word for something that is crooked or wrong. Gran has a long list of things that are kookamatoo: the internet, men, the prices at Whole Foods, *Game of Thrones*, electric can openers...

I glance sideways at her. "It's a hospital for the criminally insane, it's supposed to feel kookamatoo."

Shoal is behind us now, and I'm shivering from the cold. The fog hangs over the water, which has suddenly become choppy.

"Want to go inside and get a coffee?" I ask.

She turns toward the doors that lead inside the ferry, beelining to the snack kiosk and warmth. I know she is struggling to understand my reasoning for this. I'm past trying to understand it, years past—I'm at the acceptance stage. It is a nice place to be, unless you're Gran.

I follow her inside as she silently rumbles. She is wearing jeans and the sweatshirt I asked her not to wear: *I'm with Crazy*—which at the moment insinuates *me*! Hiding her shock of white hair is a knitted Seahawks hat, the pompom on top bobbing viscously.

"Gran, can you slow down?"

She speeds up.

Cal says that when Gran and I get like this we act like children, which is a humbling statement from an eight-year-old. It doesn't stop me though.

"The Seahawks suck, Gran! And everyone but you knows it!" She doesn't turn around, but her middle finger shoots up. I laugh, because man, do I love Emele Dickinson.

# 4

**GRAN WAS WEARING** her work clothes: a floral blazer over a black dress. Her shoes were the same coral shade as her lipstick. Her face wasn't just pale, it was gray. She'd only just arrived, ushered into the room by a female cop and seated next to me. She grabbed my hand, searching my face for some clue as to what was going on. I didn't know what they told her. I looked away, ashamed, and waited for the guy detective, Audrain, to speak.

"Mrs. Walsh—" Audrain started.

"Ms. Walsh," Gran interrupted.

"Excuse me. Ms. Walsh, are you Iris's guardian?"

"Yes. And Piper's—her twin sister who is missing."

"Of course..."

I don't like his tone. I look at Gran; her hands, veiny and age-spotted, are trembling.

He stares down at his notes. "Your granddaughter says she saw two boys—"

"Men, they were men." My voice was scratchy but loud. I knew that because Poley flinched. I reached for the Dr. Pepper, taking two long swigs. It was as I screwed the cap back on that I remembered their clothes as suddenly as I'd forgotten them, and then their names came back to me as well: RJ and Angel. The movie I didn't want to see, Dupont—and the soda! They must have put something in the drinks they carried in for us. It all came tumbling out of my mouth, and Gran's face got whiter and whiter as she listened.

"Are you sure she didn't go with them willingly, Iris?" Poley repeats.

I'd already told them she hadn't. I glared hard at the female cop with the round face and slicked-back hair.

"Maybe they left you behind, huh?" She tilted her head to the side, coaxing. "Or maybe they were into your sister more than you, and now you're angry...you want to get them in trouble..." She left it open-ended, her eyes trying to wedge something out that wasn't there.

"No," I said. I was not on trial here.

She lifted her rear from where it sat on the edge of the table and walked toward a water cooler in the corner. Tag, you're it—her partner moved to fill her spot, standing above me instead of sitting.

"This is ridiculous," Gran said. "If she says it happened that way, it happened. My granddaughter is not a liar." Her voice was clipped.

The guy cop—Audrain—looked at Gran. "We're just trying to help, Miss Walsh..."

"Why don't you make it sound like it then?" Gran snapped back.

"I'm certainly trying, but you're going to have to answer a few questions, Iris." He turned to me.

I nodded as if I hadn't been answering questions for the last few hours.

"Did she walk out of the theater, or were they carrying her?"

"She was walking but they were holding her arms."

His face didn't change, and he wrote something down on his yellow pad. "Does she have a boyfriend?"

"No."

"What about drugs…does she drink? What drugs…pills or—"

"Weed, she smokes weed sometimes…"

Poley and Audrain exchanged a look.

"I don't see why any of this matters." Gran looked between them. "My fifteen-year-old granddaughter is missing. She was put in a car by two men and driven away." The five seconds of silence that followed felt loud. I could hear my own jagged breath and theirs.

"It matters very much, Mrs. Walsh," Audrain said. "Our job is to determine if she was abducted or if she's a runaway." He was leaning back in his chair and casually bouncing the pen between his thumb and pointer finger as he looked at her. "We can't use the department's funds and time on runaways, you understand what I'm saying?"

"No."

I was on the verge of crying again.

"Mrs. Walsh, your granddaughters willingly went to the movie theater, purchased tickets, purchased snacks, and sat down to watch a film with three boys."

"None of that means she willingly left with them," Gran snapped back. "This granddaughter said she didn't."

They all looked at me.

"What about my phone?" I blurted desperately. "Can I press charges for them stealing my phone?"

Audrain's eyes lit up as he pointed a pen at me. "Now, that we can do."

Hope began pulling my lips into a smile. If they were to go after them for my phone, we could get answers about Piper, as well.

"Give me the full names and contact information of the men who stole your phone."

My smile melted away. "I—I don't know."

His eyebrows pulled together, pained.

We were getting nowhere. They didn't believe me, either way.

"Pull the video then—the theater, the gas station across the street—someone has to have video of my granddaughter being pushed into that car."

"These things take time."

"She's a missing minor!"

"She could be a runaway."

Gran's face was pink now. They weren't listening to her, either. I could see the tremble in her hand as she gripped the table edge and used it to stand. She was tired, the skin sagging beneath her eyes.

I felt the guilt again. This was my fault. If Gran had another stroke, that would be my fault too. The room smelled of stale corn chips and bleach, and I breathed in through my nose and out through my mouth to avoid the incoming panic attack. I thought of something then—the drinks RJ and Angel handed us. Giant, sweating cups of soda. Had I mentioned this already through this merry-go-round of questioning?

"They put something in her drink," I rush. "And probably mine too, but I didn't drink much of mine."

He stared at me hard and then turned to his partner. "Send someone over to collect the cups."

Puzzled, I watched as she left the room. How would they know which cups were ours? Was he patronizing me?

He made his eyes big when he looked at us again, his lips folded inward. "Anything else you can remember, Iris?"

"Dupont," I said suddenly. "He goes to our school, Chris Dupont." I had to be chill, or they wouldn't believe me. They'd continue patronizing me, wasting time, when they could be out there looking for Piper. "Chris Dupont introduced us to Colby and those guys, Chris will know something. His mom works in the deli at Farmer's Market."

Gran looked at him expectantly. "Call that young man and find out where my granddaughter is." So straightforward. So point-blank. Simple.

Yet he sighed and positioned his pen over the yellow legal pad. "What did you say his name was again?"

I slapped my hand over my face as Gran literally spelled it out for him.

Gran and I sat side by side in that little room for what seemed like hours, just waiting. I offered her the doughnut they'd given me, but she shook her head and stared at her hands. It was unbearably hot in there, and I started worrying about Gran when she took out her pill case and pushed a white something between her lips. She wouldn't tell us what they meant or what was wrong, but I'd snuck into her medicine cabinet once and found pill bottles lined up neatly like her perfumes.

I never told Gran what I found, but ever since then I'd been watching her carefully for signs of sickness. So far, she seemed normal, and that had somewhat made me feel better. But now, sitting in the meanly lit room with my sixty-seven-year-old Gran, I could see she wasn't well.

I was about to ask Gran if she was okay when Detective Audrain came back into the room. His face looked all wrong, and I knew something was definitely not okay.

"We spoke to Mr. Dupont…"

Mr. Dupont. I lifted my eyes to his face, both afraid and anxious; Gran grabbed my clammy hand with her dry one.

"He says your sister seemed fine when he saw her in the mall. He said he didn't go to the movie with you and has no idea who you were with or why."

"He's lying! He introduced us to those guys. He knows who they are."

Audrain shrugged apologetically—possibly patronizingly, as well. "It's your word against his. There are no witnesses who saw what you saw."

I was speechless, flabbergasted. Was I not enough of a witness?

"I'm going to put out a bulletin that she's a runaway."

Gran and I stared at him, not understanding.

"But she didn't run away, Iris has told you that. *She* was a witness—she was right there!"

"And we will continue to investigate, but at least getting her picture out there and on law enforcement's radar—"

"Gran," I said, gripping her sleeve, desperate to be heard. "She didn't run away."

She placed her hand over mine and nodded. "I believe you." Her voice was final. I believed her. We both looked at Detective Audrain, who stood unflinching; his conviction was as strong as ours. They weren't going to look for my sister because they thought she was a runaway. Piper would never not tell me if she was planning on going somewhere.

"What about the cups?" I said urgently, marveling at the irony that what I once thought was a ridiculous stretch was now my last hope.

For a moment he looked lost—like he didn't know what I was talking about. His dark eyes blank, like he'd already moved on to something else, some other case.

A thought so painful flitted through my already overcrowded brain, almost doubling me over in pain—they were never going to find my sister. They weren't even going to look for her.

Cognizance finally blinked in his eyes. "The cups! Yes, we will look into that and let you know."

But he knew as much as I did that they'd probably cleaned the theater by now, thrown out the drinks that RJ and Angel brought from the concession stand. It would have been easy to sneak something in before they came back. I pictured the only evidence buried in a dumpster of other cups, hopelessly lost.

"Here is my card, ladies. Call me right away if you hear anything from Piper—anything at all."

The patronizing. It was thicker than the despair.

# 5

PRESENT

**TWO WEEKS AFTER** our ferry ride past Shoal Island, I retire my therapy era. That side of things is done. Finished. Kaput. For the first five years after Piper was gone, I needed therapy, but after that I wanted it. It made me feel better to talk about Piper every week. The therapists were dedicated to teaching me how to carry on after my entire world fell apart. Had I learned to carry on? Yes. But it took a vast amount of work to want to, and I had to change who I was as a person to desire life. Most of them told me that I was the lucky one—a bizarre, bold thing to say to the sister of a kidnapped girl. There were definitely no winners in my situation. Nevertheless, I am stuffed with perspective, fattened with self-awareness—shrink-wrapped. Pun absolutely intended. I am ready.

The restaurant where I've been working for the last two years throws me a goodbye party. I eat a large slice of sheet cake and take a final shot of tequila before stepping outside—a jobless woman. For now. Soon I'll start my work-study at Shoal. I'd be paid—mostly in experience, but there is a small wage, as well. A miniscule bonus to my ulterior motive.

I pull into Gran's driveway at eight o'clock and reach to the passenger side floorboard to grab the leftover cake they sent home with me. The paper plate is buckling with the weight of it, and as I'm trying to figure out how to unlock the front door without dropping it, the door flies open.

Cal stands in the doorway, arms at his sides, his face ashen. It takes me two breaths to notice the cell phone dangling from his hand—Gran's.

The balls of his cheeks are flushed and damp like he's been crying.

*Sniff, sniff* "—Gran—" *sniff, sniff* "—fell—"

The sirens sound a second or two later. My son's face confirms that he was the one who summoned them. *No, no—no!* I think. His blue eyes are vacant as he stares at me, cherub cheeks wet from tears.

"Where is she?" I manage.

He points to the door that leads to the garage, his finger shaking.

"Go wait in your room!" For once he doesn't argue, scampering around the corner. He shuts the door with a bang.

I drop the sagging plate of cake and run for the garage, flinging the door open with so much force it bounces back and almost hits me in the face. My vision swings like a pendulum as I step into the two-car garage. The lights are on, but I can't see her. I run around her car to the far side of the garage where she keeps her gardening tools and the Christmas decorations. The first thing I see is the ladder on its side. Behind it is Gran's body.

My knees land hard on the concrete next to her. She's not conscious, but she's breathing—barely. "Gran! Gran!" I put my fingers on her pulse, feel the dying tap of her heart, and leap to my feet.

The high-low of the sirens gets shorter—they're close! It

takes me ten seconds to reach the garage door opener, hurtling myself over the hood of Gran's car. I slam my fist against the switch, and the motor kicks on as I race back to her side.

The ambulance bounces into the driveway seconds later, and there is a spotlight shining on my face. Shielding my eyes, I call, "Over here!"

Doors open and close. There's the scuff of feet and voices. I let go of her hand and move out of their way, keeping my eyes on the chaos as I take three steps back until I'm out of the garage and in the driveway.

I don't realize that I'm rocking until someone grabs hold of my shoulders and squeezes gently—Gran's casual boyfriend, Billy Ross. He owns the craftsman-style house three houses down. As head of neighborhood watch, he was probably out the door when he heard the sirens.

Billy is an old guy who works out. Lost his hair and found his muscles; a finely aged meathead—Gran's words, not mine. He stands behind me until the stretcher passes, and we get a look at her face. It isn't good. We turn to follow as Billy looks toward the street where anxious faces are gathering—Gran's neighbors. They have good intentions, but I cannot deal with this right now.

"Billy." My voice is hoarse. "Can you ask Mary-Ann if she can come over and watch Cal? I need to follow the ambulance." I wonder if he was asleep before he ran out.

"Go with the ambulance," he says. "We'll take care of it..." A first responder is holding the door of the ambulance open. Behind him I can see the vulnerable lump that is Gran lying on the stretcher. I'm tempted to jump inside.

"I can't. I have to talk to Cal before I leave. He's inside, afraid." I look at the man holding the door. "Go," I tell him. "I'll drive."

He closes it without a word, and they're gone.

I run inside while Billy talks to Mary-Ann—another neighbor friend whose face I spot in the growing cluster. Cal is in the living room sitting on the couch. He looks so small and afraid, I burst into tears. It's the wrong thing to do, of course, because he cries when I cry. I hold him on my lap and tell him it's going to be okay. A mother's lie—nothing is ever okay, but they need to believe it can be. I hold his face in my hands, look into his big wet eyes.

"I have to go to the hospital. Mary-Ann is coming over to stay with you."

"No! She's my gran too! I want to go with you!" He throws himself against me as Mary-Ann opens the front door and steps inside, wiping her feet. Cal, who doesn't like people to see him cry, wipes his face on his sleeve and stares at the blank TV screen stoically.

"I'll be back. Everything is going to be okay," I lie again. He ignores me. It's hard to get up and walk to the door; I'm leaving one person for another—it's a terrible feeling. I try to catch his eye before I leave, but he's stubborn.

Mary-Ann turns on the TV and nods at me to go. "Let's bake cookies." I hear her say before I close the door.

The doctor, a woman in her fifties who resembles Dana Delany, tells me that Gran had an ischemic stroke, which is caused when an artery to the brain is suddenly blocked by a blood clot.

"We administered tissue plasminogen, which dissolved the clot, allowing blood to reach the brain. Due to her age, we can't know the full extent of the negative effects the stroke will have on her. I'm going to keep her here for a few weeks to observe her, but she's going to need weeks—maybe months—of physical, occupational, and speech therapy. It's a long road from here, unfortunately."

Time becomes a strange, painful warp of worry and guilt. The next doctor I speak to is an animated man in a bow tie and colorful socks who gives me further warnings in a singsong voice, like we're in a musical instead of the ICU.

"You're going to need help. She needs in-home care and someone to drive her to physical therapy sessions. Long road…" he says. The nurses give me sympathetic glances as they squeak by in their practical shoes. They bring boxed apple juice and animal crackers for my shock. I'm touched, but I don't want any of it.

I don't remember the drive home; I'm suddenly in the driveway, aching all the way to my bones. I walk through the door for the second time at midnight. I'd been texting Mary-Ann updates from the hospital, so she opens the door before I can take out my key. It looks like she wants to hug me but doesn't. I'm glad. Kindness feels like too much. Everything feels like too much.

"He's asleep. I let him keep the TV on. It seemed to take his mind off things a bit." She paces to the dining table and grabs her bag and sweater.

I look toward Gran's room and see the flickering of light through the crack in the door. "Thank you, Mary-Ann. I don't know what I would have done without you—truly. It's late, and I know you have to work in the morning."

She flips her blond hair out from beneath her sweater and beelines for the door. Waving off my thanks, she touches my shoulder. "It was fine. I graded tests. Gary is sanding our floors, so it was nice to get away from the noise for a few hours." Her husband was retired, having passed the family business to their son. "He was great as always," she says, nodding toward where Cal lies asleep. "Any more news on Betty?"

I tell her what I know.

Her face grows serious. "Iris, I talked to Gary about it, and we'd like to help with Cal for the next few months. I can take him to school with me in the mornings and bring him back. He can eat dinner with us and do his homework. We have the spare, and he will be able to hang out with Bryan on Friday nights. Just until Betty gets better." She squeezes my hand. "You'll need the help."

I don't know what to say. I haven't even gotten that far ahead yet, and she's already giving me a solution. Bryan is her nine-year-old grandson, and Cal absolutely loves playing with him. But spending such long periods of time away from home, and without me or Gran?

"You've been through a whole lot. Why don't you sleep on it and let me know?" She positions her bag on her shoulder and swings open the door. I almost call after her—I don't want to be alone, could she sleep over maybe just tonight...?

A selfish thought. Mary-Ann has done enough for one night. Besides, I'm a big girl with a little boy to take care of. I thank her again and lock the door behind her. It feels strange being here without Gran, like being in a Walmart after it closed—so full of things but empty of energy.

I check on my cherub-faced son, covering him with Gran's duvet. He'd camped out in her room to feel close to her, and it sends a pang of sadness through my heart. I'll have to explain everything tomorrow morning; what a horrible thing to wake up to. I drink two glasses of water standing over the sink. I'm trying not to panic, but my world is collapsing. There will be medical bills, and medical transport. There is a chance I'll have to be her full-time caregiver.

Not tonight, I tell myself. My emotional capacity is on empty. I need sleep. I shower and crawl into Gran's bed with Cal, turning the volume all the way up on my phone.

I can't deny it; I'm being triggered. Because on top of the stress this sudden turn of events has inflicted upon me, I can't stop thinking about the last time this happened...those cata-strophic days after my sister disappeared in that car. The de-pression associated with that time lingers on those memories like grime, no matter how hard I try to douse it. If I choose to remember, I am also choosing to hit refresh on my trauma and feel it all over again.

Some things can't be avoided, I think as I fall into jumbled dreams where strangers stop to tell me that it's going to be a long road ahead.

The next morning Cal stumbles into the kitchen, sleepy and rubbing his eyes.

I sit him across from me at the table and tell him what happened while cinnamon buns bake in the oven. If someone is sad, you feed them. Gran's take, but I'm willing to give it a shot. I explain everything the best I can, but when I get to the part about him staying with Mary-Ann and Gary—he loses it.

"If you told me who my dad was, I could go stay with him!"

I shouldn't be surprised Cal is using this as another opportunity to bring up his father, but I am. I take a moment to steady my voice before answering. "No, you couldn't, Cal. That's not the way it works."

I can't stand the idea of him hating me and thinking his father is out there being a hero. That narrative has somehow taken root in my son's brain in the last few months, although I knew this would happen eventually as he got older. He's been more inquisitive lately, asking after a man I'll never forget, but want to.

Cal is approaching manhood without a man to show him the ropes—a reality for a lot of little boys, but it makes me feel deeply guilty, nonetheless. I haven't been able to produce a substitute father for him, I've been too busy tracking the men who took Piper. It stings for him to see his friends and their dads together, a feeling to which I can relate. When Piper and I were little, we'd tell people our dad's name was Tom Cavendish. We didn't know a Tom or a Cavendish, but we liked the way it sounded—a news anchor name.

The timer on the oven dings. "Look," I say, getting up and grabbing the kitchen mitts. "You've got a mom who is crazy about you, and the coolest great-grandma in the world. This isn't permanent, it's just until Gran gets out of the hospital and my work-study is over." My voice sounds overly cheerful. He's not buying it.

"Bryan will be there on the weekends," I offer.

He cracks a smile. *That's all you need.*

"You're going to be a really good dad someday. As for your dad—I don't know where he is. That's something we have to work through together, so talk to me about it when you need to, and we will be sad together."

He nods, a good boy, and he is pressing back the tears, trying to be strong for me. I don't want him to have to do that— be strong for me. He is the kid and I am the adult, and I want to make sure he always knows that. Even though I don't feel like an adult right now. I want someone to cry on, someone to stroke my hair and tell me everything is going to be all right. She is in the hospital.

I sit beside him while he eats. My son, my sweet son has no idea how hard I'll work to keep him away from his father. I'd kill.

# 6

PAST

THE SKY WAS dark when we pulled up to the mailbox on East Cherry Street. I rolled down the window, squinting at the numbers.

"It's the right one," I said to Gran. Before she could stop me, I opened the door and hopped out, my Chucks splashing through the deep puddles in the driveway.

I couldn't see much of it, but the house was squat, tucked behind a row of overgrown hedges that separated house from sidewalk. The driveway was to the left of the house, leading to a detached garage, and when I turned toward the door, I immediately heard voices trailing from the open window. A bunch of scraggly tennis shoes sat in a tumble beside the door.

I knocked, still looking at them…looking for my sister's shoes. The door swung wide, and a woman in a dirty black baseball cap stood staring at me. She was wearing a Farmer's Market polo with a badge that said *Manager Ruth*. I'd seen her behind the counter shaving turkey and scooping macaroni salad into containers.

"What?" She ducked her chin, her eyes grazing over my face like she was seeing something nasty. She looked like a female version of her son.

"Is Dupont home—I mean Chris?"

Her scowl only got deeper; she grabbed the doorknob with one hand and cocked the other on her hip.

I asked again, in a way Gran would approve of. "Ma'am, may I please speak to Chris? It's very important."

"Are you pregnant?"

Her question hit, and I was unarmed. Mouth open, I blinked at her a few seconds before violently shaking my head. "No, ma'am."

She slammed the door in my face, but I heard her calling, "Someone at the door for you, Chris. Get your ass out here."

When the door opened again, Dupont looked surprised to see me. He was still wearing the same ridiculous outfit he'd had on earlier.

"Whadduwant?" He smelled like weed.

"Where's Piper?" I looked him over closely like Piper's whereabouts were hidden somewhere on his body.

We shared the slab of concrete in front of the door; food smells were starting to drift out of the windows, and I realized with dismay that I was hungry. How could my body think of eating right now?

Dupont was wiry but he was a lot taller than me. I stared up at the smattering of pimples along his jaw and knew with certainty that he knew something. He was being shady. His eyes were darting between me and the street.

I looked over my shoulder and saw the glow of Prius headlights.

"Who the fuck is that?" He stared toward Gran's car, the muscles in his jaw jumping. He was acting strung out, and when I looked closer, I saw that his pupils were dime-sized.

"Chill out, dude," I said quietly. "It's my grandmother."

Dupont shot another suspicious look at the car and wiped his nose with the back of his sleeve.

"I don't know where your fucking sister is."

"Bullshit!" I'd seen the way he was talking to RJ and Angel or whoever those guys were. He knew them. "Come on, Chris…"

He narrowed his eyes at me when I used his first name.

"She's my sister, man. Those guys you set her up with put her in a car and drove away. She's missing."

"I didn't set her up with those guys. Colby came to me asking about her, just like I said. I hooked him up, but I don't know him like that, and I definitely don't know his friends." He was lying. I could see it all over him like a nervous jitter.

"Then what was in it for you?"

He shrugged. "I help out, that's what I do."

"You don't help out for free…"

I got the feeling he wanted to hit me as he tucked his hands in the pockets of his pants, staring at a spot over my shoulder. He wasn't going to tell me anything. Had I really expected him to? Kids like Chris Dupont worked for themselves. I had nothing to offer him, no trade to make.

"I just need to find those guys…Angel and RJ. They have Piper. I'll owe you one, okay?" What did that mean—to Dupont…to me? I knew what Piper meant when she said it, but I was small and weird, and my lips were always chapped. I felt stupid and ashamed right after I said it, but he wasn't looking at me, he was fixated on Gran's headlights. I wished she'd just turn them off.

Dupont's jaw started working as he backed into the house. "You called the police already," he said. "They called. You think I'm stupid? Now get the fuck out of here!"

Fearful, I backed up until my heels bumped against the pile of shoes. Out of the corner of my eye I saw movement through the living room window—his mother. In seconds he'd be slamming the door in my face. If I knew anything about moms, it was that they didn't want the cops called on their kids.

"You either tell me something or I'm going to the police again. I'm not kidding, Dupont!" I raised my voice, standing on tiptoe so my words could reach his mother. Sound travels in small houses.

"The police." I said it louder.

Dupont froze, then quickly stepped back outside, closing the door quietly behind him. "I'm going to fuck you up." He pointed a finger at my chest.

The rain had picked up and was starting to soak through my shirt; I was so cold, I had to force my teeth to keep from chattering.

"I'm giving you the choice of talking to me or the police," I said. Bold words for someone as scared as I was. I lifted my chin to look at his face and immediately saw what was about to happen.

I barely had time to brace myself; one minute I was standing on the stoop, and the next I was on my back in the grass, the rain hitting my face in tiny gasps. I lay on the grass behind the hedges, the wind knocked out of me. Before I could grab a good breath, Dupont put his foot on my chest, pinning me down. I wheezed—pain exploded through my lower back and sternum where the bulk of his weight pressed down.

"Gah!" I clawed at his foot with my hands, but he was leveling his weight on my chest, his left leg keeping balance as he leaned toward my face.

"Lucky for the old lady there are two of you." After one last thrust, he took his foot off my chest, and I rolled to my side, gasping. I heard Gran's voice calling my name and the slamming of a car door. No! I wanted to call out to her, but I struggled to catch my breath. I pushed myself to my knees, and as I stumbled to my feet, I caught sight of Dupont's front door slamming closed.

*"Lucky for the old lady there are two of you…"* What had he meant?

Gran was still calling my name. I walked toward the street, righting myself with my arm stretched toward her. "Get back in the car. Let's go."

She was in their driveway. "Did that boy do something to you?" I stopped walking so she wouldn't see me limp, but it was too late.

"Get in the car."

"Gran, *NO!*"

She didn't just knock; she pounded her closed fist, jackhammering where I'd rapped so timidly.

Piper was like Gran, and I'd always been jealous of their bond—their sameness. We called her the wild librarian, alluding to the fact that she paid for her degree by stripping. By the age of five, our mom was her bookkeeper, counting her tips after every shift and writing the amount in a little notebook. Gran gave up stripping as soon as she graduated, but by then she'd started dating married men. She lost custody of our mother when she was nine after being arrested for beating up her boyfriend's wife. She'd walked the straight and narrow since getting custody of my mom back, and then when our mom failed as a mother, she raised us too. On the outside she wore a pink cardigan, but on the inside, deep where she kept it hidden, she was the woman who slammed her lover's wife into the wall in a laundromat until she passed out.

The door opened more aggressively this time, and Dupont's mother stepped outside, forcing Gran down a stair.

I glanced at the car; she'd left her door open when she hopped to my rescue. I began hobbling toward it when I spotted a light on to the rear of the house. Turning toward it, I slipped between the garage and the house, picking my way down the thin alleyway the buildings made. I could hear Gran's voice, loud and assertive behind me, while Dupont's mother tried to talk over her, saying, "Hold on now, hold on. You said what?"

The window glowed warm, and soon I heard another voice. My back was to the wall next to the window, close enough that I could peek around and look inside. My eyes took inventory: a bunk bed and a dresser, Dupont sitting on the edge of the bed facing away from me, the phone to his ear.

"Yeah, she's out there right now screaming at the old lady. You want me to call the cops? You were supposed to take both of them, man, this is bullshit. Why can't you come out—"

A scream echoed from the front yard. I heard him drop something and swear. Then we were both racing toward the front of the house.

He reached them before I did, because as I rounded the corner, I saw Dupont grab his mother from behind and drag her backwards—away from Gran. Gran, who was walking toward her across the grass pointing a finger, lurched forward. "Shit—" I reached Gran in time to yank her away before she got kicked.

"You crazy old bat!" Dupont's mother screamed. "I'm calling the police!" I speed-walked Gran to the car and shoved her inside, keeping an eye on the driveway as I ran around to the passenger side.

"Go! Go!" I yelled. Gran peeled out, zigzagging into the traffic, and thirty seconds later, when she steered the Prius onto the freeway, I started crying.

She reached over and gently squeezed my knee. "Iris…later. We can't do that right now. Tell me what you found out from that boy…"

I told her everything that happened from start to end, and when I was done, she stared straight ahead like she wasn't seeing the road. I realized then we'd passed our exit five miles ago, and she was speeding—she never went more than five miles over the speed limit.

"Gran…where are we going?"

She didn't answer me; she switched lanes, passing a truck that was going at least seventy-five. The sign above the overpass said we were headed to Tacoma.

My head jerked to look at Gran again. "Are you serious?"

She was a hundred percent serious—I could see it in the set of her jaw.

"You said we never had to go back there..." I hated the whine in my voice. I sounded like a little kid. I felt a wave of anger toward Piper. Why was she doing this to us? She could never just sit still and not get into trouble. She'd been doing this shit since she was little—making Gran panic, stirring the chaos until the hunger in her eyes was sated.

"She's not going to be there, Gran!"

"You don't know that. We're like dogs, we'll eat our vomit if we have to. Even if Piper is not there, we have to tell her..."

I turned the top half of my body toward the window to let her know how I felt. "She doesn't care. If Piper goes missing, if I go missing—she doesn't care."

Gran didn't say anything to that. She couldn't. We drove in silence the rest of the way. My lips were chapped, so I opened the glove box and dug around for my lip balm.

When we reached the dingy suburbs of Tacoma, the Prius turned down the saddest street in town. Piper and I called it Mom Row: ugly cement houses painted in pastels; there were bars on the windows and yards filled with dirt and old junk.

This was the place CPS took us from when a fourth-grade teacher asked for a wellness check. Our mother was on a binge that week, and when the social worker knocked, she answered the door high and holding a bottle of Jim Beam. Gran took us in. She would have had us out of there sooner if she knew how bad it was, but our mom cut her off whenever she was using. When the social worker dropped us off at her house that day, we hadn't seen her in a year.

"You're so big!" was the first thing Gran said before she

grabbed us in one of her hugs and cried into our hair. We were limp in her arms; we'd forgotten how to be hugged.

"I should have known, I should have known," she kept saying. We didn't even know—it took months of living with Gran to understand how bad things had been. It was overwhelming to adapt to life in her little place. Three meals a day, a bedroom with twin beds and a change of sheets, constant interest and attention. *Did you brush your teeth? Why aren't you eating your spinach? Don't you girls know how to use a hamper?* We thought she was crazy when she yelled at me for answering the door without looking through the peephole first. We didn't like it, and then all of a sudden, we did. It was ours...we felt safe.

Going back to Mom Row did not feel safe. We were afraid that we'd have to stay even though our mother didn't have custody of us anymore.

Gran parked on the street outside a yellow house with a chipped brown door and sighed. She didn't want to be here either. I picked at a string on my pants as Gran killed the engine.

*"Yellow-yellow, you ugly Jell-O..."* We made up that rhyme the day we moved into the tiny bungalow, our then-sober mom grinning at us. She locked us out of the house an hour later saying we were annoying her—the first day of many lockouts. We called the house yellow-yellow, a cheerful name for the awfulness within. If I stared too long at the bedroom window, I could hear Piper crying.

Gran knocked on my window, snapping me out of my trance. I got out of the car and stood behind the open door like it could shield me, while she pounded on the front door.

"Open up, Virginia!"

If Mom was using, she wouldn't be able to hear the banging. She wouldn't wake up even when Piper and I used to shake her. But Gran kept banging, the thin wood trembling beneath her fist. The light in the living room turned on and the front door was yanked open. I wanted to throw up, but instead I stayed hidden behind the car door like a coward. A man stood in the doorway in his boxers and socks looking enraged. His hair was pressed flat on the side he'd been sleeping on it.

"What the fuck," he barked, making me flinch.

"I need to speak to Virginia."

He looked dumbfounded to see a white-haired woman standing at his door; she was clearly not who he was expecting. His gaze moved from her to me and back to her. "Who are you?"

"Virginia's mother," she said flatly. "Now get her ass to the door."

After what felt like a full minute of him sizing up the tiny tyrant that was my grandmother, he tried her one more time.

"She's sleeping. I'm not gonna wake her up right now—that her kid?"

"One of them," said Gran. "The other is missing."

He stared at her, his eyes glazed over like he was looking for the con, and then he turned back into the house and disappeared down the short hallway to the master bedroom. He left the door open—shady thing to do if you were the level of user my mother was. I shifted behind my door shield, wanting to call Gran back to the car.

A minute later my mother appeared wearing only a white T-shirt, skinny, bruised legs poking out the bottom like two pogo sticks. She was carrying her handgun, looking even rougher than her boyfriend.

I closed my eyes and smelled the rain, trying to feel Piper. It was harder being here without her. When we were little we could start and finish each other's sentences. We had the twin bond, as people so often referred to it, no matter how much we pestered each other now. And now she was gone.

"Ma?" Virginia blinked hard at her mother as if trying to clear her eyesight. She held the gun limply at her side while her boyfriend stood behind her. Coward of a giant, giant of a coward, that's what Piper would have said if she were here.

Her boyfriend and I weren't so different. I was hiding behind Gran. If we were in a reverse situation, Piper would have been screaming at our mother, blaming her for what happened, but I did nothing but cower. I was afraid of her...even right now as scared as I was for Piper.

She looked like a little kid. It was deceiving—people saw her giant, sad eyes and wanted to protect her, and she used that against them. But I knew the fury that was tucked inside of her, quiet like a mouse until she needed to use it. She'd changed her hair. The dark roots led to a charred-looking blond bob instead of the usual purple.

"What the hell, Ma—what are you doing here?" She caught sight of me and stared right through Gran, who looked like she was braced for a fight.

Gran didn't waste any time. "Piper is missing. Have you seen or heard from her?" There was no way Piper would ever go to our mother for help; that would be like jumping from quicksand into a meat grinder. Gran was going to do Gran, though, and she needed to come here to check it off the list.

I switched my weight from one foot to the other, desperate to leave...desperate to get back in the car and put the closed door between us, but I needed to have Gran's back.

"No, she hasn't come by. You came all the way out here to tell me that?" The buffoon behind her laughed three seconds late. "She's fifteen, she's probably with her boyfriend. Don't you remember how that goes, Ma?" Her voice was nasty—she was gearing up for a fight. Another favorite person to fight with was Gran. My earliest memory was of a fistfight they had in a barn—though Gran always insisted it happened in a Mc-Donald's. I couldn't see Gran's face, but I knew her well enough to see how bad she was struggling.

"She doesn't have a boyfriend," I said quickly. My mother's unfocused eyes found me and then shifted back to Gran. She couldn't look at me for long, she'd never been able to. I wanted to say more, but I couldn't convince my mouth to move.

I tried to read the expression on her face. Did what I said make a difference to her? I wanted it to. I was pathetic. I hated her and wanted her so badly. Her daughter was missing, my twin, we'd grown in her. Why couldn't she care? Didn't it mean something that we were hers?

"Gran, she's not here. Let's go!" I got back into the car and slammed the door, glaring out the window. Gran lingered for another few moments, but I couldn't hear what she was saying. I closed my eyes tight and waited. It was only when we were moving that I opened them. I could see yellow-yellow in the side mirror, shrinking. My mother was still standing in the open doorway watching us.

"What are we going to do now?" I asked once we were on the freeway. Gran was speeding, and every few minutes a streetlight would illuminate the worry on her face. I tried calling Piper's phone again with Gran's cell, but it went straight to voicemail. Piper was always on her phone, her texting game strong.

"Start texting your friends, hers—anyone and everyone, ask if they've seen her or heard anything. What were those guys' names again?"

"Angel and RJ. And you don't have anyone's numbers stored in your phone. I have no way to get a hold of anyone."

"Find someone else who knows them."

I had like…five friends, and we barely spoke outside of school. Piper was the popular one. She had hundreds of contacts stored in her phone, and she grouped them according to how relevant they were in her life. As soon as Piper and I walked through the doors of our high school, we parted ways and acted like we didn't know each other. It was a precedent she set on the first day of ninth grade: *"We're not doing the twin thing this year. I need a life—"* and so she'd gone out and gotten one while I had not.

I closed my eyes, trying to recall the names of people who knew a lot of people. The most popular person I knew was Piper's friend Molly Sharpon. Molly was in Hawaii with her family, I knew that because Piper had been griping about it the week before. We never went to Hawaii—we never got to go anywhere.

When we got back to the apartment, I hopped out of the car ahead of Gran and took the stairs two at a time, almost colliding with our elderly neighbor, Mr. Vottum. *She'll be at the door waiting for us because she doesn't have her key.* But when I reached the second-floor landing, the only thing in front of the door was an Amazon package.

I was still staring at the empty space where Piper was supposed to be when Gran came up the stairs behind me. She stooped to retrieve the package, then unlocked the door in silence. We stepped into the tiny tiled square that was the living room, staring around like we'd never seen it before. Gran was the first to move. Clearing her throat, she dropped her purse into the armchair and turned right into the kitchen.

I couldn't see her from where I stood, and it panicked me. It was stupid—there was no back door in the apartment, only a tiny window above the sink that maybe a cat could fit through. I held my breath as I passed the armchair and then the couch with the cigarette burn holes along the back cushion, and there she was, drinking a glass of water next to the fridge. Gran didn't look well. Neither of us had eaten.

I moved into action, opening the fridge and taking out sandwich meat and cheese. I made sandwiches and cut them into the tiny triangles Gran liked—tea party sandwiches, Piper called them. Gran had gone into her bedroom to change, so I set everything out on the counter where we usually ate and waited. When she emerged, she was wearing sweatpants and a T-shirt, all the makeup scrubbed from her face. She slid onto the barstool next to me and squeezed my knee.

"Thanks."

We weren't hungry, but we ate while we waited for something—anything—about Piper. My phone was gone, and Gran's didn't have texting available. Our only hope was the landline. I half expected her to come through the door at any moment, full of excuses and laughter. She'd charm her way out of trouble with Gran, and then we could put this horrible day behind us.

Or...

She might never come back.

I wiped my mouth with the back of my hand, the bread catching in my throat. Piper wouldn't disappear for a night and not tell us. She was a free spirit but a considerate one. Our mother used to disappear for days at a time when she was on one of her binges. It was an unspoken rule, an understanding that developed between siblings.

Gran called the station. They put her on hold, so she hit speaker and waited. Detective Audrain got on the phone after five minutes of nothing.

"Mrs. Walsh?"

"Yes, it's me, Detective..." Her voice was strained. "Have you found anything?"

I sat tense on my chair, waiting for him to speak. He cleared his throat, which sent bolts of fear down my legs and puddling to my feet. I knew from experience that adults cleared their throats before imparting bad news.

*Ahem...your mother is in the hospital after an overdose...*

*Ahem...we found your dog on Amherst, he'd been run over by a car...*

*Ahem...you can't go on the field trip because your mother didn't sign the form...*

*Ahem...*

*Ahem...*

"Were you at 1137 East Cherry Street this evening around 8:00 p.m.?"

"I—I'm not sure—"

"It's the home of Linda Dupont and her son, Chris Dupont—he attends high school with your granddaughters, the young man Iris mentioned in her interview?"

Our eyes met, and Gran's lips folded in on themselves. I pushed the plate of mangled sandwich away from me; I needed something to do with my hands. Did his mother call the police after we left? It didn't seem likely that Chris wanted to get the police involved in whatever this was—he'd become violent at the mention of them. I could feel the ache along various parts of my back.

"She filed a police report saying you came to their home and physically attacked them."

"What a load of bullshit," interrupted Gran. "That boy attacked my granddaughter first. They—"

"It's your word against his, and you were trespassing on private property, threatening the owner of the house. This is not a good look, Mrs. Walsh. As I recall, I specifically told you to let us do the investigating." His tone was reprimanding, but Gran didn't take the bait.

"Actually, you did not. You told me my granddaughter was a runaway and insinuated that she wasn't worth the department's time and money, leaving it up to her family to do the investigating."

There was a long pause, and then Detective Audrain sighed. I could picture the heel of his hand grinding against his chin like he'd done in that awful room at the police station.

"I heard Chris say something when he was on the phone," I blurted. "When I was…looking into his bedroom window…" There was quiet on the other end of the line, so I assumed he was listening.

Gran nodded, encouraging me to go on. Licking my lips, which felt as dry as my throat, I told them what I'd heard.

"Did you hear him use either your or your sister's names when having this discussion? He could have been talking about anything."

"No!" I said. "It was very clear he was talking about us—he was upset and—"

"If he didn't reference your names, he could have been talking about beer...marijuana. You see where I'm going with this?"

"But I heard him—he said that they should have taken both of us. That means they did take Piper. She's not a runaway!"

My breath whooshed out, and the frustrated tears I'd been holding back made a dive down my face. I stared at Gran helplessly. Nothing I was saying was coming out right. Gran squeezed my arm gently. I looked down at her pearly pink nails and lost it. Pulling my hood over my hair, I sat at the table with my head on my arms.

"Detective, at what point will you take my granddaughter's disappearance seriously?"

Stern like a librarian. Her face, baggy and exhausted, told a different story.

Another tense quiet ensued in which I could hear myself breathing.

"Have you seen the news, Mrs. Walsh?"

I hadn't. Gran watched it in the evenings, and sometimes Piper joined her; I didn't have the stomach for it.

"I don't see why anything on the news could be related to finding my granddaughter." Gran sagged against the wall, her eyes closed.

I got up to get myself a glass of water. Pulling a mason jar from the dish rack, I held it beneath the faucet. The sound of the water did nothing to drown out Detective Audrain's voice like I'd hoped. Whatever he said next wouldn't matter.

"I'm going to be frank with you. There is a mass search for

a three-year-old abducted from her driveway. Every officer we have, as well as officers from four separate counties, are looking for Lorelai and her abductor."

I put the mason jar in Gran's hand and made a drinking motion; she obeyed, taking a few birdlike sips, then setting it down.

"Kids Piper's age go missing every day. Most of them come back within a few days. I give you my word, if she doesn't show up by tomorrow, I'll file the report myself."

"If something happens to Piper between now and then, I will hold you accountable."

"You go ahead and do that, Mrs. Walsh. Good night."

The line went dead. Gran tried to cradle the phone, but she missed and it slid to the carpet.

"Piper," she wheezed. "Can you help me to the couch?"

"Gran...it's Iris. I—"

She stumbled forward, swaying on her feet like she was on unsteady ground. We made eye contact long enough for me to see the light drain out of her eyes.

Lunging forward, I grabbed her arm to steady her, but she fell sideways, crumpling to the floor. I dropped to my knees next to her, turning her onto her back.

"Gran! Get up! Please! Gran!"

I shook her by the shoulders, yanked on the pink sweater that she loved so much.

For the second time in one day, I dialed 911.

# 7

## PRESENT

**BREAKFAST IS XANAX** and gas station coffee in the prison's parking lot. My anxiety has eaten my appetite. My anxiety has eaten everything actually, the process to get here being half the battle. I had to claim her to see her, write her name out in connection with mine. Virginia Walsh. Gran had not given her a middle name, and she had not given one to us. It all seemed very spiteful: Piper and I took it hard. The loved kids at our school had middle names: Amy Lynn, Jessica Marie, Hailey Grace. Their moms proudly labeled their possessions with their full names, like it really mattered. I loved the way their lunch boxes and jackets had neatly penned tributes of love. I was also jealous.

There is a lot of buzzing in prison: you wait and walk…wait and walk. *Buzz buzz buzz* like a bored fly. It reminds me of the game Taboo, where players are not permitted to say specific words, hence the name. If you do say one of the taboo words, the opposing team presses a buzzer.

The guards wear the same "we're here now, might as well"

look on their faces. I'm buzzed into the final room. There are ten tables; I choose the closest one to me—far from the door she's going to walk through. I want to watch her walk across the room, study her facial expressions.

When the door buzzes open, I jump and brace myself. But instead of my reedy mother, a heavyset older woman wearing an orange jumpsuit walks in. I'm relieved only for a minute as I watch the stranger walk to a table where two younger men wait—her sons. I look away abruptly, thinking of Cal. What would it be like for him to visit me in a place like this? Gray and smelling faintly of piss. The thought of him being here in this dingy depressing room is too much. So why am I here? Virginia Walsh had never even tried to be our mother, and if she had, we hadn't noticed.

I don't feel healthy, maybe that's why I'm here. *No, that's not why you're here.* I'm here to see Mom... Mother... Our mother, who art in prison.

Linoleum—everything is linoleum in here, scuffed and chipped and yellowing. I crack my neck.

The door buzzes again, this time it's her. My stomach squeezes, flips over, and lands in my bladder. I crack my knuckles and hide my hands under the table in case she tries to touch me.

She nods when she spots me, proud to have recognized her own daughter.

*There she is! Sometimes I forget I have one.* I keep my face light with a hint of unaffected. She is different. I can tell right away. Her face is tan and freckled; she has deep wrinkles near her eyes like she's spent her life smiling. They somehow make her look meaner.

"I'm not using anymore, if that's what you're thinking." She slides into the chair opposite me and grins. She never smiles with teeth; she's self-conscious about the ones that are missing.

Her hair is mostly gray and short, but it's full and healthy—as is her face. Last time I saw her she'd been emaciated…using.

"Do I look different? You can say…" She waves to a guard all beauty-queen-like, then looks back at me.

I'm disarmed, feeling like my twelve-year-old self again. "You look great," I mutter.

She nods. Pauses. Waits for me to say something else. She nudges me with her eyebrows, but the Xanax has given me cotton mouth, and also—I don't want to.

"Are you…good?"

She leans back, crossing her arms over her chest as she considers me—which is different than seeing me.

"What do you think about your mama being born again, little girl?" I am silent. Stunned but not stunned. Her lips are pressed into a tight rosebud, her eyes wide like a Kewpie doll.

My mother had worshipped only one thing, though during one stint with rehab she'd hung a framed painting of a creamy-looking Jesus on the living room wall. Painting Jesus had been serenely blue-eyed and rosy-cheeked. His robe a glowing white. Whenever a laundry commercial would come on TV, Piper and I would look at the painting and whisper, "White bright Jesus keeps your whites whiter."

It hurts to think of Piper and it hurts to sit across from my mother—who has loved many things very much, but never me.

"I'm a believer," she says when I don't respond. "God cleaned me up. I believe he brought me here to change my heart, to purify me so when I get out, I can serve him." She's waiting for my reaction.

I picture white Jesus cleaning my mother up, wiping the drool and vomit from her face in his glowing robes. She is serving a five-year sentence for aiding in an armed robbery. The armed robber? Her boyfriend at the time—Joey Ger-something—I could never remember. Gran had gone to her sentencing while I stayed home with Cal. I hadn't wanted to go. What I would never forget was my grandmother's face when she came home that day—it was the same face she'd worn the weeks after Piper went missing. Empty. Vague. I already hated my mother, but that day, cradling my baby as Gran looked right through us, I hated her more. She took everything. Even now from jail, she was taking Gran from the two people who needed her. I wanted to tell Gran that it wasn't her fault how my mother had turned out, but as I looked down at Cal I didn't know if that was true or not. Piper and I were products of her upbringing, so who was to say she wasn't? Gran was good to us, perhaps not so good to Virginia when she was trying to keep food on their two-top thirty years ago. It wasn't an excuse—if I had managed to be a good mother after having her it all boiled down to choices.

I clear my throat. "I'm here because something happened to Gran."

It takes her a moment to adjust. Her eyes narrow, then glaze over. Realizing the conversation is not about her is my mother's least favorite turn of events. I watch her face fall in boredom.

"Oh, yeah?"

"She had a stroke…she's been in the hospital for about nine days and—"

"Strokes run in our family. I always thought that I would die of a stroke, but the doctors in here say I'm healthy as a horse." She dusts her hands of the worry, makes a face like she doesn't need to be bothered.

I stare at her and she stares back, unmoved. "Yes, well, Gran unfortunately is not, and I just wanted to come tell you."

"I'll have my group pray for her. We pray for Piper every meeting—every single one. I think she can feel it too, you know."

"No, I don't know," I say. "She's dead." My voice is not flat and emotionless like I planned.

What I've said does not register on her face. She has the look of a pugnacious child even at forty. "Mary prayed for Jesus," she says with conviction. "My role as her mother—"

"Holy cow, are you kidding me? She's dead, Mom." I spit out the word like it's rotten. "She's dead."

Her stare is blank. Blank because she doesn't get that one half of her twinset has been missing for nine years? Or blank in that she doesn't care?

"Mary prayed for Jesus," she repeats like she's recalling lines to a play, and I feel my eyes fill with tears. I let her talk, but I lack the energy to listen.

She doesn't say that she's praying for me. I am not a factor in her new identity. It has nothing to do with me…or Piper. She likes how it feels to have a dead kid, it makes her special. People treat her nicer because of it.

I tell myself I'm waiting for a break in conversation to bring it up, but I'm stalling. She might not remember what I'm here to ask her. She might lie, or ramble incoherently.

"I was thinking…" I begin. "About that time Piper asked you to get her birth control…remember when you told me about that…?"

I was in a fog of shock and grief after Piper was kidnapped. I can't locate the exact memory, only a handful of words said over the phone when she was high.

She shrugs. "Sure. She was at that age—I started younger than her." She laughs, and I see the dark gaps in her mouth. She's loosening up now, acting like the mom I knew and hated. I press on.

"But when she asked you for birth control, she was super into church stuff. So why would she need it?"

Her face lights up in amusement. "Are you stupid? You think people in church don't fuck?" She lets out a guffaw. I get a whiff of something sweet and rotten on her breath.

She may not be using, but she's definitely drinking. Prison hooch instead of meth, praise God!

*You have no room to judge, dry swallower of Xanax.*

"Did she mention the name of a boy?"

"Try man."

She still hasn't asked a single question about her grandson. Did I really expect her to spit out information about my sister from nine years ago? If Piper had told her anything back then, it went in one ear and out the other.

I make to stand up, and she looks shocked.

"Where are you going?"

"Home to my son. I came here to tell you about your mother, and now I'm done."

"She's an old lady, Iris, what do you want from me—tears? She has to die eventually."

I need out of here fast. The one thing I don't tolerate is Gran slander. I'm to the door and waiting for the guard to open it when she yells out my name followed by a man's. The name hits me hard. I've heard it.

"The name of the guy…"

She's still sitting at the table when I turn around. Grinning. She wants me to come back and be her audience. Her face says she thinks I'm coming back, but I have what I want.

I turn away again. No need to waste another word. I have the name. I have confirmation.

"She was my daughter! A mother never forgets…" Her voice has reached an ugly pitch: wet and accusatory. She needs me to believe that she loves Piper more than I do, like it's a competition for who owns the largest portion of grief.

The guard says, "Coming or going, lady? You need to sit down or leave…"

*"A mother never forgets…"* Her words are bouncing around my brain.

Neither does a sister.

# 8

PAST

**IT WAS EARLY MORNING**—twenty-four hours since Piper was taken; ten hours since Gran collapsed. For three tense hours I'd sat in the waiting room, dreading the moment the doctor would come out and tell me she was dead. But when tiny Dr. Orly came to collect me from the waiting room, it was to tell me that Gran suffered a minor heart attack when she collapsed, and fortunately, the medics arrived in time to stabilize her. She was also dangerously dehydrated, he told me, and had forgotten to take her medicine. He had the type of face that stayed the same no matter how dire or joyful the news; only when he was finished speaking was I able to conclude there was no bad news tacked on to the end of his speech. She was going to be okay.

"She's awake and asking to see you."

I couldn't speak I was so relieved. I followed Dr. Orly through hallways, doors, and unapologetically bright lighting that hurt my eyes. And then we were at *her* door, and he was giving me that look like, brace yourself—which I did, but nothing can really prepare you for seeing the strongest person you know looking like they'd had a near-losing fight with death.

She was not sitting up like people are in the movies; she was lying on her back, and the lump her body made under the covers was childlike. I was frightened as I tiptoed my way over to the side of the bed. She opened her eyes as soon as I was beside her like she could sense my presence, and she smiled.

I was so shocked I couldn't smile back. I gawked at her bare, pale face and frowned instead.

"Sorry I scared you…" Her voice was hoarse. Piper would have known what to say in that moment, but I didn't. I never wished for my sister's presence so hard. Where was she? How could she do this to us—to me? My words tangled on my tongue. I nodded tearfully and held her hand. She didn't look this tiny when she was standing, she filled a room with her energy. Her eyes fluttered open and closed as she tried to stay awake.

"Go to sleep, Gran," I said firmly. Her eyes closed and didn't open again. It was like she was waiting for permission. She couldn't even allow herself rest in the hospital.

It made me so sad for her, and I was sniffling next to her bed when Dr. Orly cleared his throat. *Uh-oh…here it comes…*

"We're going to keep her overnight to monitor her. Do you have someone to call who can pick you up?"

"Yes." The lie came easily; Piper and I were used to lying about that sort of thing. "My mom," I said, when he kept staring. That seemed to appease him, but he still looked off about something. His face twitched; it was just for a few seconds, but it scared me.

"I have Tourette's," he explained. "Do you know what that is?"

I did and I said so.

"Your grandmother mentioned something about your sister being missing…"

It was a sucker punch. I had to close my eyes and reset: Piper is missing—you need to find her. Gran is in the hospital—you need to make sure she doesn't fight the doctors on the treatment she needs.

"Yeah," I said, not meeting his eyes. "The police say she's a runaway. They've put out a…poster." The word was dry and stale in my mouth.

The doctor cleared his throat. "A poster?"

"A bulletin," I corrected myself. "We spoke to a detective… he put out a missing person bulletin." I was so tired I was seeing double. My tongue felt clumsy and thick as I grappled with the situation I was in—I was a minor with an incapacitated guardian and a missing sister.

"Do you live with your grandmother?"

Dr. Orly was nice, but if I didn't choose my words carefully, I'd be spending the next few nights in a foster situation. He was busy—busy adults liked to remove the problem as quickly as possible. *Focus and do what needs to be done.* Those were our words—mine and Piper's.

"Yes, but my mother lives close. I'll call her now." I patted my pockets until I remembered my phone was stolen. A wave of panic before I nonchalantly moved to the room phone and picked it up, miming dialing. It seemed to work, because out of the corner of my eye, I saw Dr. Orly nod and clasp his hands at his waist. He wanted this part to be over so he could go on his way and not think about me again. No one wants to be in charge of the smelly, sad teenager. The game was hot potato, and we were it—that is, until we were cooked out of the system. Timer went off at eighteen.

I made eye contact with him and said into the dead receiver, "Hi, Mom, can you pick me up now? Yeah, I'll tell you everything when you get here. Awesome, thanks, I'll see you soon." I gave him a thumbs-up like I had it all worked out.

"I'll send one of the nurses in to walk you down." He hesitated once more in the doorway, but finally seemed to decide

I was old enough to be left on my own. As soon as the door closed, I slammed the phone on the cradle and kissed Gran on the cheek. "I'll be back," I whispered next to her ear. She smelled like Gran—like home.

I was out of the door and down the hall before anyone saw me. The dinner tray lady glanced my way but didn't seem to notice me or care. I snatched an apple from the cart and ducked around a corner. It was five past five, and the sun had yet to warm the sky. I passed a sleepy-looking guy sitting at the check-in desk, and then the doors sighed as they expelled me into the dark morning.

There was a McDonald's half a mile down the street going left. To the right: a gas station with panels broken out of the sign. I stood under the awning as rain flecked past, trying to decide what to do when someone from inside the hospital yelled out, "Excuse me, miss! Hey!"

I flipped up my hoodie and booked it, my Converses getting soaked when I failed to navigate around the puddles. I ran farther and farther away from Gran. It felt like I was betraying her. I stopped when I was sure no one was following, bending over at the waist to catch my breath. The apartment was in a decent neighborhood, but I'd have to walk through a couple of sketchy areas to get there.

The McDonald's crowd looked dour this early in the morning. A young employee with a broom and dustpan made eye contact with me and quickly looked away. We both hated today for different reasons. In an attempt to get warm, I sat at a table near the bathroom, pulling my knees up to my chest and watching a mom trying to feed hotcakes to her pissed off little kid. I was hungry. I didn't have money for the bus.

I could see the morning traffic through the windows, cars lining up to get on the freeway like slow-crawling beetles. The sky was dark, and the rain was astonishingly cold when I stepped back outside. First things first—I had to call Audrain and Poley.

Twenty-four hours—she'd been missing long enough that they had to pay attention. But my phone was gone. It would have to wait until I got home.

My hands were so cold I could barely turn the key in the lock. It didn't feel good to be home; without Gran and Piper, the tiny rooms felt like an empty movie set—meaningless and cold. I stood on the four beige tiles that Gran jokingly called the entrance hall. If I took a step I'd be on the worn gray carpet.

My clothes were heavy and damp with rain and sweat. I peeled them off as I ran for the bathroom and stood naked on the yellow bathmat, stomping my feet while I waited for the water to get hot. A week ago, Piper had insisted on painting my toenails a neon-green color; it had looked ridiculous against my too-creamy skin, like a fungus. My big toe was chipped on one corner, and the polish on my baby toes had rubbed off entirely, but now as I envisioned her blond head bent over my foot, her face serious as she concentrated, a sob escaped my throat.

After my shower, I stopped in the doorway of our bedroom. Facing me were two twin beds on the same wall, separated by a tall dresser. My side was bare: gray comforter, white lamp, no posters or photographs to remind me of who and what I cared about. Hers was overflowing with personality: polka-dot comforter, daisy sheets, pink-and-green pillows on her bed—she even had one of those frilly skirts at the bottom that hid the crap she kept underneath.

I was fuzzy. My thoughts felt thick and clumsy. Piper's favorite hoodie was on the floor next to her bed. I pulled it over my head and found a pair of clean jeans in our shared dresser.

I hoped Gran wouldn't freak out when she woke up and saw me gone.

The phone was ringing. I bolted upright, waking in a gasp. My heart was pounding so hard it hurt. I drowned in my dreams: in lakes, oceans, mud, sometimes vats of uncooked elbow pasta. Even the good dreams ended in drowning.

The ringing stopped abruptly. The light in the bedroom was wrong, too dark. The digital clock next to my bed said it was three o'clock. *I slept for four hours?* I felt out of my mind, petrified. Squinting around the room, I searched for my cell. It wasn't next to my bed on the nightstand. A car honked outside the window, Then it all came back: the movie theater, Gran... Piper... They'd taken my cell phone before shoving Piper into the car.

My hands shook as I dialed 411 for directory assistance. A man's voice came on the line.

"Can I have the number for the Queen Hill Hospital," I heard myself say into the cordless.

"Do you want me to connect you?"

"Yes."

I jotted the number down on the Charlie Brown notepad I gave Gran for Christmas and waited for the call to connect. The hospital put me on hold for what felt like an hour. I watched Gran's Felix the Cat clock in a trance count the seconds with his eyes.

My anxiety was at a boiling point. The dead silence pressed against my ear felt like a bad omen. A voice was going to come on the line and tell me Gran was dead, I just knew it.

"Hello, is this Iris?" She didn't sound overly serious. In fact, her voice was cheerful.

"Yes...?"

"Your grandmother tried to call you before she went into surgery," she said.

I stared at my bare feet, stunned. Gran wasn't dead, she was in surgery? It took my brain a few seconds to catch up, and then a different panic set in.

"I don't understand. Is she okay? What type of surgery?"

"You can call back in a few hours and check on her. If she's awake you may even be able to talk to her."

She didn't answer my question, but I couldn't muster up the common sense to repeat it. Thanking Diane, I hung up. The thought crossed my mind to call my mother, but I quickly squashed it. She didn't believe me about Piper, and she'd make Gran being in the hospital about her.

It was time to call the authorities.

Girls went missing all the time, especially in big cities. They ran away mostly, but what about those other stories—the ones where men took them for other reasons? Audrain and Poley made it clear that they believed her to be a runaway, despite the fact I'd seen her *taken*.

I called the station and asked to speak to Martin Audrain or Amanda Poley—neither were available. I didn't know whether to be relieved or distraught.

With Gran's phone in hand—and last year's yearbook—I sat at the kitchen table with my formulating plan.

The messages in Piper's yearbook were written in fat bubble letters. They were mostly of the *have a great summer!* variety, but beneath half of those messages were phone numbers. *Call me! Let's hang out!*

I started writing down names and numbers. Someone had to know something. I had a full page of contacts when the house phone rang, startling me, and I wanted to throw up when I saw the caller ID: it was the police station.

"Ms. Walsh, it's Detective Audrain."

"It's not—" I sigh. "This is Iris. My grandmother is in surgery. Do you have news about Piper?"

There was a pause, and when he spoke, he sounded different than he had yesterday. Always sounding different, Audrain was. "I do, I would need your grandmother to come to the station…"

I was already sliding my feet into my sneakers. "My grandmother cannot come to the station, but I'm on my way!" I calculated that I could take the 202 bus and walk the rest of the way. I'd be at the station in forty minutes.

"We need to speak to a guardian, Iris. Do you have any other relatives that can come down—a mom, dad—an older sibling? Who are you staying with?"

"A friend. And no, there's no one else." My voice was flat.

Another pause, like he was weighing what to do. It was a weird situation. But there was no way I was going to call my mother. She wouldn't be helpful, she'd show up drunk or high—or both. She'd make more problems. I squeezed my eyes closed.

"I'll send a cruiser out to get you," he said.

"No!" I interrupted. "I'll get there myself." I ended the call and tossed the phone on Gran's recliner. It bounced off of her *Stay Sassy* throw pillow and landed unceremoniously on the rug. The pit in my stomach was expanding by the minute. The oily smell of the police cruiser filled my nostrils; my stomach recoiled at the memory. *Don't think about it.* I was good at that: turning off my feelings and wading through something without acknowledging it with words. Sometimes it was better not to give words to your thoughts, it deprived them of oxygen. It was a topic Piper and I disagreed on. When I saw her writing in one of her journals, trying to hide it from me, I'd think, poor, unfortunate soul…

Grabbing my things, I headed for the door.

# 9

PRESENT

**I GET OFF** the ferry at Whidbey, and my phone tells me it's ten degrees colder here than it was in Seattle. *You're taking a boat route rather than a bus route!* An amazingly cold experience. Shivering, I follow the email's instructions to where the *Water Glass* is optimistically bobbing on the waves. A small line has formed to board, colorful puffer jackets punctuating the endless gray. Every step that takes me farther away from Gran and Cal gives me anxiety. I cannot protect them from an island. It's been a full-time job to rationalize the position. The continuous operation of the hospital and the tediousness of travel require swing shifts. Three days, two nights on Shoal Island. My supplies are carefully rolled into my backpack: three pairs of white scrubs, two pairs of sweatpants and T-shirts for down time, a novel, a plastic bag of toiletries, a pack of playing cards, and snacks. The captain, a stocky man, stands on the dock unsmiling while we waddle past in our winter gear. Everyone seems to know what they're doing, so I follow suit, quickly finding a seat so I'm not a nuisance. I notice I am the only one already wearing my white scrubs; my coworkers having wisely donned warmer pants for the trip. Fifteen minutes later the *Water Glass* parts the kelp as she pushes toward a little beach surrounded by formidable rocks. The island is hilly and heavily forested. Excitement surges in my belly. I stand too soon. Silly. The motion knocks me back to my seat. Someone laughs—a woman wearing a bright red parka and dark sunglasses. She's sitting across from me and two seats over. She clutches the handrail for support to show me, and I copy her.

"Happens every time," she says. "You the new girl?"

"Iris." I show my teeth, and she shows hers. Hers are very nice teeth, straight and just the right size. Everything about her is the right size. She is wearing red lips, contrasting with the black fur lining the hood of her parka.

"That won't do," she says.

"What?"

"Your first name. We don't use those. We all go by our last names. It's a safety thing. I'm Bouncer."

"I guess I'm still Iris," I say.

She doesn't look convinced. "No shit. What's your first name then?"

"I thought we weren't allowed to say?"

"Touché." A tighter smile this time. My sister's case went cold so fast, her name never became a thing. There was no one looking for her like they did with Elizabeth Smart and Jon-Benét Ramsey. The chance that someone will recognize my name is small, but I still want to be careful.

I fall in line behind Bouncer as we make our way off the dock. At least twelve people get off before me, and there's another ten or so behind. The path to the hospital from the boat dock is paved and narrow, affording only one person at a time— or two people walking arm in arm. Unless I want to get cozy with Bouncer, I'm forced to stare at her back as we trudge the path along the beach. The smell of wet earth lifts from the ground with the mist. I cling to the straps of my backpack. The path suddenly curves left, pushing us toward the center of the island. When we finally crest the hill, my thigh muscles are screaming.

I unbutton my coat and see that I'm not the only one. People are pulling off their winter gear as we walk. I'm excited when the sign comes into view: white letters on a blue/black paint: Shoal Island Hospital. There's a large space beneath the name, where the words *for the criminally insane* used to be. I want to stop for a moment and take it all in, but I'm already lagging way behind Bouncer. *You can come back later and take a photo to show Cal and Gran.* I pick up the pace, lightheaded from excitement. The path curves again, and suddenly there she is: a strange sight. A mutt of a building, it is an architectural abomination. A Victorian-looking dollhouse is at the center, plucked from another era, neatly painted. Projecting out of either side of the house are two differently styled buildings. On the left is a lodge house, and on the right and extending toward the cliff wall is a brick building; the type of structure you'd imagine a prison to look like: imposing and bleak. It's all surrounded by the greenest grass I've ever seen.

Modern cream armchairs sit around a huge hearth fireplace. The ceiling is expansive, white with heavy walnut beams. It looks, for the most part, like a lodge. To the right of the fireplace is a wide carpeted staircase that narrows at it climbs to the second floor. My options are to go left, right, or up the stairs. Everyone else seems to be filtering left toward a set of propped-open double doors. I slow down, and the man behind me grunts in frustration. Someone tall pushes past me, their backpack knocking me in the head. I'm being herded, taken somewhere I don't want to go.

The switch happens in a matter of seconds: my adrenaline turns cold, and a flush of negative energy runs through my body. I am suddenly a fish out of water, gasping for air, eyes glossy with shock. I should not be here; my plan was silly—childish even—what was I thinking?

I smell popcorn; I want to retch. I feel pressure on my wrist, and when I look down, a hand is encircling it—red fingernails, red hair—Bouncer pulls me out of the stream of humans and leads me away. We stop near the fireplace, where she pushes me gently into an armchair. I am a frozen dinner—cold on the inside, hot on the outside.

"You're having a panic attack," she says. "Here—" She shoves a pink water bottle into my hand.

"Hold it with your other hand…"

I look at her in confusion.

"Go on…do it."

Bouncer and her bottle turn into a watercolor beneath my tears and sweat. I fix my gaze on her hair—candy-red—and transfer the bottle to my left hand.

"Switch again," she says. I do as I'm told, watching as she crouches on the cream rug, balancing on one knee as she searches the pockets of her backpack. I can hear the movement of things: keys, paper, plastic tinkling around in its depths.

The color of her hair reminds me of the heart-shaped lollipops Cal gave to each of his classmates on Valentine's Day.

"Keep doing that…back and forth."

She has something in her hand when she stands up. Motioning for me to take a sip of water, she eyes me warily.

"Kid, get it together," she says under her breath. I nod, screwing off the metal cap and lifting the bottle to my lips. I swallow two measured swigs before handing it back to her. Better. I look at her gratefully.

"Look, you can leave now if you can't handle it, the boat sticks around for thirty minutes."

I shake my head vigorously. "I'm fine. I just…" *Panicked?*

"I didn't eat this morning. I'm a little lightheaded."

"Here, take this…" She grabs my hand and presses something into my palm. My fingers close around it automatically. "You're through that way." She points, and my eyes follow the direction of her finger. I'm too breathless to do anything but nod. I try to display how grateful I am with my eyes. I'm cognizant enough to be embarrassed; the worst has passed. I look down at what she passed to me—the little treasure in my palm is peach-colored; we've met before.

"Go on, take it," she says, glancing around like someone might see us. Not people taking pills in a mental health facility, I think dryly. And then I don't think; I place the pill on my tongue and let it ride the wave to the back of my throat—down, down, down.

"Good girl," she says, looking impressed. She offers me her water bottle again. I shake my head.

"You're going to ask for Jordyn. Have you met Leo?"

"Dr. Leo Grayson?" My voice cracks. Her smile twitches, then grows stiff.

"Whoops! Dr. Grayson," she corrects herself. She lifts her eyes to the ceiling in a *silly me* gesture. Accidentally on purpose, I think. It isn't unusual for people to give the new hire a hard time, but she is clearly fishing after what I think of him. I hide my enthusiasm and shrug.

"No, I haven't met him. I've heard a lot about him though, I heard he's great..."

A lie. I know everything about him; the plan doesn't work without Dr. Grayson. He is the literal bridge to Piper.

A decade ago, Dr. Grayson was the most renowned psychotherapist on the West Coast. He was camera-shy, but the internet loved him nevertheless—his career was a conversation in the blogosphere. Not one, but two doctorates. He is the author of half a dozen books (none of which were stocked in Barnes & Noble). Back in the early two thousands, before he took the position on Shoal Island, he'd been a celebrity in the community, taking a lot of speaking gigs from what I saw online. Described as smart, handsome, charming, and a bit shy by one journalist. The same three photos accompanied his name, but then…nothing. There was nothing written about him for years until someone asked, "Whatever happened to that famous psychologist?" on Reddit. Why he took the job out here is anyone's guess. My guess is solitude. Some people are good at the spotlight but not made for it. He's probably in his mid-forties now; the last photograph taken of him and posted online was seven years ago.

I shake my head, and she nods slowly. "You're pretty." She says it like it's more of an observation than a compliment, and before I can respond, she turns on her heel and walks away.

"Thanks," I call after her, but she's already waving at someone and jogging to catch up. I didn't even get the chance to ask what she does here. She certainly knows who I am though—in a place this size, everyone probably knows. However, no one looks my way. No one seems to care in the slightest that I am here. I feel a sense of relief as I stand. Maybe no one noticed. I walk in the direction she pointed me, my spine a little more curved than it had been five minutes ago.

The email Jordyn Whyte sent had said to be at her office at nine fifteen.

I see the sign for the restroom, and beyond that is a gold plaque that says Offices/Registrar. As I approach the window, the door next to it opens.

"New girl…" A man who looks to be in his late twenties holds the door open with his hip. He glances down at a notepad. "Iris?"

I nod. He has one of those baby/man faces like George O'Malley from *Grey's Anatomy*—benignly boring, but handsome.

"Jordyn is waiting for you." His face says nice, but his tone says impatient.

I follow him through the door and down a long corridor that

smells like fresh paint. The ceilings are low, and the lights are the cheap office kind—buzzing insistently above us.

The man is speed-walking, and I get the sense that I'm late for something. But looking at my watch, I confirm I'm right on time. He stops suddenly, and I collide into his back.

He doesn't acknowledge the collision; instead, he raps twice on the door and swings it open without waiting for an answer. No one is inside—not that I can tell. The office is a mess—Gran would call it trashed. It looks like the place old files go to die, except in the middle of the stacks is a desk with a computer.

"Jordyn will be right in." My guide closes the door without telling me his name.

I look around the claustrophobic space. To my relief, a tiny window is cracked open, letting the fresh, cold air in. The window isn't large enough for an adult to crawl through, but it's something to look at other than the files.

I'd read online that the hospital had been renovated a dozen times since its opening in 1944 to accommodate its various uses over the years. Originally built as an army outpost, it was a no-nonsense cinderblock building that sat on a cliff and had an incredible view. Ten years later, it was converted into a prison. The cinderblock was razed, and an even uglier building was put in its place: Shoal Island Prison. The prisoners only got to enjoy the view for five years because in 1960 it closed due to supply shortages and funding. Another three years passed before a wealthy widow bought the island. She painted the prison pink and turned it into a home for unwed women to have their babies—aka, a place for embarrassed parents to send their knocked-up daughters. The widow built her own house—a Victorian shingle—in front of the prison so that when visitors crested the hill they'd see her mansion, which was breathtaking. It might have been a comfort to the parents of those girls to leave them in such a stunning place—where they could be forgotten about for six months until they returned slim and infant-less to their parents. Except the girls didn't sleep in the main house. They were marched off to their real home—a converted cell facing the sound. The home was shut down in the seventies after Roe vs Wade, and the free love movement put an end to the era of the sent-away pregnant woman.

And now here we are: the former barracks/prison/girls' home made into a facility that houses the criminally insane. I'd bet the five dollars in my pocket this office used to be a cell. It's optimistically scented with apple cinnamon.

The door opens behind me, and a woman I presume is Jordyn comes in carrying yet more files. She wears a harried expression, and her eyebrows appear windblown, growing every which way. When she speaks, she has a tiny accent. Maybe Boston, I can't be sure.

"That was Crede, in case he didn't introduce himself...he's a nurse, best one I have, actually." She winds her way to the desk and collapses in her chair with a sigh, motioning for me to do the same. I'm on the short side, but she is over six feet tall.

I am obsessed with tall women; I want to wear their skin quite literally. Sometime after Cal was born, I'd read an interesting article in a forgettable magazine: "Why Men Are Afraid of Tall Women." You could tell that the author wanted the article to be more intellectual than it was, and for two single-spaced pages she set out to answer the big question. I don't remember the statistics or argument presented, only that the most important part of the article had boiled down to the very last sentence: "They just don't know what to do with them." I liked that. No, I loved it—a stature of intimidation.

Jordyn opens a drawer in the desk, slams it shut, frowns, opens another one. "Aha!" she says, triumphant; a granola bar appears in her hand. She shreds the packaging with her teeth and eats it in two bites. Her hair is mousy brown threaded with gray, and she wears it parted down the middle and tied at the nape of her neck. It's still wet like she just got out of the shower.

And she probably has—I saw the sign for the dorms on my way in. She smacks her lips like she just ate a hot meal.

"I'm Jordyn Whyte. You'll hear some people around here refer to me as Y2K because of the two *y*'s in my name and I'm old—real brainiacs, this group."

She produces a yellowing bottle of Tylenol from the drawer and shakes it. Popping the lid, she scrutinizes the contents for several seconds before shucking two pills between her lips.

"I keep this bottomless pit of despair running." She swallows the pills dry and flinches. "I'm gonna tell you right now that I run a tight ship. None of that *my car broke down, my kid has the flu* shit. I'm hiring you to be here. So be here. You miss the water taxi, it's not my problem. Camp at the dock if you have to, just be here on time."

"Yes, ma'am," I say.

"Our patients are our priority, and they function better— the hospital functions better—when we stick to the schedule. There're no ifs, ands, or buts about it."

She finds a half-full water bottle among the files and takes a sip, sucking it between the gap in her front teeth.

"We have forty patients at HOTI, each one a violent offender. These individuals have been deemed mentally incapable of standing trial and thus have been sent here to receive necessary treatment for their buffet of disorders. We have rapists, we have murderers, we have arsonists, and most importantly, we have rules."

*Rules!* Yes of course. I hate that word. When you play by the rules you are deemed a team player—virtuous. I have no intention of obeying the rules. I am entirely here to break them.

"Do you have any questions so far?"

"A few," I say. "What's HOTI?"

"It's an acronym for hospital on the island. Just the nickname most of us give this place. Insider jokes, and boy, do we have them…" She drops the file she's been holding in front of me. It is textbook-thick.

"Training handbook. You read a chapter and fill out the answers without cheating. I'll know if you cheat because you'll get shit wrong—I'm very impatient with people who get things wrong. In a place like this, I need accuracy."

"I'm accurate," I offer. I am.

She leans back, and I'm pretty certain she's sizing me up, already deciding that I'm not the right candidate for the job. Thankfully she doesn't comment on my size, which is five feet two inches; instead, she says, "It takes a certain amount of mental strength to work this job. The patients are one thing, but the island itself is another. This is a dangerous, isolated place. Do not wander off, especially at night. The cliffs are less forgiving than D hall."

"The cliffs, right," I say, only now thinking about the cliffs. "So where do employees take walks—exercise?"

"We have a small gym, there are treadmills."

I think she's joking. My smile drops.

"We've had some problems over the years with erosion along the cliffs. The pathways that were walkable are no longer safe."

I feel immediately disappointed. I'd imagined myself exploring the island on my breaks, taking long head-clearing walks in the fog.

"The building itself is teetering on the edge of a cliff, the fog makes vision difficult most days, and—" she lowers her voice and her eyebrows "—there was an accident a few years ago. A patient snuck out and threw themselves to the waves. We don't want repeats of that situation, if you know what I mean, so be on your guard."

Ominous. My skin erupts in goose bumps. A dozen questions rest on the tip of my tongue, but I remember my panic attack in the lobby not even thirty minutes ago. When I close my eyes, I can still see the pity on Bouncer's face when she slipped me the pill. If it gets back to Jordyn that I freaked out during my first five minutes on the job, she might question my ability to perform long-term. I nod and smile, smile and nod, but I keep my questions to myself, making a mental note to search the subject online later.

"We don't get many paid interns," she admits. "Ten years ago, we had four or five, but the board has cut back on our funding. Dr. Grayson approves two every year, and we never heard back from the other guy. More work for you," she warns.

I shrug it off. "I feel lucky to be here," I say.

"We have a staff of a hundred, and he is the only doctor on staff, so that gets a bit tough—spread thin. They've tried to get another doctor out here but...well, you've seen what a trek it is to get to the island, and most people have families."

It's time for me to say something. "Dr. Grayson must be dedicated to his work."

"That he is." She switches her gaze to the window.

*Too small to escape from*, I think. *And then those poor pregnant girls...*

"This place is special, and we're doing special things here. We're understaffed and tired, but we're doing it. Welcome to the team, Iris."

I'm impressed when the door cracks open. The baby/man who collected me from the lobby leans in. I wonder if he'd been waiting right outside the door to be cued...

I happily stand. Jordyn's office feels like it's getting smaller by the minute.

Crede's pale blue eyes meet mine.

"Crede, take Iris on the tour, then take her over to the cafeteria for lunch." She looks at me pointedly. "The dorms are being turned over and cleaned, so you'll have to wait to put your stuff in a locker. In the future, get there early to claim a bed." The morning rush that I was caught in earlier made sense now. Bouncer probably lost out because of me.

"You can leave your backpack and jacket here until after your shift."

She glares at Crede, beady eyes pinching smaller. "You smell like my dad's truck, goddamn. You can't work in health care and smoke a pack a day."

"I hear you," he says. "She ready?"

Jordyn looks like she wants to say something else about the smoking, but instead, she swivels her chair in my direction. "You're working hospice today, so buckle up…"

Buckle down. I volunteered at a hospice during my undergrad work. I knew what hospice meant—sitting and waiting for someone to die was not the education I'd been expecting today. Jordyn smiles thinly as if sensing my thoughts. "We're short-staffed. We could really use your help."

"Of course," I chirp. I hang my jacket on the coatrack in the corner and prop my backpack against the wall behind it.

I am out the door trailing Crede, my thoughts trying to catch up to what is happening.

"Her office smells like fake pie." His voice is flat, but I hear the humor.

"My gran smoked." I shrug. "It is what it is."

His laugh is reluctant; he shakes his head. "Her gran must have baked pies…"

He leads me back to the waiting area where Bouncer gave me the pill and stops in front of the staircase. "We call the downstairs area the lodge," he says. "Over there is the newest addition to the building. We just came from the administrative offices, which are in the old Victorian part, and that way—" he bops his head left "—is the cafeteria and dorms, but you'll see that later. Come on…"

I'm calculating the chances of being able to sneak into D hall at night and find his room. If I obeyed every impulse I had in regard to Piper's case, I'd likely become a patient at the hospital. I'm here to verify the truth. It's his blood that I need.

"What happens if there is an emergency at home? How would we get back?"

He gives me a side-eye. "You didn't think to ask that before you took the job?"

"I would have taken the job no matter what the answer," I admit.

He fixes his attention on my face.

I can tell he likes my answer. "I suppose they'd call the water taxi if there was an emergency. Tuesday to Thursday, and next shift comes Friday to Sunday. Monday is skeleton crew—the ferry doesn't come on Mondays. Even the doctor leaves on Sunday night, comes back Tuesday mornings—"

He walks backward up the stairs as he talks. The scene is so Broadway I half expect him to break into song. I like him despite the Seattle Freeze vibe he's giving off. We're all like that here. I don't know why, maybe it's the moderate weather that makes us moderately friendly.

"This part of HOTI is in what we call the Victorian. It's all part of the original house as you can probably see..." he tells me. "A lot of the upper-level staff like Jordyn and Dr. Grayson have private suites up here."

We reach the top of the stairs, and I blink at the sudden change in decor. "Wow," I say, "I wasn't expecting that."

Crede takes a moment to appreciate the room with me.

"I know," he says. "It's beautiful."

It looks like we've gone back in time. High-back floral armchairs sit squarely on Persian rugs. The curved walls are lined with bookcases. My eyes follow the line of books until they reach the security doors, so misplaced and ugly. Crede leads me away from the doors, around the circular landing. I run my hand along the wooden banister as we walk, the woodgrain smoothed to a gloss.

We pass wider-than-average mahogany doors, each one with

a brass handle and lock. Old fashioned keyholes stare back at me. I look curiously at each one until Crede notices and slows down.

"If you walk by around noon when the cleaning crew are here, you can get a little peek inside."

I laugh because he's caught me. I do want to get a look inside.

"That one is Dr. Grayson's." He nods at the last door on the landing. I want to press my ear to the wooden door and listen for him.

"He has a place in the city too, but some nights he stays here."

I'm practically salivating with the information, but I keep my expression neutrally interested. I'm playing a role, being a character. I'm smart, but I'm not that smart; I'm hard-working but not an overachiever. I absolutely cannot draw attention to myself. It took years of planning and hard work to get to Shoal, and I'm not going to muck it up with stupid mistakes. Hundreds of other applicants from around the country applied for my internship, some of them from prestigious colleges. Me—not so much. I spent the first two years at community college and then transferred to UW for my last three years of undergrad work. It just so happened that one of my professors was a former roommate of Leo Grayson, and he emailed my application and résumé directly to him. I could tell that Professor Pratt liked the idea of discovering me, sending his star student for Leo Grayson to inspect. I'd let him think there was convincing to do, but I'd chosen his classes because of his association to the famed Dr. Grayson.

*He can be a tough guy to work with, but the research he's done on the effects of early trauma to the adult brain…well, you'll be hard-pressed to find anyone who knows more on the subject.* I was life's subject at the moment, but I didn't say that; instead, I wholeheartedly agreed, and Professor Pratt did the hard work for me, cutting through the red tape and dropping me directly on Dr. Grayson's desk. Leo Grayson was impressive if you were into that sort of thing.

"Iris?" We stop in front of an elevator.

Crede is annoyed. A crease appears across his forehead.

I'm embarrassed, I haven't been paying attention. *Don't mess up, idiot.*

"I'm sorry," I say. "I was distracted by the books. I'm a nerd."

Some of the stiffness leaves his face. "Oh, yeah?" His tone is different—lighter.

If books were the way to someone's heart, I had the roadmap.

"I like the darker stuff," I say. "Poe and Neil Gaiman."

Crede grins. "A dark escapist!" His winter eyes are engaged and moony at my mention of Gaiman. I might be enjoying the conversation if I were planning on being friends with him.

He tells me about what he's reading, and this time I make sure to pay attention. He's a fantasy guy. I admit that I haven't read any of his favorite books as we come to the end of our walk and stop in front of the security door.

"I probably have an extra copy lying around. I'll bring it for you."

"That would be great," I say. The book sounds interesting despite the fact I haven't found time to read for pleasure in the last few years. It makes me sad to acknowledge the fact that I don't read anymore. It was once an integral part of my personality. Small things to give up, I remind myself. I am a mother, a granddaughter, and a super sleuth. I am good at research— definitely not half-bad at planning. I am here, aren't I?

Crede tells me he reads a hundred books a year, most of them on the ferry going to and from work.

"How long have you worked here?"

"A year," he says. There is finality in his tone—he is done talking about himself. But I am not done. I need allies, even if it's this grouchy baby/man with the silver hair.

"How did you get the job? I mean, it's not exactly easy to get a position here."

"Dr. Grayson scouted me at a work fair in Miami, moved

me out here for the job, and here we are. What?" he says, look-ing at my face.

"Nothing." I wasn't quick enough to sweep my expression. God, I need to get better at that. He gives me a look that says he doesn't believe me.

"It's just… I heard Dr. Grayson was a recluse."

Crede looks bewildered, and then his face grows red.

"It wasn't him personally, someone from the hospital came out to recruit…"

"Ah," I say. We pass an elevator with a no service sign duct-taped over the call button.

I change the subject as we close the square and near the end of our second-floor tour.

"Did you know anyone out here when you came?"

"Are you always this nosy?"

"Pretty much."

He snorts. "I didn't want to. I'd just broken up with my fiancée when I went to that job fair. I was looking for a way out of there. We call this highway to hell, by the way." He nods to the staircase. "And this…" he motions to an ugly metal secu-rity door "…is the dark side. Y2K doesn't like it when we call it that, but hey…"

I feel a trickle of excitement crawl up my back and rest in the nape of my neck like a hot hand.

I like that. Hopefully at the end of the highway and on the other side is a man who can give me the answers I need about my sister.

"Behind those doors, everything changes. You read the man-ual?"

I nod.

"Good. Keep your guard up." Crede eyes me. "We've got some real personalities in this place. Here is your security badge."

I take the key card he hands me and clip it to the pocket of my scrubs.

"This is your access to…everything. Keep it on you at all times. Ready?"

I focus on his face and nod.

Crede motions for me to swipe my card. "After you. I'll meet you on the other side," he says.

I hold the card up to the reader, a red light reads the barcode, and the door buzzes open. I take a deep breath and step in far enough for the door to shut behind me. A second later I hear the same buzz, and Crede steps through. It's a glum little room. We are in a box with no windows, only the guard's cubicle, which is to my right and behind Plexiglas. I see a set of eyes staring at me through the glass.

"All personal belongings including cell phones into that basket," Crede says.

"What? Really?" I stare at him. I've worked at hospitals before, and none of them has ever separated me from my phone.

"Really," says a voice. The voice is deep, the tone flat. The source: the man with piggy little eyes and a buzz cut sitting with his arms crossed over his chest, staring at me. He is huge just sitting there, and I can't imagine what he looks like standing up. He points to a white plastic basket with my name written in Sharpie. "You get it back when you leave."

My mouth grows dry. I think of Gran lying in her hospital bed, Cal at school— "What if…there's an emergency or someone from home wants to reach me?"

"They call here, and we page you."

Pressing my lips together, I nod. Nothing bad will happen, I tell myself. I glance once more at my phone before dropping it in.

"Do you have kids?" the piggy-eyed man asks.

"Yes," I say. "An eight-year-old son."

Crede's blue eyes are bouncing back and forth between us; our conversation is clearly taking too long.

He summarizes with, "You'll be paged on the other side if there is an issue."

I glance nervously to my left, where a solid metal door leads to the patients. What if something happens to Cal or Gran?

For a split second, I wonder if I am doing the right thing. Too late, I tell myself. Too late—too far—too deep.

"Oh, yes, all right…" I fumble with my pockets, pulling out some lip balm, a five-dollar bill, and my keys. When my pockets are empty, George (I see his name tag now) eyes me suspiciously like I am hiding contraband somewhere on my body, but he buzzes us through anyway.

"Ex-military?" I ask as soon as we're out of earshot.

Crede grins and gives me a little side look. "He's actually a pretty cool guy when you get to know him."

I don't feel hopeful.

He laughs when he sees my expression. "He warms up if you bring him snacks."

"Don't we all," I comment. He rewards me with another grin. With Crede, it feels like I've just scored big in a game I don't know the rules to yet. Small wins.

We are now on the other side of Shoal Island Mental Hospital for the criminally insane, or HOTI—it seems like everything has a nickname in this place.

"This is the oldest part of the building," Crede tells me. It looks old. The ceilings are low.

"The soldiers' barracks?"

He looks impressed. "Yep…they slept in this room. It's just an antechamber to the walkway now."

I'd seen photos of the walkway online. It is essentially a glass corridor between the historic house we just left to the stocky hospital wing, rebuilt in the two thousands.

We cross the rectangular room, empty except for a couple of barrels. The air is damp and salty. I'm shivering as my eyes try to adjust to the low light. We've gone from dim to dimmer. A couple of flickering yellow bulbs hang from the ceiling. How did the soldiers live in all this wet darkness for months at a time? And then suddenly we are back in the meager Washington sunlight, standing at one end of a steel-and-glass structure—an aboveground tunnel. The floor and the ceiling are made of the same dark steel, but the rest is glass. I peer out into the dripping woods, green-and-brown leaves sticking to the outside of the glass, sprayed there by a strong wind. Below us is a thick stream, the water moving surprisingly quickly.

"That stream sustains fresh water on the island; gets pretty high, as you can see."

Our shoes echo on the grate beneath our feet. I think about how lovely it must be here in summer.

"Do the patients get to go outside often?"

"They have outside areas, but I'm sure Y2K told you about the cliff erosion. We have to be careful where we let them wander."

We reach the end of the walkway. Crede holds the door open for me. I take one last look at the canopy of green and step into a small, windowless room. There is another security door in front of us; he swipes his card and stands back, allowing me to step through first. We are officially on the other side.

"Welcome to the dark side," he says grimly. I look around in surprise. It's not what I was expecting.

It's as if we've walked onto a stage from a side door. To my left is a living room area with a couple of sofas and a large TV mounted to the wall. Ahead and to my right, a care station faces four hallways. For a moment I believe we will go undetected—two more bodies in a room of bodies, but the sight of me following Crede causes a ripple of quiet that begins at the front of the room and moves its way back. Everyone stops what they're doing to watch us. *Two, four, six, eight…* I count the group huddled around the television—they're a motley crew of mostly men; two older women stand to the rear of the group, arm in arm.

A man sitting at a card table gets up and begins to follow us; someone else makes seal noises. A woman stares from a doorway wearing a daisy headband across her forehead, one ear tucked under the elastic. Crede ignores all of it. He is the most bored human I have ever met.

My eyes scan the letters above each hallway: A, B, C...D. My fingertips tingle in anticipation. D is the only hallway with a security door.

"You won't ever be down D unless the doctor is accompanying you. I don't need to tell you why, do I?"

I shake my head.

"Good, because stupid mistakes can get you seriously hurt or easily killed."

It's cold. I know it's not my imagination when Crede pouts and makes a *brrr* sound.

Crede's hands are always moving; I watch the muscles in his forearm flex with effort as he gestures with very tan arms.

Crede gives me the C tour first. There is a large window at the end of a wide hallway. It looks out on the sound.

"This is the patient cafeteria."

The room is windowless. The skylights are the only source of natural light. A Plexiglas wall looks into the kitchen. With such great views, you'd think they'd give the patients a better view than a prep table.

The medical wing is down the hall, as well as four treatment rooms with different beach scenes painted on the walls. He's showing me around the clinic when a door marked *Hospice* opens, and Bouncer steps out. There is a basin of water propped on her hip, and it splashes over when she closes the door behind her. Her red hair is startling... Disney startling. It crosses my mind that she dyed it that way to be so... Ariel in the ocean.

I want to ask Crede if he gets it.

Bouncer greets Crede and smirks at me before disappearing through another door.

Jordyn said I was working hospice today—that means I'll be working with Bouncer. The tour continues. Behind the last door—a calm-down room, he calls it—we find two people having sex. He shuts it abruptly.

"That happens."

Right. "Are they suppo—"

"No, but we can't watch them every second, can we?" he snaps. "We turn the eye."

He takes me back to the annex.

"What about D hall?"

"What about it?"

I shrug casually.

He narrows his eyes. "You're not one of those freaks who feed on crime stories, are you?"

"No."

He studies me before nodding.

"We have five permanent patients who live in solitary year-round. Occasionally, when a patient is a danger to themselves, they'll be moved here for a time, but it's normally just those five."

I can list them by heart, have each of their names typed in the notes app on my phone, along with a link to any articles published about them. Unlike the other patients in HOTI, the ones in D hall are not here for rehabilitation. They are here for containment.

Marshal Day Monterey.

Ellis Conrad Jr.

Dalton Barellis.

Jude Fields.

Arthur Barton.

I swallow the lump in my throat. No one has to warn me how dangerous they are. One of them killed my sister.

I'd looked up all five, done my research, but there is only one I am interested in.

"Will I get the chance to sit in on their treatment?"

"Getting ahead of yourself there, new girl…"

"Sure." I shrug. "It's what I'm here for after all, isn't it? To study treatment."

"Dr. Grayson will decide what part of treatment you'll be part of."

I shrug again. Crede looks like he wants to say something but doesn't.

It's a good thing too, because the hairs on the back of my neck are doing the cancan. It is taking major self-control to act normal.

He is behind one of those doors.

"How big are their rooms?"

"Eleven by eleven. Their rooms open to a small outdoor area."

"A garden?"

He laughs. "I wouldn't say that…"

Good, I didn't want him to have a garden—or anything of beauty, for that matter. The more grave his days, the better.

At the end of the hallway is a set of double doors with frosted glass windows.

"That's Doc's office…"

Dr. Leo Grayson himself. I find it interesting that he keeps his office back here. It is quiet, and a little damp.

As Crede leads me back out the security door, I turn for one last look. There's a whip of movement. I think, at least…

Has a door opened and closed?

No. No way. I'm being paranoid.


We are about to visit the residential wing: A. Home to the patients of Shoal Island. But before we can get there, someone dies.

# 10

PAST

POLEY CAME TO collect me from the front of the station. I barely recognized her. Hair scooped back in a two-day-old French braid—she grimaced when she saw me.

*Same.*

She wore no makeup, and her black pantsuit had a couple of crusty white stains on the lapels. I guessed she didn't recognize me either because I had to stand up and wave. It took a few seconds for her eyes to register recognition. She nodded—like, oh yeah—and beckoned me over.

"I heard your grandmother is in the hospital. Sorry to hear that."

"Thanks. Has something happened with Piper's case?"

She didn't look at me; it seemed like she was trying not to.

"Detective Audrain is going to meet us there and explain."

*Okay.* I shut up and let the anxiety eat at me. She took me to a different room this time—this one had a painting of Mt. Rainier on the wall. Poley sat in a chair across from me, her legs crossed and her eyes on the linoleum. She reminded me of girls at school—unsure and on edge. Her whole vibe made me uncomfortable.

Audrain walked in a second later, carrying something. His face was grim when he set it down in front of me. I leaped to my feet.

"That belongs to Piper!" I said, "That's her bag."

"Please sit, Miss Walsh." Audrain frowned. "I need you to identify some further items for me."

I hesitated. If I sat down, he would tell me something I might not want to hear. *There's no one else to hear it, you idiot.* I sank because my knees gave way, fisting my hands in my sleeves and propping them under my chin. I couldn't look when he set the other things on the table. I heard the *plink plink* and squeezed my eyes closed. I was not in charge of what was happening. The world was happening to me, and I was not ready for it.

"Her bag was found in a trash can in Pioneer Square. A homeless woman turned it in. No phone. The last place her phone pinged was inside the movie theater. It appears she turned it off or got rid of it. Either way, we can't use it to find her if it's not on."

"*They* got rid of it," I corrected. "Piper was taken by two men named RJ and Angel. Why aren't you looking for them— or the car? Chris Dupont knows them. Ask him!"

Her mouth pulled down as she audibly sighed. "We are investigating all of the above." I felt my breath catch. If I wasn't holding on to the sides of my chair, I'd shoot out of it in frustration. Piper was just another checklist item for Poley; giving me this information was something she was assigned to do today. She didn't believe me, and she didn't care about my sister. She glances at her watch. There is a patch of dry skin at the corner of her mouth, and her eyes are bloodshot.

"Am I boring you?"

For a moment Poley looked disoriented. "What?" She narrowed her eyes like she had no idea what I was talking about.

My eyelids closed, heavy with horror. I could feel myself sweating underneath my clothes. "Was there anything in her bag?"

He cleared his throat when he sat, pulling awkwardly at his tie to loosen it. The plastic baggies crinkled when Audrain laid them in front of me.

*Don't look, don't look, don't look.*

Piper's school ID, her contact case, and a paper fortune from a fortune cookie. Evidence. My stomach dropped.

"Do you recognize these items?" Audrain asked. I nodded, my eyes swimming. Takeout from China City was a Friday night ritual. Piper was the only one who liked fortune cookies, so she'd take all three and choose the fortune she liked the most. We made it a game: Gran and I would try to guess which one was her favorite. I always won. I leaned forward to read the words on the slip of rectangular paper.

"We still don't know if she ran away, or if this is foul play—"

I opened my mouth, but he held up his hand. Would he have shushed Gran? A father? I knew things about adults: they told you what was easiest, they thought you were stupid, damaged, or both, and they swore age made them smarter than you. It didn't matter if you actually lived it—they knew more because age quantifies experience. Not personal experience—just experience. A badge of knowing-not-knowing.

"I filed a missing person's report," he says like he's offering me a cookie.

"Of course you did," I said. "She's missing. A missing child, not a person."

His wormy complexion turned pink. He was one of those guys who thought kids should speak nicely to all the adults who handled them. R.E.S.P.E.C.T.—and not the kind Aretha sang about, it was entitled. His generation favored the physical demonstrations of respect over any type of verbal truth.

"You got a smart mouth, kid."

"What about an Amber Alert? You said that kid was missing from the park—they sent one out for her…"

By the look on his face, I'd poked him in a spot he didn't like being touched. He didn't want a kid telling him how to do his job—I got it. Just like I didn't want an adult telling me what I did or didn't see.

"You didn't get the plate number. There're certain criteria to getting an Amber—"

"What are you going to do then? I have to be able to tell my grandmother something when she wakes up!"

Some humanity returned to Audrain's eyes at the mention of Gran in the hospital. He sighed. "Officers are out in the neighborhood with her picture—the one here on the ID." He tapped it through the evidence bag.

"But that's blurry. You can barely see—"

"We need some better photos of her. Can you get those to us? The sooner, the better." He leaned his head back and closed his eyes. He'd had it with me.

"What about the news?"

"Kid," he said, rubbing his temples. "Go home, get the pictures. We'll work from there."

Poley saw me out.

# 11

## PRESENT

**A SEVEN-FOOT CORPSE** stumbles naked toward me, sunken eyes staring wildly around. His bald head is spotted and gray, pink mouth gaping like a worm. I watch his skinny legs buckle as he tries to keep himself upright. There are people around—Crede, nurses, the patients watching TV—but it's me those dead eyes find and focus on. *Focus* is the wrong word; he's mildly lucid as he rushes for me. Everything moves in slow motion. His penis swings like a pendulum as he lunges, arms reaching, fingers clawed. He's going to grab on to me and pull me down with him. *Nononono!*

Someone screams, maybe it's me. And then the corpse collapses in front of me with a groan, a heap of skin and liquid as he pisses himself. The room fills quickly after that. I'm pushed against a wall as people rush from every hallway. It's chaos. If it weren't for the pill Bouncer gave me, I'd be part of the chaos. Instead, I take it all in: the wailing, the screaming, the pacing. Over the noise, three nurses bark orders back and forth. One of them, a broad middle-aged woman, kneels next to the man and pumps at his heart.

*Where is Dr. Grayson? Someone find Dr. Grayson!* A woman yanks at her graying hair with one hand, hugs her waist with the other. The group who'd been watching TV is huddled together, their expressions ranging from dark to flat. I look around for Crede and see him speaking into a walkie-talkie.

"New girl!" someone yells. I look around for the source of the voice and see a disheveled Bouncer trying to clear a space around the fallen man. "Get them out of here, clear the room!" She spreads her arms to prevent anyone from coming closer, a one-woman wall. "Everyone go to your room. Come on, guys—you know the drill!" They are pressing in without realizing it, transfixed by death. I'm aware I should be doing something, but I am also waiting for help, the trained professionals. I look for Crede's unbothered face in the sea of faces—wasn't he just standing across from me using his walkie? A man wearing an apron pushes past me, bumping into my shoulder. I don't see his face, just the back of his head as he maneuvers to Bouncer.

*Do something, Iris!*

I can't move. Maybe I don't want to move. Reality is fuzzy. Have I always been able to hear my own heartbeat when I close my eyes? When I open them everyone around me is moving— white blurs in white space. I hold my breath to make it stop, and it does.

"You coming?" It's the man in the apron. He's plain-faced with sandy hair and eyebrows. Sandy skin—not sandy, freckled—even on the back of his hands. He's managed to herd the lookie-loos out. All except one.

"Where?"

I can tell my answer is the wrong answer. He examines me closely, frowns. I've not been paying attention.

"The cafeteria…" Then, "You're in shock…"

Am I? "Who is that man?" I can't tear my eyes away. His

socked feet are closest to me, bright white like he's never walked on them.

"Was…"

"What?"

"He's dead," he says simply. "Otto. He's been in a coma for months, poor guy."

My mind is struggling to follow. I have to replay what he's said to myself before I get it. "In a coma? So, he woke up and just…died?"

He shrugs. "I have a couple trays of brownies cooling in the kitchen. They're supposed to be for after dinner, but I figure we can make an exception."

I look past him to where Bouncer and the other two nurses kneel next to the body. They are no longer trying to resuscitate the man. Bouncer wipes a hand across her forehead, spent.

Help has arrived in the form of Jordyn and two men with a stretcher. The nurses rise, making way for them, while Jordyn stands over the body, surveying it with her hands on her hips. My heart is beating so loudly in my ears that I can't hear what they're saying. *That's not him, the guy is too old to be him…*

I jump when someone touches my shoulder—it's the man in the apron.

"Come on, new girl. They got a lot to sort out."

I follow him.

An hour later, I am still sitting at a table in the patient cafeteria, a paper cup of black coffee in front of me. I don't remember eating a brownie, but the evidence is all over me in the form of crumbs and frosting. I try to dust myself off, but the chocolate smears. I feel more cognizant, but my limbs are heavy. I drink the bitter coffee, shamefaced. I don't know what happened out there, but I completely froze. It was embarrassing. I feel like an idiot. Having a job like this is all about managing crisis situations. *Good freaking job, Iris.*

The coffee scalds my tongue, and I don't care. I sip it down to the dregs and take a look around. I feel better, less in my head. Apron guy comes around with the coffeepot, and I hold my hand over the cup, shaking my head.

"I'm much better. Thank you, though, for everything. My name is Iris, by the way." I sound as disjointed as I feel.

"They call me Chef." He's in his fifties, empty face. Meager facial hair grows in reddish-blond patches around his jaw.

"It's great to meet you, Chef. Thanks for the coffee…and the brownies."

I need to pee, but I don't trust myself to stand up yet.

"Crede told me to tell you that he has a quick meeting with Dr. Grayson and will be by shortly to collect you."

"Great, I'll be ready." I force a smile. Chef studies my face, the rag he's been cleaning the tables with hanging limply in his hand. I think he's going to say something else, but he turns and walks away.

I look around. The patient cafeteria is empty aside from Chef and a small dark-haired woman who is helping him wipe down tables. I'm about to ask for a rag so I can help when Crede appears in the doorway, scanning the room like he's already annoyed. When his eyes land on me, he sighs, relieved. He crosses the room, weaving between tables. I stand up to meet him, but faster than I should, and the fishbowl wobbles like Jell-O. I sway on my feet, grabbing the back of my chair to steady myself. I'm sweating, but I feel chilled.

"Whoa! Are you okay? Easy there, slugger…"

Crede is suddenly right there, gripping my upper arm to steady me.

"I'm fine," I lie. "I stood up too fast."

His frown says that he doesn't believe me. Chef comes out of the kitchen with a bottle of water and hands it to me.

"Thank you," I say, and then I add, "for everything." Chef's face remains flat as he nods at me. He disappears back into the kitchen. Crede gives me a hard side-eye.

"Making friends, I see..."

"He was really nice."

Crede looks at me as though searching for the joke, then shakes his head. I consider facial aggressions annoying. Passive-aggressive.

"I'm behind schedule." Abruptly, he turns away and walks, expecting me to follow. I roll my eyes at his back and feel immediately childish. I run to catch up.

"Who was that man?"

"A patient," Crede says flatly. I frown, undeterred. My thoughts are running so fast I can't keep up. I try again.

"What was his name?" I know Crede mentioned it, but the memory feels hazy.

Our shoes make squeaking noises on the floor *eee ee eee ee.*

Crede looks annoyed but he says, "Otto Knott. Metastatic cancer. Seventy...we can check his blood type if you like..."

It's still too early in the relationship to tell if Crede is uncaring or efficient.

"Where will they keep his body?"

"We have a morgue."

*Yikes.*

"Will his family come to get the...body?"

"He only has one brother who is older than him and lives in Florida. He's never been up to visit as long as I've worked here. Those types normally ask us to bury them here." When he sees my face, he rolls his eyes.

"People spend their entire lives in this place. Sometimes they have no family, or family who care very little, in which case we bury them here."

"That's so sad," I say, and I mean it; a man died at my feet. I saw him leave his body. He was and then he wasn't.

"You're young."

"So are you," I shoot back.

I feel the blood rush to my face. Crede stops in his tracks and gives me a long, hard stare. I wait to be reamed out or fired, but then I realize he can't fire me—only Dr. Grayson can, and I haven't even met him yet. If I don't get to Dr. Grayson, I'll never have access to the man I really came here for.

"I'm sorry," I say quickly. "New girl nerves."

Crede is annoyed for a moment, and then his face softens. I breathe a sigh of relief when he nods. "It's been a rough morning for everyone."

I nod eagerly, and we start walking again. We reach the annex—a half circle with the care station against the flat side—and it's been cleared of Otto Knott. I marvel at how quickly someone's death can be cleaned up. An hour and it looks like he was never there. A lifetime of conflicts, love, and thoughts swept into a body bag. I think of Piper. My heart hurts.

"Hey!"

I jump. Crede is zoned in on the care station. I follow his eyes. It's a bird, it's a plane, it's Bouncer!

"Where is everyone?" Crede is speaking louder than necessary, or maybe it's the echo.

"Hey yourself."

She's been crying, and there's blood on her scrubs. I don't remember there being any blood on Otto…

Crede repeats himself. "Where is everyone?"

Bouncer stares at him.

"Where do you think?" she says finally. "Getting them settled down."

The sound of chimes causes us all to jump, and I laugh out loud. He sighs, looks at his Apple Watch, then at me. "Guess you won't be working hospice."

A phone rings behind the nurses' station. Crede looks pointedly at Bouncer. "Why don't you show Iris the filing system until I get back?"

"Wait, where are you going?" Bouncer calls after him. "I don't have time for this…"

"Boss wants to see me."

That ends her round of questioning. But I have a question for her: namely, what the hell did she give me, because it sure as hell wasn't Xanax? Crede walks to the only hallway blocked by a door and uses his key card to open it.

When he's gone, she doesn't look at me. Instead, she turns and disappears behind the door to what I presume is the records room. The door isn't all the way closed. I push it open and follow her into a brightly lit records room. It's a small room, gloomy and filled with filing cabinets. Two windows look out at the nurses' station, their sills lined with small religious statues: Mary, holding a red heart in her hands, eyes to the sky in anguish, a wooden cross with a barely bloody Jesus, a stone statue of Buddha, and a couple of porcelain crosses that look handmade.

She examines me a moment, her face contorted in annoyance. I can tell that she doesn't want to be left in charge of me. I was supposed to be in hospice today, out of the way. The resignation on her face is painful to look at.

Regardless, she shows me the filing system and teaches me how to search for records and then check them out of the system.

"Were you Otto's nurse?"

She shrugs. "Everyone is everyone's nurse here. We're short-staffed."

I stand in the doorway, propping the door open with my body. Bouncer stands at a desk, facing me.

"Yeah…" She looks over the monitor of a large desktop computer. "He's been comatose for months," she says finally. "It was like taking care of a plant."

My reaction is automatic. "Wow, okay…"

She glares at me. "You got a problem, new girl?"

I sigh. "I got a lot of problems, Bouncer, but you're not one of them." I'm not going to let some power-tripping nurse ruin my plan. I don't confront her about the pill. The last thing I want is to make enemies on day one.

We're in a stare-off. She breaks first, her expression suddenly morphing into something else. She has the alertness of a dog watching a squirrel. I follow the direction of her gaze, and three things become obvious at once: Leo Grayson is standing in the annex, Leo Grayson looks great, Leo Grayson is looking at me. It's hard to break eye contact with him—I know logically that I can, but I won't. I'm being cataloged, which is fantastic—it's according to plan, I remind myself. I try to blockade the emotion, doubling down on my facial uniform of: amicable… eager…attentive. I'm not here to be impressed by Leo Grayson, but I know from experience that a man of his educational stature will require some fawning.

I'm free to study his profile. Dark hair—too thick to be fair—nice nose, a neatly trimmed beard. He's tall but not too tall. Shrinks bore me. Their sensible, free-spirited clothes bore me; he's wearing a gray zip-up hoodie over his scrubs and white Air Force 1's—same thing as the rest of us except with cool shoes. He notices me checking out his feet and grins. I tear the remaining crescent of fingernail off my thumb. He's cute for an old guy…smirky.

Growing up, I could tell people liked Piper more than they liked me. She provided the nutrients people needed to survive: warmth, light, and energy, whereas I was a rain cloud. At HOTI, I am Piper, not Iris—the good half. With the doctor's attention still secured, I shrug and smile shyly.

The security door to D hall opens, and Crede steps out. Red-faced and sweaty, he walks over to the small crowd and stands in front of Dr. Grayson. They exchange words. I only see the back of Grayson's head, but Crede's expression is pinched. They both turn to look at me at the same time. Crede breaks away

from Grayson and walks in my direction. Grayson walks back
to D hall, disappearing behind the door. I feel delusional, obsessed, desperate. I just watched a man die, and I might have
been drugged by a coworker. My legs still feel shaky, and my
temples are starting to throb. My need to see and touch Cal—
to make sure he's okay—is choking me.

My smile feels rigid as Crede approaches. "Since your hospice training is canceled, Dr. Grayson has asked to meet with
you," Crede says.

I fill my lungs with the astringent-rich air and nod. I should
be elated, but instead I feel like a walking cactus.

"Great," I say. "Lead the way…"

By the time we reach the security door to D, I am sweating, using every affirmation in my therapy tool belt to keep
it together.

He chose me for this position, but I chose him first—not because of his knowledge of the human mind, or because being
his intern could open doors for my career. I chose Dr. Grayson
because he is the only one who has access to my sister's killer.
Her killer is behind the secure doors of unit D. *You can do this,
of course you can.*

Crede swipes his card, and there is a loud click as the lock
swings left.

D is unremarkable. Six white doors—three to a side—and
stock gray carpet. The doors are equipped with small windows
for doctors to check on their patients. There is a curtain over
each one to offer privacy of course, but I don't know how I
would feel being under the constant surveillance of one person, like a lab rat. I fall back to study each door—to feel if I *feel*
anything. Would I recognize his face? I remember him vaguely:
button-down shirts, pressed pants, and a weak chin.

Crede looks over his shoulder, impatient, and I run to catch
up. At the end of the hallway, we reach a more formal wooden
door that looks like it belongs in a house, not a psychiatric unit.

He stops to face me. "I'll be back to collect you in thirty..." His voice is chipper. "Make it count."

His words, meant to be encouraging, ring ominous.

I watch him go, fear pounding in my ears. This is it, just me and the boss now. Ready or not...

I raise my knuckles and rap twice, holding my breath until I hear him call for me to come in. My stomach lurching, I turn the knob and step inside.

He's sitting at his desk when I walk in. He stands when he sees me, holding out his hand, and I grasp it, taking in the moment. I am shaking hands with what Gran calls a fancy man: handsome, intelligent, and—according to the internet— wealthy, thanks to his family. He has the relaxed air of a man who is used to being around people.

He greets me warmly, grasping my hand in two of his and looking me in the eyes. His hair is thick and brown, and it curls up at the ends. There are threads of gray near his temples and smile lines around his eyes, but he is alarmingly youthful. The expression in his heavyset eyes is playful.

"Miss Walsh, it's so good to meet you. You're having one hell of a first day."

I've read all the articles about him, combed through all the professional papers he published. He's brilliant. I have to remind myself that I am not his patient, nor his work-study, nor his fan. I am not even really here to learn from him; it was a mere plus, the cherry on top of an experience. I have nothing to be intimidated by.

"Dr. Grayson, it is such an honor. At the risk of sounding unprofessional, I am a huge fan of your work. You have to hear that all the time—sorry, I am fangirling."

He absorbs all of this with an amused grin. We blush at the same time, and I look away as Dr. Grayson clears his throat. "Please sit..." He motions to one of two armchairs facing his desk.

The smell of a recently extinguished cigarette lingers in the air. I look for the evidence, and there it is, curling near the ceiling in a nicotine stratus cloud. A smoking psychotherapist? Very noir. As I lower myself into the armchair, I realize I must be grinning, because he looks at me pointedly and says, "Do you want one?"

I shake my head. "I'm fond of the smell but not of cancer."

He laughs, caught but uncaring. He sighs, leaning back in his chair, studying me. Like most of the male therapists I've worked with, he has relaxed body language.

"My peers see smoking as an unresolved addiction."

"And how do you see it?" I ask.

He looks at me in surprise. "Like an unresolved addiction." We both laugh.

"Iris Walsh." He says my name again.

His desk is one of those great big mahogany antiques—it would be imposing, except the only thing that sits atop it is a closed MacBook.

I'd provided my transcripts (which are excellent), two letters of recommendation from graduate professors, and a hundred and twenty volunteer hours at the teen counseling center.

I wait politely for him to go on, my hands sweating. I've gone to great lengths to conceal who I'm related to, writing about the addiction in my family instead of the tragedy.

I don't want the trauma of losing my sister to overlap with my ability to advance here. There were probably dozens of candidates, some of whom were Ivy-League-educated and already publishing articles. Not that I'm complaining.

"I know most of you go by your last names here, but I go by my first. Please call me Leo. I hate the doctor bit."

I have no intention of calling him Leo, but I nod.

"You referenced your young son in your letter. Where is he now?" He glances up at me.

"At school. He's eight years old and quite brilliant." I can't keep the pride from my voice. Cal is that sweet spot in my life, the consistent joy giver. SweeTart, Sour Patch Kid, Skittle—his nicknames are every sort of candy. We'd grown up together, my dark-haired son and I—and it's fair to say that we'd lost our childhoods as a direct cause of each other. I will never regret him, but I fear that someday he will look back on what I wasn't able to give him, and he will wish his mother were someone else.

I clear my throat in an attempt to defog the emotion from my voice.

"I was pretty young when I became a mom," I said. I know what he's thinking. Most people are shocked to hear I have an eight-year-old son. "My grandmother helped a lot, and I was able to graduate and attend college." This is the part I dread talking about; there are always pitying looks. People of the older generation applaud how I turned my life around, as if having a baby young is the same as substance addiction.

"Hey, that's pretty great. Taking care of a little person and going to school is no small feat." He says it slowly and deliberately, like he means it.

I get squirmy at the compliment. Seldom is the uphill climb toward education honored if it belongs to that of a young, unwed mother. Most people I've encountered present the attitude that getting an education is the least you can do after you've burdened society with the fruit of your womb.

"My mom did my laundry until I graduated from college, so I'm not sure how you managed all of that…"

I laugh, unprepared for that bit of self-deprecation. His eyes light up at the sound of my laughter, and it feels nice to pull a reaction from a handsome man. But there is a feeling bristling behind the nice—something like déjà vu…

"There wasn't much time for self-indulgence," I say. "The hard work came first. Now I get to pursue the things I've been waiting to pursue." That is the part I practiced. I always end my speech with a tight-lipped smile—relaxed but capable.

"I like that."

I blush even though I am proud of myself for managing the last eight years. "I think we all do," I say and then think better of it. "Well, most of us," I correct myself, dropping my chin.

Again, he laughs. He has very nice eyes, the type that warm or cool you, depending on his mood.

He turns serious then, the transition from friendly to professional jarring me a bit. "How will you manage being away from him, especially as much as this job requires?"

The heater kicks on, the sound reminding me of Gran's old apartment. I avoid the urge to shiver. I'm prepared for this question. This has been the most difficult part of the decision-making process for Cal and me. When I told Cal I'd be spending three nights of every week at the hospital, he'd grown teary-eyed, but nodded a moment later, trying to be brave. He reminds me so much of myself—the need to please, to not be a burden. I'd hugged him close with tears in my own eyes, reminding myself that it wouldn't be forever.

*"We'll make every second count when we are together, okay?"*

He liked that.

"Cal and I discussed it before I applied. We agreed that for our future this was the best step for me. He's with my grandmother when he's not with me, and there is no one I trust more."

It's Gran's age I'm worried about. She pretends that everything is fine, but I've noticed some pretty serious changes in the last year. She's in the hospital now. I won't fool myself into thinking she'll be here forever, which is why I am here in the first place, to give her answers before...she's not here.

"Wonderful," he says. "We're happy you've joined the team. I think you're going to be a great fit." He folds his hands on the desktop, and I sense that our time is up. Smiling dutifully, I nod. We stand at the same time, looking like a choreographed television show. This is the part where he extends his hand for one more shake before he sends me off. As his hand engulfs mine and I'm congratulating myself on how well things went, he says, "There's something very familiar about you. I can't place it…maybe a celebrity doppelganger…"

I hold my breath because if you hold your breath while looking at someone your expression remains frozen. *You don't look like her anymore.* Because of the lack of media attention and public outcry, very few people have ever heard of Piper's case. It's a weak assurance and entirely untrue, but the chances that he'll make the connection are slim. It takes what seems like forever before he sighs in defeat. "I'll have to think about it."

"You do that." It comes out more flirtatiously than I meant, and I blush under his gaze.

I certainly hope he doesn't.

I hustle to get out of there, Dr. Grayson's eyes on my back.

My buddy Crede is waiting for me outside. "Lunch is next," he says with a tight smile. "Though we only have thirty minutes left of it…"

I give him an apologetic look.

"It's fine." He sighs. "Today was tater tots. I hate tater tots. Dinner is more relaxing anyway."

# 12

PAST

**THE DAY AFTER** they questioned me at the station, Detectives Audrain and Poley made a visit to Gran's recovery room. I met them in the lobby, and we shuffled in the room together, hospital badges stuck to our clothes, heads at a respectful angle. I blinked in surprise. She was propped by a stack of pillows, glaring at Audrain and Poley—tiny and mighty.

Her hair was combed, and she was wearing a shade of lipstick I'd never seen before. No doubt she'd sweet-talked some nurse into letting her borrow it. Gran felt naked without lipstick.

While they reintroduced themselves to Gran, I parked myself in a chair in the corner of the room to supervise. I didn't trust Audrain as far as I could throw him. I thought the detectives kept it together pretty well when she told them what incompetent, prejudiced, half-asleep assholes they were.

"Piper has been missing for seventy-two hours." She folded her hands gracefully on top of the covers, her voice cold and firm as she gave the news. Everyone knew what law enforcement said about missing kids—you had to find them within the first forty-eight hours, or chances were, you weren't going to find them. Gran continued. "Any type of physical evidence and leads you may have gotten on that first day are gone." She let that sink in. "My granddaughter told you what happened, and you refused to believe her. What are you doing to find her?"

It was now clearly Audrain's turn to speak. Gran pressed her lips together and resumed her glare.

"What we have," he said, "is a handbag, and five seconds of grainy surveillance video from a bank. What we don't have are names, witnesses, or proof. We can't confirm that she didn't get into that car willingly." Audrain looks at me. "Sisters don't tell each other everything…"

"Are you a sister?" I asked.

"We dusted the bag and everything we found inside for prints. None of the prints on the items are in any police database."

"So you're saying the men who kidnapped Piper are criminals you've yet to arrest before now?"

"Mrs. Walsh—"

"Miss," Gran interrupts him.

"Right, *Miss* Walsh," he corrects himself. "We've opened an investigation, and we have detectives on the ground as we speak. They're canvassing the neighborhood with her photo—"

"What about the ferry? They could have taken her on there—she might have used a bathroom. There have to be cameras on those things…" Gran's hands were shaking, and she noticed it the same time I did. Unclasping them, she reached for her water. Before I could stand to help, Poley jumped up to get it for her. Handing the cup to Gran, she stayed by her bedside, blocking my view.

"We're checking on that, right now actually. I'm expecting to hear something back within the hour. Our officers are also interviewing sex offenders in the area. We've tapped your home phone in the event a ransom call comes in."

"How can I answer ransom calls if I'm here?" she snapped.

Poley nodded like she'd already thought out the answer. "We have someone near the line until we can get Iris back to your apartment."

"Iris? You expect my traumatized fifteen-year-old grand-daughter to negotiate with kidnappers for ransom?"

"Gran," I said closing my eyes, "I want to. Besides, I know their voices."

Gran stared at me but didn't say anything. She seemed to be shrinking in the bed, getting further and further away.

"We've got everything under control." Audrain looked at Poley, who looked at me. I nodded. I was getting the feeling that they were saying what they needed to say to keep Gran calm.

Poley made a sound that might indicate sympathy. "What we need from you is to rest. We might have a lot more questions in the coming hours, and you should be on your game—not exhausted. For Piper..."

"You've had a health scare, Mrs. Walsh. We're trying to be conscious of that. Also your doctors have threatened us," she admitted with a small smile.

Gran seemed fine with her answer. Fine enough—she was tired. She always made a point of choosing her battles wisely. But that didn't stop her from pushing right into the next question.

"That kid who arranged the meeting Piper had with those boys, Dupont, have you looked more into him?"

Audrain and Poley exchanged a look. "We have. He came into the station with his mother this morning. He claims the conversation they had at school on Friday was about money Piper owed him for weed."

"That's a lie!" I blurted. "I was right there listening to the whole thing. He never said anything about weed. Neither did my sister."

"Was anyone else present other than you when they had that discussion?"

"No… We were leaving school, walking out of the building. He was tailing us home trying to get Piper to meet up with a guy."

Audrain cleared his throat. Still sitting, he said, "Dupont claims that he never arranged to meet Piper at the mall, though he remembers seeing you both there. He said you weren't with anyone that he could tell."

"And you just believe him? That's it? What about Colby Crimball?"

"He has a solid alibi, and his parents have hired an attorney…"

"Why would they hire an attorney if his alibi is so solid?" I shot back.

Audrain's hands clenched. "Why don't you leave that up to us?" I could hear the implication of *child* in his voice.

Gran was released from the hospital two days after my sister officially became a missing person. She wasn't well—you could see it in her eyes, though she was making a show of trying to be. Betty Walsh was effortless in the way that she never had to think about being herself, she just always was: student, stripper, librarian, and grandmother—in that order—but she would have done it out of order too and laughed about it. She liked the color pink, could never find her glasses, and had a sharp sense of humor. She'd been my and Piper's advocate for years, barking at old dogs in a broken system. People respected her.

Once she was discharged, the hospital made a big to-do about wheeling her to the door. An orderly waited with us in the pickup area, holding on to the handles of Gran's wheelchair as if we were going to steal it. No one was there to pick us up, which depressed me. Not even for myself, but for Gran who had no one but a crappy teenager to take care of her. Piper would have done a better job of it; she did granddaughterly things with Gran: walks, shows, and Christmas crafts even when we outgrew them. I was the sour, angry one. It should have been me who was gone. Regardless, I'd done my best to get everything ready for her, like they told me.

We climbed into a taxi, neither of us speaking. The cab driver was nice, even helping me walk Gran up the stairs to our apartment.

Gran clutched a plastic bag of pill bottles to her chest as I unlocked the front door, that's all I would let her carry. She hesitated before going inside; right away I knew what she was feeling. It wasn't home without Piper…it wasn't anything without Piper. I waited with her while she grappled with it; eventually she shuffled inside. We were lost.

The first month I refused to go to school. Gran needed me at home. I couldn't look at those people and pretend I cared about things like grades and homecoming—or what they were saying about me and Piper. And they *were* saying things. I didn't tell Gran about the rumor Dupont started, because she was already obsessed with him. Besides, the rumor was boring—sluts, we were both sluts. How original. According to Dupont, we turned tricks on the weekend for oxy. It was a smear campaign that left a trail of lies for police to follow. A social worker came to our apartment to do a welfare check and referred to my sister and me as foster children. Gran called her a useless fucking *dumple*—her word for idiot—and made her leave.

Gran recovered from her ordeal in her recliner, a glass of water and the house phone always in arm's reach. There were no ransom notes or calls. Though she did a lot of work to find my sister from that chair: making calls, making threats, and making threatening calls. Dupont was the source of her anger. Without the other two, he was the only three-dimensional person for her to hate. I had nightmares about him crawling in my window to kill me, a filthy beanie on his head. And then there was that prick, Colby Crimball, who claimed he wasn't even at the movies the day Piper was taken. His brother, Matt, was his alibi. Ironic, since Matt was the one who was supposed to meet us. The Crimballs threw their attorney at the cops over and over. Dupont's mother wouldn't talk to them or let them near her son.

The other two guys—RJ and Angel—according to police, they just didn't exist. Like Gran predicted, by the time detectives questioned employees of the theater, not only had the security footage been taped over, but the guy working the ticket counter only remembered there being two men—the ones who'd later stood in line at the concession stand. They'd used cash to buy the soda and popcorn, and no, he couldn't give a good description of either of them because he was high that day. The cups with their fingerprints were inevitably thrown away. There were no cameras in the alley where the dark sedan idled, though police did confirm the broken exit door they used to leave. The footage of the Ford Taurus driving past the trash can where Piper's bag was found was not conclusive evidence. I was all they had.

They asked me to come to the station to have composite sketches made of the men, RJ and Angel. I knew realistically their names were not RJ and Angel, but that didn't stop me from repeating them to myself over and over. The air in the hulking glass building felt charged by all the bad things that were happening. Everyone was still looking for the kid who'd gone missing. I tried not to feel resentful of the attention her case was getting, or that her case was making everyone too tired to focus on my sister's.

I thought the sketches were pretty good. We left it at that. They showed a picture of Piper on the six o'clock news. I'd given Audrain and Poley her school photo, and now that I was staring at it on a TV screen, I knew she'd be furious with my choice. The depth of hatred for myself was so strong I began to cry—and then sob. Not knowing what else to do, Gran sat with me on the couch, rubbing circles on my back. I'd failed her again. I couldn't get anything right. The tip line blew up—mostly it was people spotting me one place or another. I dyed my hair black, wore my glasses instead of contacts so I wouldn't mess with the investigation. I was living some shitty noir film with no plot. My grandmother couldn't even look at me; it was like she was mad at me for not looking like Piper. I was mad at her for wanting me to. Another month passed before police found the footage. Although it wasn't the footage we were expecting.

It was a dark blue Ford Taurus driving away from the ferry terminal and stopping at a trash can a few blocks away. The man who got out and deposited something in the trash can matched my description of Angel. The trash can was where the homeless woman said she found Piper's bag. The plates on the car—stolen. I watched the footage at the station, my fingernails digging into palms, hungry to see a glimpse of my sister, but it was Angel's grainy image I saw next. I recognized him. "That's him! That's Angel," I said, not taking my eyes off the screen.

"We think they traded her off to someone else at the ferry. We're running the plates of every car that drove on or off that day. That could take a while. In the meantime, this is who we need to find." Audrain tapped the screen where Angel was running back to the driver's side door. The car drove out of frame four seconds later.

"How are *we* going to do that?" Gran, who had been quiet until now, stood up to face the detectives. Her body had been growing stronger every day. She no longer used a walking stick, and she'd put on some weight. In the evenings, she drove to random neighborhoods all over Queen County, putting up missing posters of Piper. She walked into a homeless encampment, perched on the side of the freeway with bags of takeout and soda, and handed her poster out there too.

"This is an open investigation," Poley assured her. "We're looking…"

Regardless of their promises, my sister's case went cold. After months of searching, every lead having gone dry, tips having dried up, we heard from Poley and Audrain less and less. Those were the hardest months—of not knowing. The roller coaster rumbling up and down: she's fine/she's not fine/she's fine/she's not fine. Gran and I drifted apart during those months. We crossed paths politely with "good-mornings" and "good-nights." I went back to school as an only child. She got a raise and a promotion. We lived, though barely.

We didn't hear from Piper for another year.

# 13

## PRESENT

**SEPTEMBER BRINGS THE** last days of cloudless blue sky. The seagulls and tourists are relentless in their pursuit of food and pecking. The last push of summer means the ferries are always packed. During my first week at Shoal Island, I rely on adrenaline and positive thinking, which is the new trend on Instagram. I'm certain the influencers are going to positive us all to death, but it's through their tutelage that I convince myself I'm tough enough to power through. What I am is underslept and overcaffeinated. To compensate I wear concealer under my eyes and drink more water. The Wi-Fi on the island is spotty depending on the weather, and calls are near impossible. The anxiety of not being able to take calls takes its toll on me at night. I dream of Piper when I sleep in the dorms; when I'm at home I dream of the island. No matter where I sleep I always wake up in a cold sweat.

"I had a dream you never came home like Aunt Piper and Gran and me had to go to the island to find you…"

I turn to my son, frowning. That would be terrible, my little boy around criminally dangerous humans. I try not to let the horror reach my face.

I'm only sixteen years older than he is. I don't have the whole parenting thing down yet. Older, wiser women tell me I never will. My fear at eight years old had been finding my mother dead; my only comfort during that period of time was the solid body of my sister: hugging it, hitting it, or just visually seeing it—I wasn't picky. "Come here…" I hold my arms open. He takes the hug somewhat hesitantly at first and then my boy melts in. He needed that.

"I'm only a ferry away. Four nights home, three nights on Shoal."

When I'm home for my four nights off, Cal never leaves my side. I wake up in the early hours of the morning to find him curled against me. It reminds me of the days Piper and I shared a bed in yellow-yellow. I sleep better when he's there, but guilt wraps itself around every second of every day.

On the ferry I check emails and pay bills while I still have Wi-Fi. Once I walk through the doors of Shoal, my time belongs to the hospital. *Understaffed* is a word I hear no less than three times a day as I am passed around. My job, Crede informs me, is to help wherever I can. Rush-rush-rush becomes my new language.

During that first week, I am kept away from the patients. I'm instructed not to speak to them unless they speak to me—which I find particularly odd. It's not unheard of, however, for interns to turn into glorified maids, childcare givers, or pet walkers. During my undergrad internship, the case worker I shadowed had me vacuum his car and clean his desk drawers. It was par for the course. I pay my dues and don't complain. Sometimes Crede will collect me from whatever I'm doing, only to deposit me into another mess of a situation.

During my second week of training, I work the dark side with a nurse named Janiss. Janiss is in her early fifties, give or take a few years. She has pointy features centered in the middle of a wide face, and she wears her hair in a bob, stiff with hairspray. I haven't known her for more than five minutes when she tells me that she's from the same town as serial killer Warren Leslie Forrest with pride in her voice.

I know of Warren Leslie Forrest—the war veteran turned serial killer.

She tells me with conviction that Warren Leslie Forrest is why she became a nurse. I don't ask her to expound because she stops suddenly and I almost run into the back of her.

"We have a resident artist." I follow her gaze to the twenty feet of wall space between A and B hall. There's maternal pride on her face as she studies the mural, then glances at me to see what I think. I'm impressed, I am. In the chaos of Otto Knott dying at my feet, I hadn't noticed it; but now that I am standing in front of jelly-toned colors, I am transfixed.

Six white rabbits pose along a backdrop of dark green cabbages, dead purple wolves hang limply from their mouths. The wolves are small like rats. Their bulging tongues loll out of their mouths out like eggplant. I shiver: a grape jelly massacre.

"He's really good."

I mean it. I examine the cabbages behind the carnivorous rabbits; there are faces in the leaves: horrible scrunched little faces with vampire teeth. Gran dragged me to the Seattle Art Museum every chance she got. She got as excited about art as Cal did about museums: between the two of them constantly feeding me information I was a hesitant art/sea life enthusiast.

"What's his name?"

"Peter."

She tells me cheerfully, like we're chatting on a sidewalk instead of a hospital. "He studied art in New York, even had his pieces in a gallery once. Older guy," she says. "But not that old…"

I worked dinner shifts at the restaurant with a guy named

Chris who did casework during the day; he told me stories like that all the time: businessmen, artists, moms who ended up in places like this. The mental health crisis didn't show favorites. People snapped.

"How did Peter come to be at HOTI?"

Janiss draws back like I've slapped her.

In my experience it was normal to ask about patients, welcome even. Employees, especially in a place like this, needed to know what they were up against: but Janiss gives me a dirty look.

"There's a cabbage for each of the emotions," she continues. "The basic ones, anyway—"

For a moment I think she didn't hear me, but there's a tightening around her lips that wasn't there a second before. When she won't make eye contact, I know I've offended her.

I'm so immersed in my thoughts about offending her, I don't hear what she says next.

"I'm sorry," I say. "Can you say that again?" She looks really angry now.

"He's a wonderful artist, he shouldn't only be known for *that…*"

"Right," I say. I'm trying to choose my words carefully. "I didn't mean to imply anything. It just seems wise to understand each patient's history as I'll be working with them…"

I know I've made a mistake right away. Her face does aerobics before it lands on disgust.

"Dr. Grayson had him do it as part of his therapy. He calls this piece 'Vegan.'" Her tone is noticeably chillier than a moment before.

"Vegan, he's a funny guy."

Janiss scratches her elbow, giving Peter's wall one last look over.

"He taught the art classes—well I guess I should say teaches, but he's scaled back to a few sessions a week…"

I'm afraid to ask the wrong question, but luckily she goes on.

"He's sixty-eight and says he doesn't have the energy any-more. Of course we all know that's not the case, he's spry as my forty-year-old brother, they're both artists, though Har-vey works in wood." She prattles on as we walk back to the care station.

Little beads of sweat sit like pearls along her hairline. I look up at the skylight; bracken light struggles through the dirty glass. Without windows the area feels constricting and cavern-ous at the same time: like a warehouse.

"So you were saying that Dr. Grayson had Peter paint the mural as part of his therapy..."

"You're being nosy," she says.

I lift my eyebrows. "I wasn't trying to be. I'm—"

"Sure."

The nearest purple wolf looks confused. It seems that dur-ing the last minutes of its life, it's considering why it allowed itself to be eaten by a rabbit.

Without the dead body and chaotic panic, I am able to take a better look at the care station.

Painted in hues of beige, the care station is circular, a curved desk under recessed lights. Patients are able to walk up and speak to the nurses across the desk. Nurses have to walk through a half door to get inside. "Welcome to the care station," Janiss says coldly. She's put out with me after my comment. She lurches into a scripted greeting, no longer making eye contact. I fol-low, taking careful mental notes on everything she shows me. I want to do the job well—above well. I need everyone to agree that I'm an excellent employee if I want to impress Dr. Grayson enough to be allowed around the D hall patients.

"We have a lot of patients to take care of with a lot of vary-ing needs. When you work at the care station, your priority is to be alert and available without judgment—" She gives me a dragging look.

"They're all capable of serious violence. To forget that is to get yourself injured or killed." She lowers her voice. "The females are the worst. Women make the worst patients, and you can't tell me different."

She waits to see what I say. When I don't reply, she continues.

"There is no explaining how or why, they just do. We have fifty patients at the forensic unit. The men cause violent crimes on the outside. The women cause the violent crimes inside. I've wrestled with more women than men."

Janiss doesn't seem to be in the same rush as everyone else. For the next hour I'm shown how to barricade myself into the nurses' station while Janiss shares details of her knee surgery. I learn about her conjunctivitis and chronic headaches in one sentence, and her strained relationship with her mother (who has body dysmorphia) in the next.

There's an emergency alarm button and a lock switch you can use to lock the doors to the file room. Strangely, Janiss shares the majority of the information within earshot of patients. She doesn't expect anything bad will happen, here in this bad-happening place.

The staff cafeteria is serving vegetable soup and grilled cheese for lunch. I grab a tray and get in line behind a group of two men and two women. I recognize one of the women, a nurse, from the dark side. She has tattoos up and down her forearms and one tiny heart behind her ear. I wait my turn for the tongs, looking around for an empty seat while the line chugs along. So far Jordyn, Bouncer and Crede have not shown up for lunch. I'm keeping my eyes open for Dr. Grayson too, but that seems more far-fetched. I turn back to the group in front of me. One of the men is wearing a uniform with a security badge clipped to the front of it. The guy with the badge looks over his shoulder at me, making a point to stare longer than necessary. My body freezes and my heart pounds. *He's just curious about the new girl*, I tell myself. *He does not know who you are or why you're here.* I smile at him and he turns away. I was being paranoid.

When it's their turn at the food they goof around, snapping the tongs at each other before taking two sandwiches apiece. The nurse with the tattoos tells the other three to behave, and they move away reluctantly. When it's my turn I take half a sandwich, snatch a container of soup from the warmer, and scoot to the rear of the room, where a couple seats have become available. I suddenly feel too hot to be hungry; cafeteria anxiety never went away, did it? My kid probably handles this sort of thing better than I do.

That's the way lunch goes for the first two weeks of my three days on/four days off schedule. Walk in, grab a tray, choose a foil-wrapped sandwich from one of the labeled rows, grab a side, ignore the bottled water for a sweaty cup of lemonade. After that, I'd report back to the dark side. I rarely saw Dr. Grayson, who spent his days treating patients in D. Sometimes I'd see someone from the kitchen wheeling the meal trays to the security door, at which point Bouncer or Dr. Grayson would take over. There were always six covered dishes on the cart—one for each patient and one for Dr. Grayson. I watch the meal cart with a different type of hunger, the dirty dishes the most appealing part.

The end of my training arrives quietly. If Gran were well, she would have made me a special dinner and dessert, maybe even suggested we go out somewhere with linen napkins. That night I put on sweats and one of Piper's old T-shirts. I dig an ancient box of Hamburger Helper from the back of the pantry, and Cal and I eat by candlelight to make it fancy. I have much to be happy about; the temporary success of securing the job and keeping it puts me one step closer to my goal.

"Your shirt has a cuss word on it," he says between bites.

"Yeah," I say. "It belonged to your aunt Piper."

He studies the shirt more carefully.

"Did she go to that lady's concert or something?"

I drop my chin to look at an upside-down Britney Spears. On it is the infamous snake picture from the MTV Music Awards above the lyrics: "It's Britney, bitch!" Before she got religious, Piper liked to steal things. The items were of teenage variety: sunglasses, boyfriends, lip gloss, the occasional necklace. The T-shirt was her last hoorah before the youth group bonfire, during which repentant teenagers burned things that caused them to sin. I saved Britney from the flames, plucking her out of the burn pile and hiding her in the laundry room.

"Nah, we never had the money to do stuff like that. She just really liked her music. She wanted to be a singer too."

"Cool, can I wear it?"

I eye him over my water goblet. "You want to wear your mother's T-shirt? Isn't that uncool or something?"

"It's not my mother's T-shirt, it's my aunt's…" he counters.

My mouth goes dry. Kid, you have no idea.

"I have some things of hers that you can have if you like…"

I eye the bottle of wine Gran keeps above the fridge. I'm not really a wine girl, but tonight I am thirsty for it.

"I'll show you after dessert," I say. "Why don't you go take your shower while I wash the dishes."

"We don't have any dessert. I've eaten every last cookie and popsicle in the house, and you haven't done groceries in for-ever."

"Take your shower and you can find out…"

"I feel like this is a trick."

As soon as he closes the bathroom door, I drag a chair to the fridge and retrieve the dusty bottle of house red. I pour my-self a glass and grab two bags of peanut M&M's from my se-cret stash. By the time Cal is in his pajamas, I've polished off one glass and my head is spinning. I pour the rest of the bottle down the drain. No matter how much I want to, I can't drink away the facts. I don't want my days at home with Cal to be fogged over with alcohol.

We spend the weekend goofing off at home, playing Xbox and watching movies. I try not to think about the fact that I won't be there for Gran's first day home, or the fact that I'm not going to see Cal for three consecutive nights. It is going to be hard for all of us. A nurse will see her through the transition day. After that, Billy is going to take care of her during the day, and the neighbors are pitching in to drive her to and from her physical therapy. *Check, check, check!* Cal will start taking the bus home from school now that Gran is home, and one of Gran's neighbors—a wiry, middle-aged lady named Roshana who owns her own yoga studio—will walk him to the house, check on Gran, and text me an update about both of them. Mary-Ann is making their meals and dropping by every night to eat with them. I have all eyes on Gran, but they aren't my eyes, and for that I feel guilt. I should be the one taking care of her, she deserves that after all the years she's taken care of me.

On Monday morning I hug Cal at the front door and wave to Mary-Ann before I lower myself into my car. Focus now, cry later. I chug water from my bottle, my eyes glazing over. Pretending to be fine is exhausting. I park in a lot nearby and walk to the ferry terminal, wondering for the hundredth time if I'm doing the right thing. I stare at my hands until it's time to get off the ferry and switch to the water taxi. The day is colder than it looks. Everyone stands huddled together on the dock waiting to be let on. No one speaks to anyone or makes eye contact; it's entirely too early and too cold to be friendly.

The drenched air pierces my parka as soon as I step off the water taxi. I smile woodenly at the captain, who ignores me. It's a windy day; the water is choppy. Bouncer's face is green as she gets off behind me.

My backpack is heavy, stuffed with three days of necessities. *Three days!* I focus on the guy in front of me, who has an egg sandwich in one hand and a cigarette in the other. The smell ignites a handful of memories: my mother frying eggs wearing only a stretched-out white T-shirt. The ash from her cigarette falling into the pan as she burns our dinner. I turn my face away and let the wind do its thing, breathing the fresh sea air to anchor myself to the present. My sister's body has never been found. Seven years after she disappeared, my mother filed the paperwork to have her legally declared dead. When Gran found out, she threw her coffee mug against the living room wall, brown droplets streaming against the basic white paint like muddy water. If Piper were declared dead, no one would be looking for her. My mother had done it to hurt us when we wouldn't let her see Cal.

The most I can give Gran at this point is answers. It's what I owe her after losing Piper. It's the least I can give Cal after losing his mother.

# 14

PAST

**OUR MOTHER WAS MEAN**, she didn't feel bad about it either. Her words hit harder than her hands; we liked it best when she was sleeping. She hated us with the most intensity right after a breakup. That's when she'd detail her resentment about our existence. I wanted a son and God gave me two girls, that's how I know he hates me.

We made ourselves as small as she needed us to be.

When she was high, usually passed out on the brown sofa we tiptoed around, taking care of ourselves to the best of our ability while she mumbled incoherently in her sleep.

I was in the kitchen heating a can of soup when I started thinking about our father. Piper didn't like to talk about him, but I loved the idea of a father. The kids at school talked about their dads more than their moms. Dads were funny, they built things, and they ordered pizza. Maybe our dad didn't know we existed. I liked to picture how happy his face would be when he found out that he had not one, but two daughters. I'm so happy, he'd say as he hugged us.

I split the soup between two mugs and put the pot in the sink as quietly as I could. A few feet away Mom stirred on the couch where she lay under her favorite blanket.

"She's talking in her sleep," Piper said. "It's creepy."

I lick the drop of soup from the rim of my mug. "You should ask her who our dad is." It was a joke, but Piper got a look on her face.

"Do you dare me?"

"No," I said. "She'll get so mad if you wake her up."

It wasn't the first time we tried to find out his name, but her answer was always the same: "No one."

I watched the back of Piper's head as she crept in. She had a chunk of hair chopped short near the nape of her neck due to a bubblegum accident. Scrawny shoulders poked out of her T-shirt as she leaned forward.

I heard her whisper it: "Who is the twins' father?"

Suddenly Piper jumped back, falling on her butt. She scooted backwards, and I could see Mother's open eyes, yellow disks. She half lifted herself on her elbow, and opening her cavernous mouth, she screamed, "NO ONE, you little fucks! Get out of here! Go the fuck to your room!"

We scurried away—game over, skinny dirty rat children. Iris and Piper, daughters of NO ONE! There was no tripping up that junkie; she was dedicated to keeping us fatherless.

At 4:46 a.m., the morning of November 9, one year and one month after Piper went missing, the house phone rang. I'd been a light sleeper for the last year, so when I heard the *priiiiing*, I sat straight up in bed, wide-awake. I listened for another ring, but there was none. Either Gran had gotten to it, or the person dialing hung up. I was concentrating on the silence, lowering myself back to the mattress, when I heard Gran speak:

"Virginia, stay right where you are. I will be there shortly."

I was in the living room in a flash. She was sitting upright in her recliner; she fell asleep there sometimes when she was watching TV.

"What's wrong? What happened?"

Gran hadn't moved, she was still as a stiff. I dropped down beside her to feel her pulse, and she smacked my hand away. It stung, but I was too relieved to care. Not only alive, but alive and feisty. I rested my face against the tufted arm of her recliner to hide my relief. It was short-lived relief when I suddenly remembered what she'd said. Virginia was my mother's name. It was a name we didn't say in this house. Something happened. She was processing, and I wished she could process faster. After about a minute, she snapped to. Looking directly into my eyes, she said, "Get my shoes and my bag. We're going to see your mother."

She wouldn't tell me anything on the drive. Only, "I have to see it for myself, then we'll talk about it." What the hell did that mean?

She played one of her Christian CDs on full blast to drown out my questions, so I sat on my hands, rocking back and forth as we sped down the nearly empty freeway, Gran leaning into the wheel like she needed the car to go faster.

We parked in front of yellow-yellow just as the sun cracked open like an egg, dripping light through the clouds. The front door was propped open by a deck of playing cards. Gran kicked them aside and pushed the door all the way open. It stank worse than usual: bodies, cigarettes, and a mixology of rotting take-out. She stepped inside with me glued to her elbow. I didn't want to be here; I was afraid of what she'd look like now. It seemed that every year her face became thinner, more grotesque with sickness.

"Virginia?"

I squeezed Gran's elbow, and then we both gasped—walking out of the bedroom wearing a yellow caftan, healthy, plump, and with her hair in clean waves, came my mother. She was holding something. At first I thought it was a puppy nestled in a blanket. I drew closer to her, despite myself. I wanted to see—had we driven all this way to see my mother's new dog?

But by the look on Gran's face, I knew that wasn't right. Something wasn't right...and then something cried—a hopeless wail. A pink fist pushed itself out of the blanket and held itself in the air, triumphant. My mother's arms were scarred but not scabbed, and I stepped closer.

"This is Callum." It was the first time I'd heard her voice since the night we'd come here trying to find Piper. It was too much—her voice and that flaky new fist retreating into the blanket.

Gran walked right up to her and took the bundle, staring down at it in shock. My mother didn't try to stop her. She dropped her arms to her sides and looked at me with clear eyes. She had half a smile on her face as she studied my hair, and if Gran weren't there, she'd have something mean to say about it. She jerked her chin to Gran, who had yet to look up from the infant.

"That's your nephew, girl," she said. "Piper's baby."

Something cold burst in my chest, flapping and rolling behind my rib cage. I looked from my mother to the baby, my vision blurring. I wanted her to say it again, to make it make sense. *Piper's baby.*

My mother looked smug as she watched my face, leaching my reaction. When she'd had enough, she turned her round rump toward the bedroom, disappearing into the dark, and emerging carrying a snatch of paper between her fingers.

"Someone knocked on the door at midnight. Banged on the damn thing like they were trying to knock it down. No one was there when I opened it. I was ready to shoot their ass too." She nodded at the kitchen counter where a gun lay idly next to a box of tissues and a half-eaten hot dog. "That kid was in a box with the blanket and this—" She held out the paper to me, as Gran was too busy staring at the infant to take it.

I was not comprehending. Everything smelled and looked and felt wrong. Plucking the paper from between her fingers, I read the words.

*Iris, daughter of no one, please take care of my son.*

*His name is Callum.*

It was signed:

*Twin*

I stared at those words, my eyes watering. It was Piper's handwriting. She was alive. Piper was alive, and she'd not tried to contact us. She'd run away just like the police said—let Gran and me suffer for the last year not knowing. *Alive or dead, alive or dead…* I made a noise in the back of my throat, dropping my chin to my chest. I refused to look at her—or Gran—or the baby.

I scoured the note again. That was all? No *I love you*, or *I'm sorry*, or *I'm safe*? Not a single word to explain why? There weren't enough words to salve the last year of our lives. Gran and I had been through it. And she'd been off getting pregnant and having a baby? Had she left with those guys because she was pregnant? No—the baby Gran was holding was too small. It was new.

"It's Piper's handwriting," I confirmed.

For the first time since being handed the baby, Gran looked up. She nodded at me like it was decided. Then she looked at my mother. "We'll be taking him with us."

Virginia opened her arms in a do-what-you-will gesture. "Something else for you to save, Mother?" Her tone was taunting, but Gran didn't seem to care; she was signaling for me to head to the door.

Once I was outside, Gran followed. We brisked our way down the weed-choked path and to the Prius. Virginia was leaning in the doorframe, her arms crossed over her chest.

"Don't you want the box he came in?" She cackled so loudly, a light turned on in the house next door.

"I'm going to kill her," Gran said, handing me the baby and opening the passenger door for me.

"Not today, though. We need to get out of here."

I don't know what made me turn around, or where I got the boldness to walk right up to her carrying her supposed grand-baby. I heard Gran call my name from the street, but I ignored her. Her mean little eyes were fixed on my face, daring me to say something she didn't like. She liked to get in your face and then shove you away like you got in hers. I remembered the feel of her bony hands gripping, shoving, smacking. When she was small and skeletal, she was a bully, and now full and fleshy, she was still a bully. You could change the packaging, rebrand the anger—but the rot was inside where no one could see it…rotting.

"I want the box," I said. She looked startled at first. Then she smiled her joker's grin and turned back into yellow-yellow, emerging with a cardboard vegetable crate. I held the baby in the crook of my arm and took it from her.

"You were always more like me than she was," she said. My stomach roiled. She was looking at my hair again. "People like you and me, kid—we like to hide in plain sight." I didn't know what that meant, and I didn't want to. I turned my back on her and walked to where Gran was waiting.

She drove until she saw a Walmart. I waited in the car with the baby while Gran went inside. I'd held a baby at church, the youth pastor's, but never one this little. He made weird noises and once cried out in his sleep like something was hurting him. How many days old was he? If this was really Piper's baby, why had she left him at our mother's house? *Why had she left him at all?* Unlike me, Piper loved kids. She'd volunteer in the church nursery on Sundays just for the chance to hold babies.

"Where's your mama?" I asked him. He yawned so big I

saw each tiny nub on his gums. I was suspicious. Gran had not taken a single moment to question any of it. It's like she looked down at him and knew. My mother's history as a compulsive liar was proof enough that something wasn't right. This baby could be my mother's, or it could belong to a complete stranger. It could belong to Piper too, I thought.

Babies smelled like their mothers—or maybe they knew their mother's smell—I couldn't remember. But either way, if this baby had grown inside of my sister, he would smell like her. And I would know the smell of my sister anywhere. I lifted his head to my nose and breathed him in. Once…twice… I started crying.

Gran came out wheeling a cart piled so high she had to poke her head sideways to see around it. I held him while she unboxed the car seat and set it up. It took close to twenty minutes, and she was sweating by the time she was done. When he began crying, she held him in the back seat while I made his bottle. Gran talked me through mixing the formula with the water. He grunted and snorted as he ate. I couldn't read her face as she bent over him. She was in go-mode—get it done and don't complain mode. After his bottle, she patted his back until he burped. Then she laid him on a blanket in the trunk to change his diaper. Tiny chicken legs stiffed against the air, and Gran soothed him with her voice. A black knob was stuck to his belly button.

"That's his umbilical cord," Gran explained when she saw me looking. "It falls off about a week after they're born." I didn't say anything else. I got back in the front seat and buckled my seat belt while she strapped him into his little chair.

We were on the freeway before Gran spoke.

"He's Piper's," was all she said.

"I know." Out of the corner of my eye, I could see her look at me. "He's mine now," I said. "She asked me to look after him."

Gran nodded. "We can do it together."

"Are we going to tell the police?"

"I'm still thinking on that," she said. "Give me a few hours to screw my head on straight, and I'll have an answer for you."

"Piper's alive," I said.

# 15

PRESENT

**MY FIRST OVERNIGHT** went something like this:

"I'm Benni, I'm the household manager. If you don't know what that means, don't sweat it. I don't either." She speaks over her shoulder as we walk—much like everyone else in this place.

Despite the fact she's wearing a medical boot, I have trouble keeping up with her. Her hair is a hive of curls turned to frizz, and she wears the expression of someone whose entire life has been one endless shift of trouble. She leads me away from the older section of HOTI to the wide, well-lit hallways of the staff area.

The air seems to change the minute we step through the wooden double doors. She points things out as we walk: "That's the kitchen—but it's not a real kitchen, just a couple microwaves and a fridge. Everyone takes their meals in the dining room. But look here…" She leads me to a walk-in pantry; the shelves are stocked with noodle cups and instant mac and cheese.

"My favorite foods!" I'm only half joking.

Benni grins. "You and me both." She nudges the back shelf

of the pantry with her hip, and it opens to a tiny storage room. She hits a light switch on the inside of the wall, and I gasp dramatically at her reveal—it's a Little Debbie stash closet. Satisfied with the look on my face, she closes the door.

"Speaking of the fridge! Always mark your food with your name," she tells me. "Someone has been stealing everyone's yogurt. There's not a yogurt safe in this place—not even the nasty kind."

I think all yogurt is of the nasty variety, but I keep my mouth shut about that too.

We leave the kitchen, and she points left. "That's the lounge area. There's a TV and a pool table. Everyone pretty much keeps to themselves."

"Do you live on the island full-time?"

"Yep. Right-o, this is you…" She unlocks the door with her key card, and we step inside.

The dorms have high ceilings with cedar beams and finished concrete floors. Bunk beds form two rows along each wall with a broad center aisle down the middle. At the end of the aisle is the bathroom. It's a large space while still managing to feel cozy.

"Like adult camp!" Benni waddles into the room on her booted foot, checking the temperature on the thermostat before adjusting it. "It gets cold in here at night—they were cheap with the insulation, is what I say. Bring warm pajamas."

"Warm pajamas, check…" I adjust my backpack slung over one shoulder, and she points to various things before we stop to face the bunks.

I see her looking at me out of the corner of her eye. "What are you anyway—nineteen? Twenty?" She sighs. "You young ones have no reason to be here. It's not good. They're selfish is what they are. This place eats people up, makes them disappear."

"What happened to your foot?" I'm eager to change the subject. Ominous warnings are my least favorite way to start a job.

"Accident going down the stairs."

I can tell that she's lying, but who am I to complain? Lying is what women do to get by—not even for anyone else, just themselves.

"Find a free bunk, set the code to your locker. If you need anything like extra blankets or sheets, there's a storage room to the left near the bathrooms. Toilet paper, toothpaste—everything you need is in that storage room. Keep your stuff in here." She hands me a beige tote bag with the hospital's initials on it.

"Don't be shy about using the products, either. They take it out of your paycheck, so might as well lather up, if you know what I mean."

I look around at the two rows of neatly made bunk beds. The sheets are crisp white; a gray blanket is folded across the foot of each bed with a pillow sitting neatly atop it.

The first bunk is a few feet away from where we stand. "How do I know which beds are free?"

She points to a clear credit-card-sized envelope attached to each bunk. "There's a green side and a red side. Green means the bed's open, red means it's been claimed. Find yourself a bed and put the red side out. It's your lucky day because you get first choice."

Simple enough.

"One more thing before I leave you to it: when your stay at hotel HOTI has come to an end, strip the bed and take your dirty bedding over to the laundry chute—it's right over there." She points to a metal door in the wall. "It just got fixed. Works kind of like a trash chute, but instead, everything shoots out the end into a giant hamper. No need to strip your sheets every day, just the last day you're here so we can get it ready for the next crew." She is walking me over to a room marked *Storage*. "Get a clean set from here and remake it at the end of day three. Got it?"

I survey the shelves of crisp white sheets and another of plaid blankets. She glances up at me to see if I'm following along. I've been nodding all day, I feel like a bobble head.

"I gotta go." She taps the face of her Apple Watch. "Shoot, I'm already late." With a quick wave over her shoulder, Benni is gone.

Some curtains are already pulled around their beds. I find it unsettling; has its occupant merely shut the curtain to hide an unmade, or is there a human back there? Benni hadn't said the dorms were closed during the day, so they very well could be occupied.

*It's kookamatoo!*

Gran's word makes me sad. The fact that I might not hear her say it again…

I bite down on my tongue to shock myself. I'm tired—not thinking clearly; the lack of sleep is making me feel cagey and morose.

The schedule board is on the wall near the admissions office. There are always a couple people crowded around it, looking disappointed or pissed. And then I see it—*Walsh/Iris* next to the letters *ds* or *dark side*. A rush of excitement passes through me. It feels as if I've passed a test. And then I realize that whoever made the schedule has done it on purpose—written out my full name. My stomach drops.

"Doing the fun stuff today, Walsh. Don't get used to it."

I look over my shoulder at Bouncer. She's uncomfortably close, leaning in as if she has something to tell me. She doesn't tell me anything, however, just stares at the whiteboard, her eyes hovering on my name. She's not wearing her eyelash extensions, and her naked eyes are alarmingly lizard-like. Foundation is caked around her mouth and nostrils, and her breath smells five days old. I turn back to the board, fuming. I'd lied to her by telling her my last name was Iris. Had she found out my full name and googled me? Panic rises in my throat, clogging my breath. I think about all the files piled on Jordyn's desk; my information could easily have been in one of them. Had Bouncer seen my file?

"It's Iris," I say through my teeth. "I told you that."

I snap a picture of my schedule and casually put my phone in my pocket. I don't want her to know she's upset me. She doesn't move; I feel her frenetic energy buzzing behind me.

"You're going to be his plaything for a while, we all were. It's not going to last, and I promise you it won't end well."

I turn around now so I can fully see her.

"What?" My hackles are raised.

"Don't play dumb, Walsh."

The way she says my name makes me want to laugh: *Wol-shh*. I hover between flight and fight like a bee caught in the wind. The Iris who did nothing in the movie theater that day is frightened into a state of frozenness, the Iris pissed that she did nothing in the movie theater that day wants to punch Bouncer in the face. I study her more closely. She's high…maybe drunk by the smell of her. We are alone. I step quickly to the board and use the back of my hand to erase *Walsh*. The chance that someone will make the connection between Piper and me are slim, but I don't want to take any chances. When I turn around, she's grinning like she's caught me. I feel a flash of anger, the urge to take back control of the situation.

"Go take a shower, sober up."

The grin slides from her face, and the vein on her temple begins to pulse like an inflamed worm. "Fuck you, bitch."

A run-of-the-mill insult, a little trashy and hardly offensive. I refrain from reaction. Instead, keeping my voice low, I say, "I don't know what you gave me earlier, but I'm warning you right now, if you pick a fight with me, I'm going to win."

I don't stick around to see her reaction. I shove past her, my mind already on the next few hours of work. Supervising activities and group therapy with Dr. Grayson was the double rainbow in my sky.

"Didn't your mother teach you not to take pills from strangers?"

Her words pierce like cold water, and I feel my heart react, swelling painfully behind my ribs. I climb the stairs, swipe my badge, drop my phone in the basket along with a couple Hershey kisses for George and bury the anger for later.

I'm to assist with the patient-led classes: art, then dance, after which I will sit in on group therapy led by Dr. Grayson. I meet Peter—an art prodigy, who teaches painting as part of his therapy plan. He is the one responsible for the disturbing scenes decorating the walls. Janiss introduces us, her hands clasped at her waist like a proud mother. He is a delicate-looking man who wears thick, square-framed glasses too big for his face. His thin, mousy hair is desperately scraped into a ponytail at the nape of his neck.

Ponytail Peter says very little as he supervises finger painting. He moves around the room like a cat—expressionless and unpredictable. I think I hear him murmur into someone's ear at one point, but I never actually hear his voice. He is the rabbit in his paintings on the wall—or maybe that's too art student of me. I'm glad I only have to look at his art when I'm on the dark side.

After lunch, a man named Lucian plays soft music and leads us through a swaying meditative dance he calls tree ritual. A handful participates—arms waving, hips swaying—while others look on listlessly, unimpressed by our willow arms. The whole thing makes me sleepy.

The patients are indifferent toward me; I am another chip in the bowl, a medically minded triangle they must tolerate because they have no choice. There is an hour until group therapy. I decide to retrieve my phone and call home, check on Cal and Gran. I cross the glass walkway, swipe my badge, smile at George as he hands me my basket. The chocolate is gone. A sliver of foil wrapper remains in the bottom. I pluck out my phone, collecting the trash as an afterthought, and re-enter the world of Wi-Fi.

An hour later, after FaceTiming Cal, I do the process in reverse. I am surprised to see that George is no longer there. A thin-faced man pushes the basket toward me instead, his eyebrows as unruly as his hair which reaches out in every direction.

"Is everything all right with George?" I ask.

"Who?"

"The guard who worked before you. Quiet…very tall."

He shrugs. "I don't know a George."

I frown. Behind me the door opens as people return from break. I hurry to empty my pockets. The wrapper from the chocolate I brought George rolls between my fingertips. There is no trash can in this little room, so I put it back in my pocket.

When I arrive in the therapy room five minutes later, it's empty. I check the other two and the cafeteria before Janiss tells me that Dr. Grayson canceled group for the day. My disappointment is huge. Ever since I was accepted for this job I have waited patiently, hoping I'll be able to shadow the doctor, earn his trust—that's the next part of my plan.

That evening, I decide to take a bottom bunk closest to the bathroom door. No one wants to listen to flushing toilets all night, so it seems like the humble bet. At the foot of each bunk are twin lockers standing side by side. I hang up my scrubs and put my makeup bag and brush on one shelf and my jeans and T-shirt on another. Then I put the red side of my bed card facing out and check out the bathroom.

There are four shower stalls and four toilet stalls in the women's. The shower stalls come equipped with shampoo, conditioner, and body wash, and there are fresh stacks of white towels on a metal rack in the corner by the sinks. It smells like fresh paint and wet concrete. I hear the tinkle of voices; the staff must be trickling in for the night.

Cal and Gran are probably having dinner. I send both of them a text letting them know I'm okay and settling in for the night, and another to Mary-Ann, who is making their dinner.

It's really cool here! Like a giant cabin.

I snap a few photos of the bunk beds, thinking Cal will get a kick out of them, and try to send them. My texts go through, but the pictures don't.

All good here, Mary-Ann answers. We are watching Gravity Falls.

Cal sends me a bunch of nonsensical emojis, which means he's in a good mood. I send Gran a voice message. Cal will help her play it, so I have to be careful with how I word things.

"I know you don't like the way I'm doing things…" The clatter of feet and voices grows louder. I lick my lips, and hurry. "I hope you're feeling better…it's all going to be over soon… I love you so much. I'm being safe and careful."

I hit Send, picturing her face as she hears my carefully worded message. Gran could call my bullshit every time. Being safe and careful was relative, wasn't it? A toilet flushes, and a minute later, I hear the splashing of water in the sink. The person above me coughs as they roll over. I tuck my phone under my pillow and take out the pink foam earplugs Mary-Ann gifted me. There was a time when I thought I could move on, be the healthy sister, the good mother, the granddaughter that was enough—but I just can't… I can't. No matter how much I convince myself that I've moved on, I eventually end up right back here—looking for answers, one way or another. I might as well get it over with.

Dr. Grayson is in my periphery as I refill my iced tea at the drink station at dinner the following evening. "Anywhere beneath the Mason-Dixon line, this is the nectar of the gods. We only get it once a week."

I glance up. "You sound a little bitter about it."

He nods, his face solemn. "The household manager has it out for me."

"Benni?" I laugh as I close the spout, and iced tea drips on my hand.

He hands me a napkin because he's closer to the stack. "She hates me," he admits. "I may have submitted a few criticisms in the suggestion box. Big mistake. Huge. It's not a suggestion box at all apparently. She only accepts compliments."

I hand the napkin back when tea drips on his hand. He smirks as he dabs it off. "Thanks, friend…"

"You're welcome, Boss."

"Ouch…" He makes a face, pretending to be offended.

We're in a slow walk, carrying our trays in the same direction. No one seems bothered that he's in the cafeteria, outside of the typical glances and skirting around him. If he were eating dinner in the fishbowl, it would be another story. Out here he is a boss; in there he is a savior.

We find seats opposite each other at the end of a table. I'm lightheaded from his attention. Even as he looks at me, I feel the needy pull for more of it. My daddy issues are so mean.

"Aside from a man dying at your feet, how has your experience here been so far?"

He's wearing a faded gray T-shirt and gray jeans. His belt is designer. He looks like a casual guy on a casual date, which sends heat up the back of my neck.

*Why did you even think that?*

I spear a forkful of coleslaw into my mouth, chewing slowly. "It's definitely been an experience," I say. "I'm looking forward to it though…"

He nods. "A futurist."

"Is that a bad thing?"

He takes a bite of his pulled pork sandwich and shrugs, one arm slung over the back of his chair. He's one of those guys who looks at home doing…whatever. Like every situation fits him just right. I want that.

"You miss the present in a chase for tomorrow. Your brain says, 'Soon, soon, soon.' Soon becomes an obsession…" He looks up at me. "Am I wrong?"

He can see on my face that he's not. We eat in silence for a few minutes. Every so often he nods at someone in greeting, but no one approaches him.

"Is this what it's like to have a session with you?"

His answer is to look into my eyes. The attraction I'm feeling for him is diabolically dangerous, not to mention stupid, stupid, stupid.

"Don't worry," he says. "We all have obsessions…" He gives me that sideswept grin again, and I feel winded by it…again.

"What's yours?"

I don't expect the answer he gives me, or the way he looks at me when he gives it.

"You're going to have to tell me that…" He wipes his mouth and tosses the napkin onto his empty plate. He's about to stand up, and I feel desperate to keep him. I don't know what he means.

"That's why you're here—to learn and observe."

Fine. Sure. But is he giving me permission to learn…him? I feel flirted with, but I've never seen him interact with any of the women here—except Bouncer, and she threw herself at him. Was Dr. Grayson the one she was warning me to stay away from? Like it's any of her business who he flirts with.

"I—I thought I was here to observe the patients…" I'm flustered, and he can tell.

He picks up his tray, his eyes lingering on my face for a sweltering five seconds. "You are. See you…"

I watch him walk out, along with everyone else in the cafeteria. The boss has left the building. It's only after he's gone that everyone stops what they're doing to stare at me. Which makes me wonder in horror—have they been staring at us since I've been at the drink station with him? I'd been so preoccupied with his attention that I hadn't noticed. Before, I was the new kid; now I'm the new kid Leo Grayson ate dinner with. By the look on their faces, it isn't something that goes down often.

I could use that to my advantage—if he is attracted to me, that is. Leo Grayson is exactly the right person to get me in the room with the man I've come looking for. I want to process everything he said in detail, get away from the curious eyes and get some fresh air. I'm in a hurry when I grab my tray, not bothering to look behind me as I push my chair back.

I feel the impact before I hear the voice. "Hey! Watch it!"

From behind me—the clatter of falling plates and silverware. Something splashes on my ankles. I've done it now. Goddamn my clumsiness. *You were being moony, not clumsy,* I remind myself. I want to crawl inside my own body and dry up from the embarrassment. *Let me turn into a husk right now!*

I set my wobbly tray back down to face her—damp, human, and contrite. She's taller than me, but not much older, her dark hair braided in pigtails so tight her eyes stretch catlike toward her hairline. I'm so embarrassed. My rush into apologies doesn't faze her.

"I'm so sorry, I don't know what I was thinking. I should have looked behind me! Oh man, look at your shoes, here—" I reach for the napkin holder—one of those stupid silver rectangles—and frantically begin pulling. It's been overstuffed and I can't get the paper to come out. I yank desperately until I've secured a triumphant handful, which I offer her like a bouquet of flowers.

She looks from my offering of napkins to my face and back again. Then she just turns around and walks away.

I eye the overturned tray, the plate, the fried chicken leg that skidded several feet away, and wonder—should I clean it? She's had a bad day, and I probably pushed her over the edge—or at least that's what I tell myself, bending down. By the time I have everything cleaned up, everyone has gone back to their dinner. I decide to take that walk.

Being on the island makes me feel close to Gran and my sister. We never visited it together, other than the ferry ride I took with Gran. It's hard not to think of her out here though; the smell of the air triggers memories faster than any of Gran's albums. I've always been a smell girl.

The San Juan Islands are an archipelago with three main islands and literally hundreds of smaller islands scattered through the Salish Sea. In summer, tourists drag their kids and coolers onto the ferry at Anacortes and rush the coveted cords of beach for the best spots. San Juan, Orcas, and Lopez Island are popular among outdoor enthusiasts like Gran.

Every summer after we went to live with her, we were either on a wildlife tour or a kayaking excursion. Once, in the early hours of the morning, we'd left our tent and biked to a remote part of San Juan Island to whale watch. We'd set up on an outcropping of rocks while Gran used her camping stove to make us oatmeal. For hours we sat huddled together under the chilly morning air, talking about nothing and everything. I preferred the times it was just us and Gran doing whatever zany thing she'd thought up, but Piper, being the more social one, had preferred the camping trips we took with Gran's church friends.

Those are the memories I cling to—the few precious years Piper and I had together that were not filled with trauma.

On a clear day, I bet you could see Mt. Baker from the beach—snowcapped, if you're lucky. I walk the trail to the ferry, visions of Piper blowing through my mind openly, softly, and popping like a bubble when the next one arrived.

Hours of therapy have taught me to celebrate the time I had

with her—to focus on those memories rather than the last one. But there it is—the last one.

Rubbing my arms and wishing I'd grabbed my hoodie from my locker, I push hard up the incline, my thighs starting to burn. It's dark outside, but the moon and the ferns outline the trail well enough to provide direction.

I'm cresting the hill when I look up and see someone walking toward me from the beach. Not walking—jogging. I see wide shoulders and stop abruptly. A strange man running toward you is never a good thing.

"What are you doing? Get back inside." A barked order.

I stare dumbly; he can't possibly be talking to me. Perhaps I've wandered off the trail and am walking somewhere I shouldn't be, but no—this is the same path we use to get to and from the dock where the water taxi picks us up.

"Are you talking to me?"

"Do you see anyone else around here?"

I drop my chin. I don't like his tone.

He's an arm's distance away from me when he stops; his scent arrives a second late—beer and cigarettes. I can make out a snub nose perched above rubbery, swollen lips.

"Who are you?" I swipe the hair out of my face, confused… a little scared too.

"I'm security. Who. Are. You?" He jabs a finger at me. He reminds me of a city cop in the movies, flashing around his East Coast accent, trying to act all old-school tough. He isn't drunk, but he's soggy around the edges like he's getting there.

"I work here." My whole body is flushing hot then cold, hot then cold. Men are dangerous. Men are more dangerous when they're drunk.

"Funny," he says. "I've worked here a long time and I've never seen you before, so you're either new or stupid, or both."

He's trying to intimidate me. Years advocating for my sis-

ter in male-dominated spaces familiarized me with this spe-
cies of anger.

"What's your problem? I'm trying to take a walk."

"If you worked here, you'd know you're not supposed to be
out here."

"No one told me that," I snap, taking a sideways step away
from him. He is one of those guys that gets right in your face
if you let them.

"Go back." He points a finger in the direction of the hospital.
I eye the scraggy patches of hair on his chin; he has a hunted,
wild look about him, like a hyena.

I clench and unclench my hands to get the blood flowing.
I'm scared, and I'm furious he's making me feel that way. "Are
you trying to scare me?"

"I'm trying to get you back inside… You're picking a fight
with the wrong person, little girl…"

"I'm not picking anything, I'm trying to take a walk, old
timer." My stubbornness keeps me glued to the spot. I should
just go back, but I can't—I'm committed to the fight he started.

My bad man alarm is screaming, and bad men make me
angry.

*"You pick fights with men who remind you of the men who took
your sister."* My therapist, announcing the obvious, wasn't something to get excited about, in my teenage estimation.

*"Yes,"* I'd said easily. *"So what?"*

*"Soo, if you pick a fight with the wrong person, you could poten-
tially end up hurt."*

Isn't that the point? Why does anyone fight? It isn't to feel
good, it's to feel.

*What's the point of what you're doing right now?* I ask myself.
*Because this isn't going to help your sister…*

*Nothing can help your sister, you idiot, she's dead.*

Some of the air goes out of me.

"What's your name?" I ask him.

He lets out a short burst of laughter. "You gonna report me to the higher authorities or something?"

"No. I'm going to memorize it for later." I feel like a silly little woman with paper-thin threats.

He doesn't touch me, but our bodies are close. With his half-closed eyes he looks drunk and sober simultaneously.

"Sol." He grins, tiny oval teeth like popcorn kernels. "Sol of security."

It takes concerted effort to turn my back on him—every cell in my body vibrates with the possibility of a surprise attack. My sister's nightmare—a man grabbing…taking…

I go over the options as I trot downward: strangulation from behind, a shove between the shoulder blades that sends me tumbling down the steep part of the hill, a knife in the tender part of my neck, or a gunshot to the back of the head. All things I'd pictured happening to my sister. I am so close to answers, I can't risk fighting a pointless battle. I make it to the bottom of the hill, high on adrenaline.

A woman is eating corn chips and reading a Stephen King novel in a chair by the fire, crumbs collecting on her shirt. She doesn't seem to notice me when I pass.

My run-in with the Clint Eastwood knockoff has shaken me. Replaying what happened is only leaving me more confused. Had I made up his tone—imagined it being more aggressive than it was? When people say to trust your gut, it always goes over my head. I don't know what gut instinct is supposed to feel like. Since the day Piper disappeared, I've considered my gut to be dysfunctional, like some people's intelligence. If it were an organ, I'd want to have it removed like a gallbladder or a rotten appendix.

I turn the corner. Two people are making out—her back pressed against the wall, his hand on her hips. I scurry past them beetle-like, wanting to look but not having the guts to. Away from their families and friends, people are probably hooking up all the time. No biggie. I reach the end of the hallway right as one of them starts to moan. This isn't exactly what I had in mind for these overnight shifts.

# 16

PAST

**PEOPLE WHO LEFT** you were easy to hate—easier to blame. They didn't care to defend themselves, so you experienced your abandonment in silence. You tended the garden of bitterness in silence. Eventually you started making your own assumptions about why they left. That's when the garden really got to blooming. My garden was never dreary; on the contrary, my resentment was colorful, my anger bright and binding like a choking vine. There were so many variations of anger that I didn't know where to look most days.

Cal made sense to me even when the world didn't. It was easy to understand him. He was helpless. He didn't choose to be left in a box on someone's doorstep. Piper chose that for him, and by choosing that, she made it a part of his history. I was raising him having barely been raised myself, and she was where?

In the rotting center of my anger was my mother. She picked the fight by abandoning us first.

The moment Cal was in my arms, I wanted to protect him. I was mad at my sister for not sticking around to do the same.

Why hadn't she come back—or at least given us a reason she left? The note she'd written me had been patiently penned, her neatest handwriting—an order without explanation. *Here's my son, take care of him.*

We called Poley and Audrain as soon as we got back to the apartment. It was one of those days where it was easy to track them down. An hour later, they walked in smelling of the outside and of coffee, looking just as awkward as always. We hadn't seen them in a while—Audrain had grown his hair into a midlife crisis while Poley cut hers short and dyed it jet black.

They handed us each a paper cup of coffee and bent to coo over the baby, who was sleeping in his car seat. Gran was polite, but when she answered their questions, her words were clipped.

"We'll head out there to talk to Virginia tomorrow. You say she just left the baby on her doorstep in this box?"

"We don't know who left him, just that he was left." Gran's coffee sat untouched beside her. She was perched on the edge of her seat, ready to leap up if the baby made a sound.

"It's Piper's handwriting," I said, showing them the note.

They ordered a DNA test for Cal and took the box and note as evidence.

I didn't want to give them the box; it was the last thing my sister touched other than her son. I had no use for the police, no patience for the saturated niceness. I didn't need the DNA tests to confirm who Cal was. I knew who he belonged to when I smelled his head. He wasn't going to be another kid without a mother. Gran knew the truth, my mother knew the truth, the police knew the truth, but to everyone else, he was mine.

I signed up for a homeschool program so that I could take care of Cal. That was the deal Gran laid out—I could stay home, on the condition I finish high school. I managed to scrape by with C's in most of my classes and lost so much weight I barely resembled the photos from the year before. Gran and I took shifts: me in the day, her at night—neither of us sleeping enough. We survived on Hamburger Helper, frozen waffles and coffee. Piper's little boy was our emotional sustenance. Even what we did for ourselves was for him. We ate and laughed and played music in the apartment to keep him healthy and happy. I cried in the shower, silently as to not wake the baby.

Being a mother settled over me like a Washington mist: it left me chilled and damp. And then, as suddenly as Cal arrived in our lives, his presence became normal: the bottles and bouncing and exhaustion were what we did now. It was a welcome distraction; the baby giggles rolled light into the midst of our darkness.

I barely understood my own existence before I was given a brand-new existence to attend to. Cal's life was to be my apology letter to Piper for letting her down, for not protecting her. For a year I'd avoided looking at my own face in the mirror because my face reminded me of Piper, but I couldn't avoid looking at Cal's, and his face was perfect.

I graduated high school when Cal was four. Gran took us to a fancy restaurant to celebrate. Cal wore a little white suit, I ordered steak, and Gran had a glass of wine with her dinner. It was a happy time.

A week after Cal learned about the human skeleton at preschool *(knee bone connected to the thigh bone, thigh bone connected to the…)*, they found something that changed the whole case—broke it wide open.

During a drug bust in Tacoma, officials seized a hundred pounds of meth and four firearms modified for automatic firing; among the trafficked drugs and weapons they found an envelope of Polaroid photos. Poley called and asked me to come to the station to see if I could identify Piper in one of the photos. When I asked why she thought it was Piper in the Polaroid, she told me the girl looked like me.

I brought my study notes for biology and tried not to think on it until I knew for sure. Poley came to collect me from the front of the station, and she wore her hair in a pale blond bob this time, uneven bangs like stacked Legos across her forehead. She looked older and perhaps more guarded than the last time I saw her. She wore blue, except for her shoes, which squeaked against the floor as I followed her to the elevator.

"Where are we going?"

In the past I'd always been taken to one of the little rooms on the first floor of the building.

She pointed to the ceiling as we stepped inside. "My desk. They keep us on the second floor."

When I looked at her in question, she added, "The interview rooms are for more current cases." When she realized what she'd said, her face went red. She cleared her throat, pressing the button for the second floor.

"You in college now?"

I nodded.

"Good for you," she said. "What are you studying…?"

We made small talk as she led me to her cubicle. In a flat voice she informed me that Audrain was gone, and that she had a new partner—a guy who transferred from the New York precinct. She didn't sound too excited about it. I was relieved I didn't have to see Audrain; his dead-eyed stare unnerved me. I didn't ask where he was or why, and she never offered an explanation.

I didn't believe I was going to see my sister that day, and then there she was. I was stunned, my reaction slow to arrive. I choked out, "That's her…"

Poley asked if I was sure. I was sure. I was looking at myself, my mirror image. We both knew it too—she couldn't meet my eye after that.

In the Polaroid, Piper was lying naked on her back, eyes closed. I closed mine in response. For a moment the panic swelled so large in my throat I couldn't breathe.

"Iris, are you okay?"

Poley's voice pulled me out of it, I cracked my eyes open to see her pale face hovering in front of me like a ghost.

"It's her…" My voice was barely a croak. She nodded once I forced my eyes back to the photo, focusing on the things around her: the blue-and-white chevron-patterned quilt, the corner of a chipped white dresser. She was on her back, posed. It was awful, she was a child and someone—presumably a man—arranged her limbs while she was unconscious, and took this photo. A dark blur marred the inside of her right thigh: a heart tattoo she'd given herself with India ink. I looked away.

"Are you sure?" Poley's matter-of-fact face made me feel worse. There wasn't an ounce of care in anyone in this building. I nod.

"She's young," I said. "This was maybe right after it happened…that's her tattoo."

Her breasts were modest, the way mine had been four years ago, her stomach unmarred by signs of a pregnancy. I pointed that out, and Poley nodded in agreement.

"The photos are what they use to traffic the girls, but we have no idea of when they were taken…yet."

"Like a catalog?" I closed my eyes, the image of Piper pinwheeling in my vision. I would never be able to unsee that. "Oh my god," I say softly. Four years didn't make a difference. It hurt just as bad as the first day.

"Yes."

"Who took the picture?"

"We're investigating that." Her words are clipped. She took the photograph back. I was glad to be rid of it.

"That Polaroid is part of a new investigation, so this is good—no, great news, Iris." She looked like she really believed it. She was more likeable without Audrain around, but sometimes she used his phrases. Audrain always had good—no, great news!

"They're working out a plea deal with the guy who was found with the photos. He's not talking until it's in writing, but we're pretty confident that he's gonna sing." Poley was sitting on the arm of the chair opposite me. It bugged me that she could never commit to sitting all the way down in a chair. Even when she came to Gran's apartment she perched on the furniture, ready to leave. She was worse than Cal.

"A plea deal?" She'd been gone for five years, and they were just now working out a plea deal for information on a photo that was older than my son. "How many girls were photographed?"

"Twelve. We've identified three of them so far—four, with Piper."

"So you get him to sign this plea deal and then he tells you what he knows about the photos?"

"It's a start."

"This started five years ago."

"I understand how you feel, but police work takes time."

My laugh was ugly. Did she really expect me to be dancing with glee? The Polaroids came to her because she got lucky. There was no good police work involved.

"What's the name of the man they arrested?"

I stab her with my eyes as a sick eagerness twists in my belly.

"He's a street jockey, Millar Polar. Runs drugs, sometimes watches the goods—he was there the day of the raid. He's claiming the photos were left with him by someone else. He won't tell us who."

"Millar Polar," I repeated. Another name to add to the investigation—hers and mine.

"Take a look, tell me if you've ever seen this man before." She set his booking photo down in front of me. I was too afraid to look at it. The duvet my sister was lying on in the Polaroid was still swimming in my vision. Even when I closed my eyes it was there, floating across my eyelids like a light show. I wanted to be sick—and I probably would if Poley didn't give me space. She hovered like a mosquito.

"Give me a minute, will you…"

When she didn't back up, I stood abruptly, almost knocking her over, and walked to the doorway. It was glass and I could see other glass doors, people going in and out of them. Poley cleared her throat behind me, but I ignored her. We'd waited five years to hear something, agonized over the lack of police work, and she was rushing me?

I turned to face Poley. Her eyes were pressing me so hard I felt choked all over again. Sweating, I stiffly returned to my seat, and she tapped the photo with her finger, trying to get me to look. I braced myself for the worst, and the worst was what I got.

My throat closed twice before I could get the words out. "He looks just like RJ." He was ragged, meth-faced. I'd thought him older back then, maybe in his early twenties, but I'd been so wrong. He looked to be at least forty in the photo.

"He looks older," I said.

"It's been five years, Iris."

My eyes snapped to her face. "Thank you, Amanda, for reminding me. My son and I are quite aware how long my sister has been gone. I mean *a lot* older—like twenty years. Does this guy have a kid?"

"I don't know," she said, bored. "Why?"

"Because this isn't RJ. It looks just like him, though…"

"Oh."

She was disappointed. She double-checked the photo herself, large, empty eyes glancing over Millar Polar. I had the feeling she'd been hoping to walk out of here a hero.

"Maybe that's where he got the photos. It would make sense that he's trying to protect his kid."

She made a face. "I'll check it out."

It was then I noticed the sizable diamond on her ring finger. It was too pretty for the bitten-down nails and short sausage fingers.

"You're engaged." I could hear the accusation in my voice.

She must have heard it too; she didn't look at me when she said, "Yeah."

"Great," I lied. *You're engaged and my sister is still missing* sat heavy between us... I hoped her mother was planning her wedding; Amanda didn't excel at putting things together.

"I have to get back to my son," I said, standing up. "You'll call me?"

"As soon as we question him."

"Which will be when?"

The V between her eyebrows activated. "Have a nice day, Iris."

She was still the same uptight bitch she'd been the first day I met her. I stomped out to my car, slamming doors and muttering under my breath. We didn't just deserve answers about my sister, we had Cal to think of. Cal, who'd have his own questions when the time came, and as of now, I couldn't answer any of them.

His paternity haunted me at random times—when I brushed his dark, wavy hair or tickled him and heard his raspy laugh— a laugh that wasn't in our family. Would his father come back for him? Would my sister?

# 17

## PRESENT

**I'M HAVING BREAKFAST** in the patient cafeteria. The food is mushy, but the coffee is better than in the staff cafeteria. I'm contemplating why—because it's something nicer to think about than the alternative. Which is that I couldn't sleep—*can't* sleep in this place. There are too many people in one space all breathing, dreaming, grunting, and sweating. Which therapist had said that sleeping was an act of trust? I can't remember because I'm tired. I would have been a lousy soldier.

I sip my coffee as two patients trickle in, then three. It's my second morning eating here; these were the same three who came in first yesterday. Heading for the buffet, they pile sealed containers onto red trays. I glance down at my congealing oatmeal. It's still dark outside; I slept for a few hours, but the foot traffic to the bathroom woke me, then kept me awake.

The patient cafeteria has purple tables and bench chairs. The air is less charged. Everyone does what they're here to do: eat. No one takes any pleasure in it; there's a mechanical spooning, the sound of chewing, and an occasional grunt. Here, no one speaks, but everyone watches. It's a gift lost to the neurotypical.

I eat my oatmeal with raisins—big mistake. Huge. After one breakfast, the fifty or so people who witnessed my meal choice have all dubbed me Raisin. Once you're called something like raisin, everyone wants to know why. Once they know why, there's no going back. What I've learned is that people think there's something wrong with you if you eat raisins for fun. Two guys—who were also here the same time yesterday— elbow each other as I walk by.

"Hey, Raisin!"

I wave. They laugh like hyenas, but a few tables down, the older crew—the ones who ate raisins in cookies and candies as kids—nod at me. I dump my trash and return the tray. I like older people, maybe it's because I was raised by my grand-mother; they just have the best stories.

"Raisin... You're making an impression."

A jump, skip, and beat of the heart; I know his voice. Leo is dapper in a gray suit, white shirt, and glasses. I close my open mouth. He laughs at my apparent surprise, grazing his chin with his fingertips.

"Cool kids don't like raisins," I say to cover my surprise. "You didn't even warn me."

His eyes light up playfully. He's beautiful from the nose up, and the nose down—it's hard to know where to look. Heat starts in my belly and works its way down. The feeling is so distracting I don't hear what he says next, and he has to repeat himself. Raisins verses chocolate. I know I'm in a losing battle, but the friction is fun.

"I honestly didn't think I would need to. You look like a woman who knows the power of chocolate."

I make a face. "I eat raisins in my chocolate too—"

He flinches. "Stop. That's too far. Now I'm sad for you." He looks upset enough to make me laugh. He has nice teeth.

We admire each other for another few seconds before he looks around self-consciously. He has a scar on his chin, and the only reason I can see it is because he's taller than me. People are noticing us noticing each other. Dr. Grayson leans in.

"They're going to think I'm flirting with you…"

"Are you?"

He's a gorgeous guy, and he's blushing. It's endearing. He laughs from the belly and lifts a hand to wave at someone across the room.

"Come on," he says. "If we don't leave now, we'll be stuck here for another thirty minutes listening to Burt talk about his dreams."

I look over and see a man in a bathrobe making his way toward us. I loop my arm through his and steer him toward the door. Once we're through the cafeteria doors, I let him go.

We fall into step walking in the direction of the nurses' station.

"Hey, thanks. That was excellent." He glances at me appreciatively.

I blush, realizing how assertively I touched him without his permission.

"Sorry…" I step away, and put a foot of space between us.

I can smell his aftershave as we walk side by side. He sets the pace, and he's in no rush.

He glances at me out of the corner of his eye. "I went to the staff cafeteria first to find you…"

My heart rate spikes. "Oh?"

"That tends to be where the staff eat."

"You're not in there very often," I throw back.

The look he gives me is amused. "You've only been here for two weeks. How do you know where I eat?"

"Three," I sigh. "I assumed you eat in your office." I know he eats in there. I've counted the trays on the meal cart Bouncer wheels in twice a day.

Speak of the devil.

Up ahead, Bouncer catches sight of the doctor and starts heading our way. She ignores me entirely, wedging herself between us. She's showered, I can smell her shampoo. Looking past her shoulder, I can see one of the carnivorous bunnies. Run…run…run…

"You canceled our meeting today?"

"I did."

When he doesn't say more, she slaps the side of her thigh with her palm. "That's it?" She shakes her head. "For someone who claims to be my savior, you weaponize your fake incompetence. That's all you're going to say?"

Whatever is happening leaves me feeling embarrassed. It feels personal. I turn my back to give them privacy, pretending to study the staff bulletin board. We are far enough away from the nurses' station that no one has noticed them yet, but with Bouncer's voice swinging toward hysteria, it won't be long.

"You said we'd talk about—"

He cuts her off. "Caroline, you need to go home. You're not yourself."

When I look back, he's leading her away, his arm around her shoulders.

Her response is muffled, but I hear the sniffling of tears. They've disappeared toward the bridge, where I assume he's sending her to bed or to home. When I blink, he's walking back toward me, impressively bored.

"You're with me today, by the way. We're conferencing."

It takes me a few seconds to catch up, and then my eyes get big.

"With D?" I'm trying not to freak out. The big D—the only D I am interested in. This is happening faster than I thought. I didn't have access to the lab yet, and—

"No. Not today."

I have to work at keeping the disappointment off my face.

"Oh?"

He grins. "I think you'll learn a lot from this patient, he's a very interesting man. Marshal. He spent ten years in D." For a moment I don't think I've heard him correctly.

"Marshal Day Monterey?"

"Yep, that's him…"

Marshal Day Monterey. It rolls right off the tongue. I've seen his photo online: vacant eyes, reddish-brown hair that melts over his head like a dead animal.

Dr. Grayson stops at the care station before I can ask questions. "Janiss, tell the other nurses to make sure to keep the art room locked. Someone's been eating the paint again…"

"Oh no, I'm so sorry. I told him not to—I can't believe—"

Her voice cuts off when she spots me.

"That sweater is not part of the uniform," she says, tartly. "You have to wear white or cream."

I look down at my cardigan, which is admittedly yellow.

"Noted," I say. She raises her eyebrows before resuming her typing. He leads me toward D, walking briskly while pulling his key card from inside his collar.

"I have questions," I say.

He glances at me out of the corner of his eye, a little smile on his lips.

"Shoot."

"Was it the painter who ate the paint—bunny-wolf guy?"

"Yep, he's had to have his stomach pumped before. Luckily this time he only managed to eat a quarter tube of white paint before someone caught him."

"My next question is… Marshal. He's not…in D anymore?"

"You know about him?"

I nod.

"He's living in regular population," he confirms.

We stop at the door to D hall, and Dr. Grayson swipes his card.

"We aim for rehabilitation if it's possible. And in some cases, it's absolutely not possible."

"And is it possible for him to be rehabilitated?"

"He'll spend the rest of his life here. His delusions have stopped due to the extensive therapy and medication we provide him. He's able to live a normal life inside these walls. He does better being around people."

"Who pays for him to be here?"

He shoots me a look. "His very embarrassed wealthy brother."

We've arrived at the door to his office.

"Does he communicate remorse?"

"You tell me after conference."

"I hope he had a big breakfast," I say.

This makes him laugh, which makes me laugh. I'm distracted when we walk into his office, and not entirely by Dr. Grayson.

Something else has struck my interest, something even worse than doing conference with a rehabilitated cannibal.

I want to ask him who in D hall is not able to be rehabilitated, but there's a knock on the door.

"You okay?" Dr. Grayson asks. I nod, but my throat is convulsively swallowing. I'm sitting on his side of the desk in a chair he pulled next to his, hands in my lap like a schoolgirl. Marshal is intended to sit across from us.

"I need to warn you, he does this thing with his fingers…" Dr. Grayson snaps his fingers three times.

"It's a compulsion."

I nod.

"Come in." Janiss hustles a man into the room, her face stormy. She gives Dr. Grayson a meaningful look leaving. MDM is not what I was expecting. At five feet seven inches, he's hardly imposing; he's slight and hard like he's made of wire. He's wearing a button-down flannel shirt over black sweatpants. His hair is buzzed, face clean-shaven, expression penitent as a monk.

"Marshal," Dr. Grayson says, "this is Iris. She will be leading conference today."

I'm not sure if I've heard him right. I glance at Dr. Grayson's face and he nods encouragingly. Blindsided, I feel my posture turn stiff and I don't know what to do with my facial expression. I'd led group therapy at an outpatient mental health center as part of my undergraduate work, ten people would sit in a circle with me at the helm; and while I opened and closed the sessions it was the patients who did most of the talking. Most of their treatment was for addiction. Murder was not my forte.

Marshal snaps his fingers three times before nodding at me. He looks at Dr. Grayson as he sits down, a smirk propping up his little mouth.

He is alert, clear-eyed, and very much...functioning. Normally, in a situation like this I'd have an understanding of his diagnosis as well as his medical history. I can feel the doctor's eyes on my face. A flush rushes up my neck. This is my audition, I realize. Grayson wants to see what I've got.

"Tell me about yourself," I say. His hands are folded in his lap, gnarly, crooked fingers with thick blue veins. Tattoos crawl like errant bugs up his neck, symbols I don't know the meaning of. His mouth twitches like he wants to laugh. Marshal glances at Dr. Grayson, who nods.

"All right," he starts, looking back at me. "I like long walks on the beach, vigorous walks—"

He knows exactly how scared I am. It's not a surprise that either of them is testing me.

There's a tiny accent attached to his words.

"Are you from Australia?"

To my relief he nods, his expression lightening.

"Lived in Sydney my first twelve years. My mother immigrated after she divorced my father."

We go from there. I ask Marshal about his parents, his life in Sydney. I do not like the way his small eyes linger at my neck, my hands, my legs. He is a multitasker, he sneaks the looks between his story, his voice never faltering.

Marshal is so close in proximity I could pluck a hair from his head. His DNA is accessible. If Leo trusts me enough to sit in on a session with Marshal, it's only a matter of time before I am in the same room as *him*. The thought gives equal amounts adrenaline and dread.

I'm relieved when our time is up. Janiss retrieves her patient and after they're gone Dr. Grayson turns to me.

"You did well. Were you nervous?"

"Very," I confess. "I felt unprepared. I haven't seen any of your notes about him."

"You don't need to," he interrupts. "If you ask the right questions you'll hear the truth in their answers. Even when they lie the patients are revealing something about their inner life."

I bite my bottom lip, nodding in agreement.

"He idolizes his childhood and his father, he sounds the most dishonest when he talks about his feelings, it's like he's trying to say all of the right things but he's off mark."

Dr. Grayson smiles, and then he tells me Marshal's story.

On a hot evening in September, Marshal Day Monterey drove to Aurora Avenue and stopped outside of the Krispy Kreme Doughnuts to let one of the working girls into his car. I am familiar with the stretch of road: women stand around wearing lingerie and stilettos. Most of them look bored, staring at their phones instead of into the long line of traffic that moves at a snail's pace. The articles online don't specify if he chose the girl randomly. There are a lot of details in between I don't remember, but the story ends in a hotel room a few miles down the street. The manager called 911 when he heard screaming coming from room nine. Police kicked down the door to find the woman Marshal was with in the bathtub: she was alive, bleeding, and without one of her eyes. Marshal had eaten her other eye before he left her in the room. They found Marshal a few blocks away, wandering down a street, covered in blood.

It's spaghetti night in the staff cafeteria. The pasta is swollen and mushy, the meat gray. I rest my chin on my fist as I stir the mess around my plate. I am technically on a break. Four hours to sleep, or read, or play Xbox in the rec room. I'm too strung out on lack of sleep to sleep. My next shift starts at 10:00 p.m. on the dark side. I am to man the nurses' station from 10:00 p.m. to 6:00 a.m., after which I will be on my way home on the nine o'clock water taxi.

I can't stop thinking about the session with Marshal. I don't want to small talk with strangers tonight. I need to think. I am dazed, slightly dazzled and anxious. I did not expect to be attracted to my forty-something-year-old boss, I definitely don't want to be. But the fact is, I thought I'd seen it all, the full buffet of shrinks. They're predictable—that's the stability of therapy. You know what they're going to say, you know how they're going to say it. There was none of that in the session with Marshal. Dr. Grayson sat with his back to the falling rain doing the opposite of what I thought he'd do. His methods were controversial…aggressive. *Intensive* may be a better word? Is that why he is here, on Shoal, to practice the way he wants to without outside involvement? If the world knew what he was doing he'd lose his license, possibly face jail time.

*That was just one session.* I could learn so much from him, but the knowledge would be unethical. Do I care? Who am I to take the high road when my own reasons for being here are unethical? I finished high school with a 4.0 GPA, I went to college, got my bachelor's, was accepted into a master's program—all because my sister was kidnapped. Piper is the driving force behind my perseverance.

If Cal were my biological son, I'd only owe him my life,

but he is not my son, he's Piper's. One day he will ask for her full story, and to not have it for him… I don't want to think of that. I've come this far.

Marshal Day Monterey.

Ellis Conrad Jr.

Dalton Barellis.

Arthur Barton.

Jude Fields.

The man in D is going to tell me everything.

# 18

PAST

**IT TURNED OUT** that Millar Polar did have a son, but his name wasn't RJ. The twenty-two-year-old man who posed that day as RJ was really named Millar Polar III. He was currently serving time in a state penitentiary in Nevada for trafficking weapons.

The Polars were your basic brand of criminals—nothing impressive, nothing clever. Dad was in prison for drug possession, mom served time for identity theft and fraud. I couldn't find an address for Shana Polar, but that hadn't deterred me—her date of birth was listed next to her booking photo.

My mom went dark for months at a time; the only one who knew how to find her was Gran, and that was only because my mother needed money. Gran always gave it to her. I found Shana's Facebook page and scrolled until I found a string of birthday posts. Two years ago, MichaelLisaHeppernam posted a gif of balloons on her wall—*Happy Birthday from Mom and Dad* typed underneath in the comments. No one had liked the post. Michael and Lisa were easy to find. Old people were bad at the internet. It always alarmed me how accessible they made themselves. Once I had their address, I looked up their house on Google Earth. Not much to see—a mossy roof, rectangular in shape, and surrounded by patchy grass. The house was smaller than yellow-yellow. RJ/Millar spent time there growing up. I wanted to see where a sex trafficker grew up.

The next day, I caught the bus to their neighborhood, then walked two blocks to the dingy brown single-story. The yard was ripped up, mostly weeds, mud, and broken toys. I don't know what I was hoping to find other than RJ's origins. His grandparent's house wasn't going to give me any answers. Shana Polar, formerly Heppernam, had RJ when she was fifteen if I was doing the math correctly. Now in her forties, the gaunt cheeks and gray skin reminded me of my mother, except Shana wasn't as pretty. She had a crooked nose, crooked chin, crooked fucking son—I hated her with all of my crooked fucking heart. If she hadn't brought her kid into the world my sister wouldn't be missing. Logically, I knew that wasn't true, but it hadn't mattered at the time. It took a team of human filth to traffic women; RJ was a single turd in the sewer. I needed someone to blame other than myself. Shana was visually accessible.

No one noticed me on the first day. People in the neighborhood were as damp and dirty as the streets, eager not to make eye contact. A needle lay in a pile of brown leaves. I kicked it into the gutter to get it away from the kids. Who was I kidding? The kids in this neighborhood probably lived with needles in their homes: Piper and I had. I hung out on the steps of an apartment building across the street and looked at my phone until it got dark. Other than a light turning on there was no activity. On the second trip I arrived later, just in time to see an old man shuffle to the mailbox. RJ's grandfather. I recognized him from the MichaelLisaHeppernam Facebook profile.

I promised myself that my fifth visit would be my last. It was on my sixth that I saw Shana. I wasn't sure it was her at first: I held my breath when the door to the squat brown house opened and a woman walked out. Leaning on the wall next to the door she pulled a pack of cigarettes from her back pocket and lit up. The front door was still open. She yelled something into the house, and a second later a kid came running out. He couldn't have been older than three; was he hers? He darted past her and ran for something in the yard, his arms in front of him. For real, was this her kid? I stood up, incensed. How dare she bring another one into the world. She barely acknowledged the little guy was there, pacing the patch of sidewalk in front of the house with the phone pressed to her ear and gesturing wildly with her cigarette hand. He played with random objects he pulled out of the mud, holding them up for her to see: a stick, a rock, an old piece of toy. Nothing caught her interest. Eventually he wandered to the corner of the yard and climb on top of an overturned bucket. Her back was to him when he fell. He sat in a heap in the dirt, crying and staring up at her hopefully. When she finally noticed he was crying, she acted annoyed. She walked over and yanked him up by one arm, dragging him back inside the house. Whether she was that kid's mom or not, she wasn't the cuddly tender type, and I felt sorry for him. I was being too harsh…maybe…but probably not.

When the police finally got around to questioning RJ about the Polaroids, he played dumb.

I held him responsible—aside from being the oldest person there that day, he'd been the one to manhandle Piper into the back seat.

Dupont was living in New York with his dad's family. I kept tabs on him through social media. Dupont's role had been less, the intermediary for mischief. Did he know what he was arranging when he hooked Colby up with Piper that day? He knew *something*, definitely more than he was saying.

Six months after Piper went missing, a tenth grader accused

Colby Crimball of sexual harassment. His parents scooped him and his brother up and relocated to Florida—a privilege of the wealthy. They were both currently attending FSU. Matt looked just as basic as I remembered him to be—square face with an all-American confidence. Colby was sleazy—narrow-shouldered with all his features pinched in the middle of his face. In his photos, he always had his arm slung around a girl in a bikini. It seemed the only purpose of his social media. He wore his sleepy eyes, backward cap, and a frat boy smile with more entitlement than his brother. I hated him. Why should he get to live a carefree life? He was there when she went missing, as far as I was concerned. He was working with RJ—Millar, or whatever his name was—and Angel that day.

Colby denied everything of course, and without the other three guys, he couldn't be linked to her disappearance. I'd hit a wall. The investigation hit a wall. The case went cold again.

It was ninety degrees the day I climbed into Gran's attic looking for Piper. Gran had moved into her house by then, and Cal and I were living in student housing two blocks from campus.

Moving out was one of the dumber things I'd done in the last year, but I wasn't ready to admit that yet. In my triumphant march to independence, I'd forgotten that I was still a kid dealing with trauma...raising a kid. I needed my Gran; I needed my sister. The loneliness of caring for a four-year-old alone was overwhelming. Moving out on our own had only compounded my issues, and Cal was stuck in daycare more than was good for him.

Gran had us over for dinner a few nights a week. It was after a Sunday lunch of chicken and biscuits that the tide went out and the depression came in. Cal was napping in the spare bedroom. His naps were sweaty and deep; he always woke up in a good mood, which was more than I could say for myself. I beat Gran at Scrabble and made an excuse to go to the attic for my old books.

"What are you up to?" She sighed. "I don't like it already."

I knew she wouldn't. She thought that when I looked at Piper's things I got depressed, when really, I got depressed and looked at Piper's things. I'd stopped trying to explain that to her; she didn't get it. She had photos and mementoes of Piper everywhere—all over the walls.

"I want to look at some pictures and notes of Piper's." I opened the closet where she kept her games and stacked the Scrabble box on top.

"Why?"

"Do I need a reason?"

She thought about it. "No." She turned to the sink and picked up the blue sponge.

That was it? That was all she was going to say? I took it as a good sign.

Access to the attic was in Gran's bedroom. It had a pull-down door that released a rickety old ladder. It was an adventure getting up that thing. Due to the low ceiling, I had to crawl to the plastic tubs that held what was left of Piper's life. Black with red handles.

Outside the sealed attic windows, it was a sweaty summer. By the time I unclipped the lid off Piper's tub, my T-shirt was damp. I knew exactly what I was looking for. It took me a few minutes to paw through the books and stuffed animals before I found it. The shoebox labeled *2010–2012 Pious Piper*—which was mean of me, but at the time I'd been mad at her for disappearing.

I took the box down the ladder and set it on the kitchen table. Gran was in the backyard with her shears. I knocked on the window and told her to put sunscreen on. She held up her arm to show she already had, and I gave her the thumbs-up. Sometimes I didn't know who was mothering whom. I sat at the table and flipped off the lid. I'd seen all this stuff before;

it served the dual purpose of shrine and investigation. If Piper touched it once, I'd touched it a thousand times since.

Particularly, I was looking for the notes she'd written to her church friends. Sometimes they passed scraps of paper back and forth in services. Other times they used the notes section on the back of the church program.

There was something in particular that was bothering me. A sentence. Piper hadn't written it; her friend Susannah had. It was scribbled on a church program, the writing getting more and more cramped as it neared the margin. It surfaced in my memory like dreams sometimes do—maybe it was Scrabble that triggered the thought, but once I had it, I couldn't make it go away. Call it an itch. I found what I was looking for and spread it flat on the table, running my palms over the creases.

*Oh Susannah, oh Susannah, oh Susannah valentine! Hope he likes me, hope he writes me, hope he gives me what is mine.* Her handwriting looped dramatically. She was being silly—but not. *It's not really yours, is it?* What I presume is Susannah's handwriting is small and crowded like her teeth. I lift the page closer to my face to make out the words.

*What is that supposed to mean?* Piper was pissed.

Susannah drew a smiley face and a heart. *Not yours yet,* she wrote underneath.

My sister responded with a sad face.

*Soon,* Susannah wrote next to the sad face, then underlined it. *You were made 4 each other.* I presumed the series of hearts drawn at the bottom of the page was made by my sister. She was very agreeable if you said what she wanted to hear. From what I recall of mousy-faced Susannah, she liked to challenge what my sister said and then backtrack when Piper called her out. The girl could play victim better than most people could play themselves. "Susannah." I say it out loud in an effort to peel forgotten memories from that dismal period of my life. Had people called her Suzie? Suz? She was privy to Piper's secrets.

Gran kept her photo albums in her bedroom. When we lived in the apartment, she kept them in the living room on her bookshelf, but after Piper went missing, she grew protective of them. They were a visual shrine to my sister, and to look was to remember. They disappeared one by one, and then one day their shelf held only dust. The albums were a tribute to our childhood; even before she got custody of us, she'd take us places and use an entire roll of film to record what we were doing.

There were gaps in the albums, spaces of time when our mother wouldn't let us see Gran. In one photo with her, we're toothless and standing outside of the zoo; in the next we're at a Seahawks game and we have not only our two front teeth, but also the beginning swells of breasts. I remembered the stranger who took our photo exclaiming how beautiful we were, and Gran's face had visibly changed, her pride in us so evident she was still beaming as the shutter clicked. It was a relief to be loved that much. The hollow was still there from our mother, echoing and empty, but a new chamber had formed in the space next to it—a carved-out tunnel that led to the light. Gran.

There were certain photos that I wanted to see, particularly the ones from the summer before Piper went missing. We'd spent a week in either June or July, camping with her church—that was the summer everything changed. It was so subtle no one really noticed until it was too late.

We were excited to go; we'd planned our activities and researched the campground for weeks before the trip. But Piper ditched me two days in to hang out with a bunch of holy rollers who memorized Scripture for fun. I didn't get it. It was like she forgot how to be herself after that, and consequently forgot how to be my sister.

The albums were in Gran's closet. I had to wait until she went to the grocery store to sneak in her room to get them. She'd bought them in a set of four: olive leather with white stitching around the edges that was meant to be trendy. She'd stacked them upright so she could pull them out easily. I ran my finger over their spines, deciding which to pull first. The cracks branched like a palm, leather veins crisscrossing and then abruptly ending. Gran may have been a librarian, but I knew she wouldn't arrange them chronologically; she'd put her favorite first.

I took the first one out and sank to the carpet. Ha! It felt good to be right when everything was so wrong. The album I held was a full year of us being together, the after-custody photos. It was moments like this that I felt closest to her—when I could predict how she did things. I paged through the happy times, all neatly labeled: twins at the pumpkin patch, twins getting their ears pierced at the mall, twins camping with church. We were not Piper and Iris, but "twins." I knew that Gran felt guilty about our mom and the way she turned out—that's why having two girls was better than one—two girls was double the penance. She took that bull by the horns and mothered the hell out of us.

I put my finger on the photo of the three of us at Thanksgiving dinner, sitting around her small kitchen table. We were all cheesing before the prayer, holding hands and looking over our shoulders at the camera—which Gran had propped on the kitchen counter and set with a timer. A turkey, a tureen of gravy, mashed potatoes and green beans and rolls—the best spread we'd ever had. Our cheese was genuine, and that meal was the bomb.

Later that night our mom called, and we took turns letting her blame us for ruining her Thanksgiving. Gran had invited her, but she never showed. Not that we wanted her to—spending holidays with Mom always ended with her drunk and us hiding in our room while she sobbed on the living room floor about how her life hadn't turned out like she thought it would.

I didn't like when my oily-haired mother crept into my memories; the thought of her shuffling from room to room, her smell following everywhere she went, made me feel queasy. I turned the page fast. She wasn't in my life, so she didn't deserve to take up space in my memories.

The next pages were of the three of us on a hike to Franklin Falls, and then Christmas happened with stockings and presents, New Year's Eve when Piper and I stood holding sparklers on the little balcony, the parking lot behind us. I skipped ahead until I came to the Easter photos.

The same group we'd gone to camp with later that year was gathered in front of the church for a group shot. I remembered the slinky feel of the dress on my skin as Gran pulled us in. She always squeezed once we were tucked against her. Piper and I had never dressed alike—our mother hadn't bothered—but Gran bought us the same dress in different patterns that year. It was the closest we got to being matchy-matchy. Piper's had bold navy flowers on a white background, and mine was a watercolor design of lavender and pink. We'd worn our hair differently though; hers was up and mine down. I remembered that she'd insisted on that, and we'd tossed a coin for who got to wear theirs up.

When I'd had my fill of Piper, I studied the faces along the back row. They were the older teens who helped out in youth group. I vaguely remembered some of their names: Skylar had baby bangs, and Max always wore red shorts, though you couldn't see them in the photo—only his face was showing. I remember him being tall and kind of goofy. Nice. Had Piper had a crush on Max? No—that didn't seem right. Max was funny, but she hadn't paid special attention to him. Someone else occupied her thoughts back then. On the other side of Max was Ruth Byers, Gran's friend, and her husband Neil— both who did most of the event organizing and came along as volunteers. Below those five were three rows of youth, tiered at random. Gran had labeled this one: *Easter Sunday with the MCC crowd*. There was one person missing from the photo, perhaps the most important person: the youth group leader.

I kept turning pages, but after that Sunday it seemed that we did most of our activities with or around the church. I stopped turning pages when I reached the camping trip. There we were packing the trunk of Gran's Subaru, me wearing a baseball cap and Piper in sunglasses—stuffing gear wherever it would fit.

"Jam it in," Gran would say. "If there's a will there's a way!"

The next photo was of us setting up our tent. Gran had talked someone into taking it because she was in this one, posing with a tent peg while Piper and I were bent over the flopping canvas, trying to figure things out.

There were a couple photos of us fishing, wearing silly hats— *Twins catch nothing but have fun!* Gran's captions were hilarious. Neither of us looked very happy, but I was downright miserable, my surly teenage face turning away from the camera to spite her. My mood had to do with her forcing me to give my hat to Piper. She hadn't brought her own per usual, and I was over prepared with my two, so I had to lend her the one I hadn't worn yet—the one I bought with my own money— since it "fit her head better." Ridiculous. We had the same head and they both fit me fine, but when she took the argument to Gran, I was told to *just let her wear it*. "What does it matter?" she snapped. "Just give her the damn thing."

Nothing was safe from Piper's bullshit. If she could take something from me, she would. I handed the hat over. The look on Piper's face was triumphant and bored like a racehorse. She expected things to go her way.

Piper lost it in the lake.

The next page was empty, the pictures gone and the caption scratched out with blue pen. Odd. Gran would never vandalize a book—and if she needed to cover something up, she'd use Wite-Out; she had bottles and bottles of it in the junk drawer. The plastic sleeve crackled when I turned it to find one more missing photo and then a group shot on the last day of camp. This was much the same as the first except everyone was in shorts and T-shirts wearing sunburns on their faces.

Piper wasn't standing with us this time; she was in the second to last row with the pinched-faced friends she'd made at camp—the ones she ditched me for. Funny, after all these years I still felt salty about what went down. Words like *left me* and *abandoned* flew around my head like cartoon crows. Except she didn't look happy. Her eyes were flat.

The next page was missing another photo. I flipped ahead—more missing photos, more scribbled-out captions. It looked like doodling? I flipped the page to inspect the backside, and the paper pillowed beneath my fingertip. Someone had made those marks in anger. And why? I tossed the album aside in frustration, then thought of that day at camp, when Piper had betrayed me to go stand by her new friends—and didn't even look happy about it.

"Don't let it bother you," Gran had said when I shared my distress with her in the tent later. But there was a whole generation of women who told themselves not to "let it bother them." They said it to their daughters, and their daughters said it to us. I was bothered and I wanted to be—had a right even. Sisters weren't supposed to sell each other out, especially after what we went through together.

"You're growing into your own people. It's okay to do things separately—and together of course."

*The band is breaking up*, I thought, dully.

Gran wouldn't say it, as picking through her words, mincing around to defend Piper. Gran had the best of intentions, but she was playing peacemaker on the front lines and there was something insulting about having my own twin explained to me.

I wasn't growing into anything, I was the same Iris I'd always been. Piper was the one who decided to be an activist one week, and a hater the next. Teachers, parents, leaders treated her like she was whimsical instead of untrustworthy and fickle.

"The girls she is hanging out with are stupid, slack-jawed, religious sluts. She's becoming one too."

Gran's eyes did the dancing, widening then blinking rapidly like my words had blown directly into her eyeballs. She looked down at her hands like she didn't want me to see her expression, and flexed her fingers, something she did when her arthritis was acting up.

"First of all, I didn't teach you such meanness. There is no call—"

"Your daughter did."

"What?"

I felt like I was on a roller coaster. I'd rattled to the top. Now there was nothing left to do but tip over the edge.

"Your daughter taught me. If you don't like me, you should look at the way you raised her." My glare was first-class. I'd been storing the anger for weeks, letting the pressure build as my thoughts soured.

Gran suddenly looked very alert, her eyebrows picketing to her hairline, her rosebud mouth turned in on itself, and I couldn't tell if she was shocked, hurt, or as angry as me.

When she spoke again, her voice shook.

I looked away, ashamed but buzzing from the energetic sting my words had on her. I liked that she felt as bad as I did in that moment, but I couldn't look at her or I'd cry. She hadn't saved us in time. She was the reason my mother was a monster. She preferred Piper over me just like her daughter. She only raised us because she had to.

Sometimes the truth didn't need to be said out loud. My mother had a generalized lack of empathy. She was spiteful and mean and lashed out at her mother like a regularly scheduled program. It was boring and exhausting. In that moment I felt like my mother's daughter. Shame crept in. My eyes were filled with tears when I faced her again.

Gran looked at me with her sad eyes and her neat bob and nodded. "Fair enough. But she's not here, so I have to talk to you."

I sat crisscross applesauce on the floor of our tent, sweat beading on my nose, the devil heavy on my back. I wanted to say sorry, but I was angry at Piper, angry at myself, furious at Gran for being right.

Just as Gran was about to launch into her lecture, Piper burst through the opening of the tent. She made a beeline for her air mattress, flopping face-first onto her pink-and-green sleeping bag without a sound. Gran's voice faded as we stared at Piper's heaving back. What now? I wanted to scream. I couldn't even get disciplined without Piper butting in.

"What happened, my love?" Gran's voice was so gentle it made me want to cry. This was how it was: my feelings came second to Piper's. I knew what my role was: shoving my feet into my shoes, I left them alone so they could talk.

I never did find out what caused her to storm into the tent that night—or why her entire personality changed after the camping trip. As I stared at the missing pages in Gran's albums, I had a vision of sitting on our bedroom floor the day after she went missing, searching through her things. There had been photos among all of her other stuff—some of our mother, a couple of Gran during her wild years, and there were photos taken at church. At the time they'd seemed like mementos, but now I wasn't so sure.

At that point in my life, the mysteries outweighed the truths. I continued discovering strange things, like the missing pictures, that I knew were clues that would lead to Piper, but nothing ever did. Nothing. The next few years were the most despairing of my life. As the days, weeks, and months trudged by with no sign of Piper, I told myself that Piper was dead.

All these things I discovered, the things that continued to worm through my mind, eventually crystalized and formed the smallest, craziest theory. This theory led me to eventually (and dishearteningly) apply for an internship at Shoal Island a few years later.

# 19

## PRESENT

**DURING THE MONTH** of November, HOTI lays off ten members of the staff. It sends the hospital into a tailspin that doubles everyone's workload. As a result there are less eyes watching what I do, but hardly a free second to do anything but work. I bounce around the hospital doing jobs wherever I'm needed. At night I toss and turn, my sleep shallow and my skin hot.

I'm having breakfast with Crede in the staff cafeteria when Jordyn steps up to the buffet holding a plate. In the weeks I've worked at Shoal, Jordyn's appearance has changed dramatically. Her face is waxy and swollen, her gaze vapid. She stands motionless for a full minute, contemplating the teriyaki, before putting her plate down and walking out of the cafeteria.

"What's wrong with her? Is she sick?"

Crede doesn't look up. "Same as everyone else." He shrugs. "Burned out."

I open my mouth and close it again. I could say it the nice way or the blunt way.

I drop my toast. "Crede, are you being serious? Have you looked at her lately?"

He won't meet my eyes. "People have personal lives. So long as she does her job it's none of our business."

Crede looks at his pager. "I have to go. I told Janiss I'd take her a muffin, and then I have a call with Dalton's attorney."

"I'll take Janiss her muffin," I offer. "Are you talking about the Dalton in D hall?"

"Yep."

"Why do you have to talk to Dalton's attorney?"

"He's been unable to stand trial due to incompetency. The judge has asked for a reevaluation."

He hands me a napkin-wrapped muffin and I blow him a kiss.

If I'm on the dark side, I have two shadows following me around. I'm quite flattered that they've taken to me. Alma—the woman/child—and a thirty-two-year-old guy named Vespa who killed his mother when she asked him to turn his music down. Though the crime happened a decade earlier, Vespa either lives in the time before his mother died or after. He gravitates between all-consuming grief, and when he forgets—paranoia that he is going to do something wrong. He follows me with clasped hands and bed hair, fretting—he is always fretting. On Vespa's bad days he wakes up asking one question on repeat: Is my mother dead? He can't make eye contact on those days; he doesn't want to see the answer in our eyes.

I drop my phone and a Kit Kat in the basket for George. In the weeks that I've been here, he's grown a beard, and beneath the scraggly graying hairs I see the corners of his mouth turn up. George smiles at the chocolate—not me; I've learned not to be offended.

Vespa in his plaid robe is the first thing I see. When he's upset—which is almost always—he chews on one end of the belt. It hangs from its loops, one sodden end in Vespa's mouth, the other in his free hand like a pet snake.

He lunges forward, and I brace myself. Listening to Vespa is like listening to the side-effects-may-include portion of a drug commercial. I don't have the heart not to listen, he is always so distraught. His medical knowledge is impressive, so much so, he turns it on himself almost hourly. If he can't find something wrong with himself, he'll obsess about one of us dying.

One of the first things he said to me was, *"Crede isn't going to die of lung cancer like everyone thinks, he's going to die of throat cancer…"*

It is exhausting for everyone involved as he often has to be sedated when he became aggressively upset. To Vespa, a skin abrasion indicates cancer; a headache means meningitis. Crede told me that he accurately diagnosed one of the nurses with melanoma—early enough that it saved her life. With plenty of knowledge and none of the symptoms, he's been diagnosed with HA—health anxiety—hypochondriasis.

"What's wrong, V?"

"Something bad is happening…"

Hovering close to my right shoulder, he squints at me, his expression flickering between negative emotions: fear, then sadness, then anxiety.

"Like what?"

He knits his eyebrows, frowning so deeply I stop walking.

"If I tell you they'll kill me. Don't stop walking, they're watching us. Act normal."

I walk slower this time. We weren't supposed to get drawn into the patients' drama, potentially feeding a delusion. I needed to keep him calm and get help.

Crede warned me that Vespa purges his meds when left unsupervised. The short-staffing issue made it impossible to keep your eye on everyone all the time. I spot Crede behind the care station and try to make eye contact, but his gaze slides right off of me and goes back to what he's doing. An elephant show plays on the TV. Three female patients sit together on the couch wearing paper crowns they painted in art class the day before. There is a remotely competitive game of Ping-Pong happening in the common area; a handful of onlookers lurk around the table. No one is looking at us, of this I'm sure.

Vespa is breathing hard. I can tell he's grappling with what to tell me.

"You can tell me," I say, soft enough so only he can hear. "Nothing bad is happening. You're safe here."

"I heard them talking about it. They said it—not me. They're lunatics… You should ask them about it before everyone ends up dead."

*Dead?* I stop walking. "Ask who, Vespa? I don't understand…"

He takes a step toward me. Both sides of his belt are dragging on the floor. The next thing he says sends chills down my spine.

"Marshal… Jude…"

I could be anywhere at all—in an airport, at a concert, in a grocery store—and if I hear someone say the name Jude, I will stop everything and look.

"What did you say?"

Vespa's face twitches, and he reaches for his robe. I rein in my reaction, smiling through clenched teeth and mental profanity. The name itches beneath my skin—*Jude, Jude, Jude.* I dig my nails into my palms, trying to ground myself. Vespa knows something's up. His yellow/brown eyes grow wide. Gran once commented that a strange light came into my eyes when someone said his name.

"Did you just get the chills?"

"No," I lie. "Jude from D? That Jude?" I look at the door for D unit, and Vespa follows my eyes. I feel a spurt of excitement and squash it down. Not now. We're almost to the care station. If Vespa doesn't answer me now, I don't know that he ever will. Something or someone has scared him.

"Vespa…?"

He nods suddenly, and then his eyes go flat. He studies the ceiling with a pained expression, his lips working silently. I don't want to push him too hard and make him shut down.

I lick my lips, then ask him one more time, my heart pounding in my ears.

"V, does Jude come out of his room? Have you seen him?"

Lynnie, a nurse I've only worked with a couple of times, comes barreling out of A hall, her eyes glued to my face. *Uh-oh.* Underneath her bleached pixie cut, her expression is exasperated. The closer she gets the less chance I have of Vespa answering me. I grab his arm and feel the damp string of his robe under my palm. Ignoring the urge to jerk back, I look in his eyes with such concentration he can't look away. His Adam's apple bobs mercilessly under my scrutiny, but I refuse to look away.

"He's so afraid of having nightmares he won't sleep."

I try to keep my face neutral, but he smacks a hand over his mouth like he's angry with himself. "I've said a bad thing."

I shake my head casually. "No, you're just chatting with me. It's fine." I'm trying not to mess this up.

"I've said a wrong thing…" he repeats, looking unsure.

"No, you haven't." My tone is firm. Lynnie is on top of us. I lock my jaw and smile stiffly.

"What are you doing out here? I thought I told you to go straight to the cafeteria. Goddamn, I need my coffee…"

"He's having a bad morning," I say quickly. She opens her mouth to say something else, but I cut her off. "I'll walk him over. Why don't you get that coffee and I'll take over for you."

Five minutes later, I have Vespa seated at a table with two boiled eggs, tomatoes, toast, and a glass of milk. I stare across my watery bowl of oatmeal. He hasn't said a word since we got to the cafeteria, and I'm worried he's shut down entirely without telling me what I want to know.

He grimaces as he peppers his tomatoes, glancing up every few seconds to glare around at the occupied tables. "It's a death march in here. Everyone stinks."

I watch as he cuts his tomatoes into little pieces, then eats them one at a time.

"So, you can smell auras?"

"What I do is not psychic, it's purely scientific."

"Predictive knowledge?"

He shrugs, looking pleased that I'm asking. "There's no voice in my head telling me things." He examines his boiled egg before he bites into it.

"Okay," I say. "I believe you. How am I going to die?"

He glances up. "Is that really what you came here to ask me?"

This time I shrug. "One of them…"

"Fair," he says. "Pass me that butter…"

I slide the plate of condiments over to him, and he grunts. My leg is bouncing under the table where he can't see it. I want to get back to the topic of Jude, but I'm also curious about how he'll answer my last question.

For a moment, I see myself absorbed into the totality of his answer. How he says I will die, I will die. We've both lost it.

"I'm not a fortune teller," he insists.

"I don't think you are a fortune teller, V, I think you know things."

Pleased with my answer, he dusts the egg from his hands, nodding decidedly. What's left of his hair clings to the back of his head in wispy tassels. "I've thought about this a lot actually. Some people have bad health written all over them. I know a gut parasite when I see one. Thyroid problems—don't even get me started…" He makes sure no one in the vicinity is listening, then in a low voice says, "My grandmother read tarot. I loved my grandmother, she was a no-bullshit kind of lady. I believe in a little woo-woo," he admits. "Don't tell."

I zip my lips.

"Sick people have a stink about them. Rotten livers smell different than, say…prostate cancer."

"I don't know what facial expression to make," I say. "I feel awkward."

"Healthy people have a smell too—like roses," he continues.

"Really?"

"No, actually they smell like my childhood friend, Meredith. She liked roses."

"So your nose is psychic."

"No, that's not it." He frowns. "Will you let me finish?"

I zip my lips again.

"You don't have a smell at all, dead or alive—there's no pulse to your smell."

"I feel that," I say. "But also, what are you actually saying? Am I dead already?"

I'm only half kidding.

"No…"

"You're lying."

Tilting his head sideways, he considers this, then shakes his head. "No…it takes a long time for a broken heart to die."

"Sounds like you're on the fence. Why was Jude out of unit D?"

Vespa doesn't falter. "I'm not on the fence…" And then, "He lets himself out."

It seems that the cafeteria has gone silent in that moment. "How?" My voice is barely a whisper. He stares at his almost empty plate, his lips twitching.

"I don't know," he says. "But you're probably going to kill him."

I stay until 8:30 a.m., when the cafeteria closes for the morning, then send the stragglers to the common room for their daily activities. It's hard to focus on anything other than what Vespa said about Jude. Could he be telling the truth? My mind keeps turning it over. There is the possibility that he's lying—this is a hospital for the criminally insane, is it not? We are reminded of that everywhere we go: on signs, in our contracts, and by each other. Be aware, be alert. Would Vespa lie about something like that? I don't think so—he killed his mother, but he's always admitted to it. The fact that my sister's murderer could be wandering around the hospital at night catapults electricity through my legs, into my chest and up my throat.

I'm almost back to the care station when I hear his voice. It's embarrassing to admit that my whole body reacts to it. My thoughts about Vespa and Jude minimize to a whisper. Dr. Grayson is wearing his white coat, chatting with Jordyn and Crede near the foot of the stairs. Bouncer is there too, swallowing him up with her eyes. Dr. Grayson is polite to her, but I've never seen him show favoritism that might suggest they were something more. There does seem to be a familiarity between them—not lovers or friends, but something else.

I pretend to ignore them, going to the assignment whiteboard even though I know my name will not be on it. I go home today. The conversation that was happening between them has ended suddenly. Then he's beside me, and we're both looking at the whiteboard like we're studying the value menu at McDonald's.

"We don't have much time," he says softly. He's less than a foot away. If I scooted an inch to the left, we'd be touching.

I shift my gaze to his face and give him a questioning look. Erased of seriousness, his face looks boyish…naughty. He holds back a smile, the heat of his eyes making me blush.

"If I stay in this spot for longer than twenty seconds, someone will see me and come over to talk."

"Well, you better get moving, then…"

"But if you come with me, they'll think I'm busy and leave me alone."

I can smell his soap and his cologne, and somewhere behind both of those things—his skin. "So, I'll be doing you a favor?"

"Absolutely. Huge favor…" His eyebrows lift to his hairline. I can't help but laugh.

"Want to take a walk?" he asks. There's enough shock on my face to make him laugh this time. "What?" he pretends to be offended. "You don't think I walk?"

I bite my bottom lip to keep from smiling.

He is better at flirting than I am. When he's around, I forget why I'm really here. *Piper*, I remind myself. *Jude*. My priority is getting into D hall, and I am becoming painfully aware of the cost of his attention. Everyone is looking at him and thus at me. Sneaking around got harder if people were aware of your presence.

"I can't," I say. "I'd love to, but—" I make eyes at Janiss, who is watching us from the care station.

"You can tell me the truth," he says, dipping his head. "Is she scarier than I am?"

"I'm afraid so."

"That's what I thought." He pauses before becoming serious. "The very last thing I want is to get you in trouble with the nurses. If that happens, you might as well just go ahead and quit."

"I'm glad we're on the same page."

"I'll tell you what." He glances at his watch. "There's an hour and a half before everyone heads home. Meet me in the greenhouse in ten. Wear a jacket, it's chilly outside."

"The greenhouse?"

He dips his head, speaking in a low voice. "If you go out the back door in the patient cafeteria, there's a hill. Crest it and follow the gravel path. You can't miss it."

"Doctor…" A female patient wanders over to us, her hands outstretched like she's greeting her savior. She's barefoot, which isn't allowed. "I prayed for you when you had black eyes."

"Is that so, Fern? Who did you pray to…"

Their voices drift off as he steers her toward the care station.

I feel *the mush*, as Piper would say: crush adrenaline. I wait for the feeling to go with him, but it doesn't.

"Iris, you have a boat to catch, don't you?"

I jump. Behind me, standing in the open security door, is Jordyn. She's staring after Dr. Grayson, a weird look on her face.

"Yep…" I obey without thinking.

She lets the door close behind her and steps sideways, positioning herself to watch me scan my card. I can feel her hovering; her wasplike energy is making me nervous. I try not to react, but the urge to run screaming is tempting. I can't summon the confidence to look at her, so I stare at the camera to the right of the door, wondering if George is watching this all go down; I would.

"You really should eat in the staff cafeteria." Her tone is sharper than her breath, which smells of alcohol. It's not a suggestion. My mouth goes dry. Was she watching me? If she wasn't, someone else was and they were reporting back to her. That was stupid. There were cameras everywhere. Everyone was being watched all of the time.

"I didn't know we weren't allowed to eat in the patient cafeteria."

I have to scan the card twice before it works.

"It's not encouraged. Your people are out there. These are patients."

"I understand," I say.

"Good."

I come back to my senses as soon as I cross the glass walkway. That was a weird morning. In the span of two minutes, one of my bosses asked me on a work date, and the other chided me. Part of me thinks that I'm imagining his attention, but most of me knows I'm not. I'm suspicious of it and yet I want more.

I have to use my key card to get outside. The greenhouse, as it turns out, is a beautiful, warm place. Beds of vegetables grow on one side, and on the other are dozens of plant variations, all watered by a timed mist. He's waiting inside, looking at the vegetables, when I walk in. I watch as he plucks a cherry tomato from the vine and pops it into his mouth.

"Hi," I say.

"Hey there." He smiles; it reaches his eyes, and I'm a little breathless. We're standing two feet away from each other.

"Who tends this?" I ask, looking around in wonder. There are lemon trees and lime trees, green peppers, potatoes, squash, cabbage…

"The patients. It's become a passion project for some of them. They're doing great, as you can see… Alma planted those tomatoes. She seems to really like you."

"I'm a granny's girl," I tell him. "I think maybe I'm just good with that demographic."

"Don't be so humble. You're good with the patients, everyone says so. And besides, I'm not sure Alma fits into a demographic."

"True."

His hair and beard are collecting tiny droplets from the mist.

"Do the patients from D hall ever come out here?" I pick one of Alma's tomatoes and pop it in my mouth.

It's the first time he's looked uncomfortable. "We used to. There was an incident a few years ago. One of the patients had a violent regression."

"Did anyone get hurt?"

He hesitates. "Yes, actually. They attacked one of the security guards with a spade and killed him."

"Okay. Wow. I wasn't expecting that."

"Violence in a place for the violent?"

"Well, when you put it like that…"

He grimaces, his eyes going dark. "There were two patients from D who collaborated the attack…" He looks ahead to the tree line and frowns. "I have something to confess. I googled you."

I'm thrown by the change in topic, but once his words sink

in, I stare at him and say nothing. I don't do nervous talking; on the contrary, I get lock tongue.

"You look like you want to kill me," he admits. I swallow the lump in my throat.

"No, it's just my face."

He laughs.

His face is mostly concealed by his beard. I always thought it unfair that men could hide their weak chins and acne scars beneath a beard. His eyebrows are well-groomed, and he has full lips resting under a nice straight nose. I can't tell what he's thinking at the moment.

"Is that what you wanted to talk to me about?"

I clench my teeth so hard my jaw hurts.

"It felt dishonest not to mention it. I'm sorry about what happened to your sister."

"We don't know what happened to my sister," I say truthfully. "We're still trying to figure that out…"

I'm the wax version of myself: stiff, slick, and robotic.

"Do you think she's alive?" His voice is the opposite of mine, so warm it could melt chocolate.

"No."

"No?"

I register his surprise, then turn away to hide my tears. Touch pulls me back into my body. I feel hot fingertips on my wrist. He rubs circles with his thumb where the softest skin is. My love language is touch. I thought that's the way it was for all twins until Piper told me she hated being touched. I stare at a row of empty terra-cotta planters, lulled by Leo Grayson's fingertips. The rain outside sounds like traffic if you listen just right.

"I didn't mean to upset you." He regards me plaintively before letting go of my wrist. My hand drops to my side, tingling where he touched me. Outside of the greenhouse, everything is fluorescent green—Hulk green, Cal would say. I slip my hands into my pockets.

"I'm not upset," I say automatically. My thoughts meander off course, distracting me enough to trip on my own feet. Leo's reflexes are fast; he reaches for me, but I catch myself.

"Tell me about Piper."

Hearing Piper's name coming from Leo Grayson's mouth trips me up in a different way. I break eye contact to think of her. Rain falls harder, but we don't speed up. Somewhere nearby the soft *plink plink plink* of water dripping on metal.

"That's the shrink in you talking."

He laughs, flashing straight teeth. "No, it's the human in me talking. But good job changing the subject."

"What do you want to know?"

"Everything."

We follow the path to the end of the greenhouse and step out into the rain. Our clothes soak up the wet like plants. The smell of the sea air mingling with the rich dirt reminds me of Gran and Piper. I give Leo a heavily censored version of my life, pulling strands of my hair from my mouth as the wind picks up. We've walked all the way to the woods. I stop short of the tree line. Leo listens attentively, watching the ground as he walks. When I'm done, I feel exhausted. It doesn't matter how I'm telling it or what I'm leaving out. Slicing yourself open for the purpose of examination keeps your heart in a perpetual state of trauma.

"So that's it?" he says when I'm done. "They put her on the ferry, and she—what? Disappears into thin air?" He looks upset by this, which touches me. I am upset every day, every minute, every second of my life. Piper and I sliced apart by human wickedness.

"Pretty much." I take a steadying breath. I am alone. My sister left me alone to raise her boy. I miss her. I hate her. More than anything, I love her.

I have the sudden longing to be with Gran and Cal, the people I have left. What am I doing here anyway? I turn away from him to hide my face, homesick and embarrassed.

"Iris…"

It startles me when he says my name. He says it with the intensity of a man proposing marriage.

"Dr. Grayson…"

He winces. "Leo. I don't like the way it sounds when you say my name like that."

All of a sudden, I'm laughing. "Like what?"

"Like I'm your boss."

"You are my boss… Leo."

I'm rewarded with a genuine smile. We're only a foot apart again, and I can't remember how that happened. We keep drifting toward each other. I feel like a dumb kid with a crush. There's nowhere to look but at him, so I do.

And then he kisses me, and it's the softest, nicest kiss I've ever had. When he pulls away, he's looking me right in the eyes.

"I know why you're really here."

# 20

## PRESENT

**I AM PRACTICED** in the art of acting indifferent. But when Leo says those six words to me—*"I know why you're really here"*—I cannot control my breathing. I open my mouth to say something, but instead I draw in a jagged breath I then have to blow out through my nose. I'm lightheaded with panic and so dizzy I'm sure I'm going to pass out. Of course, he figured it out. He is a therapist trained to figure it out. Words pile on top of each other in my mind; I try to find something to say, but I'm too flustered to make sense.

"I'm here for the same reason," he says. I stare at him blankly.

"You couldn't help her, so you've dedicated your life to helping…"

"Yes." I sound strained, but I am collapsing on the inside, falling to a mental floor in relief. Leo cannot know why I'm really here…even though he's right about that part—the part about me wanting to help—I'm not here for that this time.

"Wanna hang out later?"

His voice is just for me.

"Yeah, I kinda do…" I say, surprising myself.

His eyes travel my face slowly like he's sipping me up. I feel the look from my fingertips all the way to my toes.

"Good."

I stare at his mouth since he's staring at mine.

"Good," I say back.

He hands me his phone and I put in my number.

We part ways in the woods near the back door of the staff kitchen. It's more cheerful than the courtyard behind the patient kitchen where the men gather to smoke. As soon as the door closes behind him, I follow Leo's directions, walking through the woods around the side of the building until I reach the security gate. This one has space for an actual key—which he took off his key chain.

"Give it back to me later," he said when he handed it to me. "There's a plum tree just outside the gate, sweetest plums you will ever taste."

I unlock the first gate and then relock it behind me. A fenced corridor leads to another fenced corridor. I'm in a maze of wire. I let myself in and out of one more gate. I see the plum tree but I don't stop to pick fruit. I cannot miss the water taxi. I walk along another portion of the building, and then I'm on the front lawn of HOTI, at the bottom of the hill that leads to the dock. I am surprised to see Bouncer standing outside the door, wearing her red parka and smoking a cigarette. She barely looks at me when I pass by, her attention on the dirt at her feet. I go to the dorms to pack up my things. There are a bunch of people stripping their beds, calling out to each other to hurry up.

"The sea boat waits for no one," a male voice says.

"Bet it would wait for Grayson…" another voice says back. I dump my linen in the chute and grab my bag from the foot of my bunk. It's the first time I've not wanted to leave Shoal Island since I started the job. I find a seat inside. I've barely sat down when Leo texts me a playlist.

He likes music from the nineties—Matchbox Twenty and Third Eye Blind will still be good decades from now, I think. Aside from his stellar taste in music, Leo is also naturally interested in people. And he is considerate. *He's also at least sixteen years older than you*, I remind myself. *That's sixteen years more mature than any man you've dated.*

At the center of Seattle's waterfront are nine historic piers, built at the turn of the 1800s to serve the railroads and the Alaskan Gold Rush. I park across the street and make my way toward the aquarium where we agreed to meet. Cal texts me a picture of his friend Luke's golden retriever puppy with a praying hands emoji. He is at a playdate at Luke's house..

Nice try, I send. Then, He's cute.

I dodge dopey-eyed men and their enthused wives, almost trip over toddlers as they dart around and then abruptly stop. The pier is lined with shops and food. I walk past the ticket booth to the Ferris wheel and the signs advertising sailing trips around the sound, asking myself what exactly I thought I was doing meeting him here. I feel stupid and foolish, until I spot him. He hasn't seen me yet, but he looks nervous too, glancing up every time someone walks near because he thinks it could be me.

He's waiting for me in front of the aquarium, wearing a gray coat and a black scarf over blue jeans. His face lights up when he spots me.

"Hey, stranger…" He smiles.

We walk back the way I came, toward the restaurants. Leo suggests we eat at one of the fast-food restaurants that serve fish and chips and world-famous chowders. It's dark outside and cold, but the pier is busy. People mill about taking photos of the wheel as it changes from neon pink, to blue, to yellow. We make our way over to a table, our breath visible in the cold.

"This was a dumb idea." He sets the bag of food on a picnic

table and looks around, rubbing his hands together for warmth. "The temperature has dropped ten degrees in the last half hour."

Despite trying not to think of Piper, I think of Piper—about how close we are to the trash can where the homeless woman found her bag. He's a handsome distraction to my dark thoughts. Producing two cans of Coke from his pockets, he slides in next to me.

"I've seen you eat those nasty cafeteria fish sticks, figured you had to like real fish and chips."

"I didn't know I had a dinner audience," I tease.

"You're hard not to look at."

I'm not a self-conscious person, but I've also never had a man of his caliber interested in me.

I like the way he takes over and does things so I don't have to. He always seems to know the right things to do and say.

"You remind me of my sister," I say.

Leo's eyebrows shoot up. His mouth is full, but he speaks around his food. "How is that?"

"My gran always says to take the compliment and shut up."

He chokes on his sip of Coke. I laugh as he pounds his chest with a fist, eyes watering.

"How do you imagine her?"

"Who? Piper?"

He nods.

"Charming. She'd wear dresses in winter…she'd be into live music and eating oysters, and she'd buy the trendy toothpaste—you know, the one that's two bucks more." I lick my lips. It feels good to talk about her with someone other than Gran.

"She'd throw dinner parties but forget to cook the dinner…" I laugh dryly. "But it would be the funnest party because she'd have some ridiculous solution like making pancakes. Everyone would be eating pancakes in formal wear."

"What would one of your dinner parties be like?"

He had me there. I hadn't really…had I ever pictured myself hosting a dinner party of any sort? In my daydreams, I attend Piper's parties.

"Well…they would be costume parties…jolly gnomes. Or like a sad winter party where everyone has to come in wrinkled clothes and bring a Crock-Pot of soup."

"I'd like to come to one of your parties."

"Oh? And what soup would you bring?"

"I'd bring a big pot of Campbell's chicken noodle and then innocently eat the better homemade soups."

I don't tell him that Campbell's chicken noodle is my comfort food—that and a Hungry Man meal. Instead, I start crying like an idiot. I grab a handful of napkins to sop up the flood.

He must not notice my sudden onslaught of tears, because he says, "Do you want to get a drink after this? I know a place up the street."

I'm so embarrassed I can't look at him. I thought I had my emotions under control after all these years. I manage a nod. Leo, the pier, a nearby homeless man with his dog—they are all blurs of color. Maybe he does notice, because he gets me more napkins, and I pull myself together enough to take a couple more bites of my food.

The bar that he takes me to is called The Honky Tonk. It's nestled between a mattress store and a teriyaki restaurant in an eighties-esque shopping plaza. The stools at the bar are bolted down, and the cracked red leather leaks stuffing. Leo orders me a vodka ginger and himself a bourbon. I must look distraught because he rubs my back in big circles and asks me if I'm okay.

I'm not. Everything that has to do with Piper is weighing on me. I'm not doing enough, I've been distracted by my feelings for Leo. I feel like I'm walking around wearing a coat of wet fur. Her murderer is Jude Fields, D hall resident, considered not competent to stand trial. I want to blurt it out, ask him questions, touch his beard, taste his drink. My head is in a tangle with my heart.

He takes my hand and squeezes it.

"Why don't you think she's alive?"

I shake my head. "I know…" My voice cracks. "I know that she's dead. If she weren't, she would have come back. She would never leave her son."

My voice is strong for how weak I feel. I've told Piper's story to therapists with such regularity that my execution is expert. Telling Leo feels different than the other times. He's not sitting across a desk with a pen and paper, for one.

Leo's expression gently pushes me for details. But we're in a noisy bar that smells like beer and has questionable stains on the carpet. We're sitting at the bar—knee to knee. His head is bent toward me, and our joined hands are resting on my thigh.

"What do you think happened to her?" His tone is gentle, but the topic is violent and gutting. I can't talk about Piper without thinking about her death. And since there were no bones, no grave, no answers—no closure—all I could ever do was imagine the many ways she could have died.

It is a sad reality that a person can be anything and everything and still be defined by the horrific way in which they left this life.

I finish my drink and plonk the glass down on the bar top. "You'll think I'm crazy." I'm not drunk yet, and I'd rather not let him see me that way.

Leo laughs good-naturedly at my comment. "Will I, now?" His eyes are dancing. "Strange thing to say to a psychologist, isn't it?"

"True. You're the last person who'd think I'm crazy," I admit.

He bows his head in thanks.

"Four years ago, I was going through my grandmother's photo albums. She'd written little captions and dates next to everything. I noticed that some of the photos were missing, and the captions were scratched out...pretty aggressively."

The bartender comes by and Leo orders for us.

"So," I continue, "I remember seeing photos when I was going through my sister's things and seeing photos like the ones missing. I haven't had the guts to look through that stuff again, but I'm pretty sure there's a common denominator between the photos that stayed in the album and the ones she took out."

"Where were the photos taken?"

"Church, church concerts, church picnics, church camping trips. My grandmother never missed a Sunday."

"So what's the common denominator?"

Two identical drinks appear in front of us. Leo slides one over. We click glasses before I take a sip, wincing as the bourbon hits the back of my throat.

I look around. There are a handful of drinkers—three men in construction gear with pints in front of them, and an old guy in a fedora staring into a glass of red wine like he's looking for a fly. Leo is still waiting for my answer. I take another sip and try not to make a face; I am more comfortable making drinks than drinking them.

"He was the youth pastor."

"You think she took all of the photos of the youth pastor out of the album? Why would she do that?"

"I think they were having sex. The caring youth pastor and the love-starved girl. He groomed Piper, and he had plenty of time to do it. She spent weekends at his house babysitting his kid. I thought it was weird that she wanted to go over there. These people didn't even have a TV in their house. They were super Christian."

I'm down to the last sip of my drink and feeling it. Leo is looking at me with a mixture of worry and pity. I don't like it. I feel the need to defend my case.

"His wife was young—like not pedophile young, but almost. She couldn't have been more than nineteen at the time—eighteen when she got pregnant with his baby."

I lick my lips. I think of the notes Piper scribbled to Susannah in the margins of church programs…the way her entire personality changed right before she disappeared. She was my twin, my good half, I knew her better than anyone on the planet. Something happened between that doughy-faced youth pastor and my fifteen-year-old sister. Overwhelmed to tears, I toss back the last of my drink and immediately regret it. My stomach rolls and I break out in a sweat. Leo, who has barely touched his drink, looks at me in concern.

"You okay?"

"I don't feel great," I admit. He studies my face and nods. Turning to the bartender, he motions for the check.

"Let's get out of here."

He pays the tab while I go to the bathroom. He's waiting for me near the host stand. Under the dim, warm glow of the lobby's chandelier.

We leave my car parked on the street, and I give Leo my address. He types the address into his phone and shows me the screen to make sure he got it right. The hospital tries to call him. Surprisingly he sends it to voicemail. He drives me home. It only takes a few minutes to get to Gran's at this time of day. When I open my eyes, we're on Gran's street.

# 21

**I TELL LEO** not to pull into the driveway. He slows on the street and I hop out, lifting my hand in a reluctant wave before I head up. I'm embarrassed. Drinking and oversharing, could I be any more charming? I don't see it until I'm right in front of the door. Stuck to the black paint with a bit of tape is a white envelope with *Piper Walsh* printed on a label. Color drains from my vision and my knees feel weak. Spinning around, I put my back to the door, my eyes scanning the small front yard.

Hedges taller than I am run the length of the property, so thick they create a soundproof panel between a bus road and Gran's rambler. It wasn't possible that someone squeezed through the hedges, so whoever left the envelope on the door had to walk up the driveway, then around the side of the house to get to the front door. I get chills. The envelope is thin and flat. I'm grappling with opening it now or waiting until I have a moment alone inside. I feel sick, but I have a feeling that whatever is inside of the envelope will make me feel worse.

Cal decides for me, throwing open the front door, and I jump in surprise. The smile drops off his face as he looks at me in question. My heart lifts a little at the sight of him.

"Hi," I say, stuffing the envelope into the side pocket of my backpack. I can't have Cal asking questions, not yet.

"Why is your face like that?" His hand is still on the door-knob, blocking my way into the house.

I smile big, big, bigger—and tickle him under the arm to make him let go. He laughs half-heartedly and steps aside, frowning.

"I was in deep thought and you surprised me, that's all."

He takes my backpack from me and carries it inside, dumping it on the floor near the garage door. It's going to be hard to act normal until I know what's in that envelope. But before I can do anything about it, Mary-Ann walks out of the kitchen, drying her hands on a dish towel. Next there is the hullabaloo of feeding me since they've already had their dinner. Pushing me from behind, Cal steers me through the living room and into the bright warmth of the kitchen. I don't have time to say hi to Gran before Cal navigates me into a chair at the table while Mary-Ann gets my food. It feels silly to be served this way, but I'm too preoccupied with my thoughts to argue.

Mary-Ann makes to go home, and I stand to hug her. "She was talking a bit today," she says. "It makes her tired, but I could tell she was happy with herself."

I eat chili and cornbread at the kitchen table while my son fills me in on what I've missed over the last three days. Cal's head is propped on his little hand, and it reminds me of my sister when she was his age.

His mother.

"Hey, why don't you get your shower in now so we can watch an episode of that YouTube show you like before bed."

He considers my offer carefully; Cal hates showers, but my rare willingness to watch a screaming millennial play video games is enticing.

"Can we eat a snack while we watch?"

Gran makes a noise from where she sits, which probably means he's already eaten too much sugar for the night.

"Carrot sticks and cheese," I say. I cross my arms over my chest to show him I mean business.

"Fine." His expression is happier than his tone when the bathroom door closes. I open the Ring app on my phone and then remember that the camera is broken and I've been too broke to replace it.

I hear the shower turn on as I stand to rinse my bowl. I can't wait any longer. Drying my hands, I reach for the envelope. My initial trepidation is gone, I just want to get it over with.

I was right—inside is a single sheet of unlined paper, its message written in the same writing as on the envelope. I glance at my elegant, levelheaded grandmother who is trapped in her limited body.

"Gran," I say. "Someone left this on the front door for me."

I sit across from her on the edge of the coffee table and show her the note. I watch as her eyes narrow. My vision blurs as I wait for her to say something, the gingham pattern on her curtains dancing in front of my eyes. She opens her mouth, but the door to the bathroom bursts open and Cal barrels out, talking a mile a minute.

I catch Gran's eye over the top of his head, and she nods briefly. I know what she means; we'd do what needs to be done and talk later.

When Cal is in bed, I draw the curtains across the window in the living room and turn off the TV. The only thing we can hear now is traffic. Luckily my kid is a heavy sleeper.

"What does it mean?" Gran says as I kneel beside her. Her voice is slurred like she's speaking through a mouthful of cotton. I help her stand.

"I don't know."

"Let me…see it…again." Her nails are painted lavender.

Mary-Ann must have painted them for her, which was really sweet. I feel an overwhelming sense of hope and hopelessness at the same time.

I know why you're really at Shoal Island. You're looking at the wrong man.

I watch as she reads it again, then I take the paper from her, and we begin our slow walk to her bedroom.

"Who…knows?"

She's breathing hard as we shuffle forward. Her right foot is out of sync with her left, like they're trying to do two different things.

"No one knows," I say.

"Iris…"

"Gran, I'm telling you. No one knows what I'm doing there but you and me."

Her eyes are blue pools of worry, the creases around them fine as paper cuts. She is worn and beautiful, and her face has taught me that it is possible to be both.

"It isn't very often that visitors come to Shoal, and if they do, the hospital insists they schedule it." She doesn't look convinced, but it's true. Most people send their loved ones to the island for the purpose of making them hard to access—out of sight, out of mind.

"Someone…"

"Who, Gran? Think about it. He doesn't have any family left."

"S—someone…" Her word is quietly loud, and it hits home.

"Someone is trying to scare me, that's all."

We get to her bedroom, and I flick on the light. She does her bathroom things on her own, so I sit on the bed and wait while she uses her walking stick to carry her the rest of the way.

"We should probably be prepared for the worst," I say from the bed.

Seventy years old and she's still preparing for the worst. What have I brought to her front door? Gran is the strongest woman I know, but she doesn't deserve this. Not after everything else...

She comes out a few minutes later, and I help her into her nightgown. When she's in bed, she looks especially small. I look away from her face—which is bloodless—and stare at the books on her bookshelf, their spines color-coordinated. She'll probably never read those books again.

"I'll take care of it," I tell her.

She looks at me long and hard, some of the color returning to her face. Then she points to her notepad. It's equally as tiring for her to write, but she's used up all her speaking energy. She writes: *I love you, Iris, but we need to have a serious conversation about what you're doing and the danger it's putting your son in. And all in the name of what?*

I feel heat build in my chest like an aggravated wind. "How can you ask me that? You know why I'm doing this."

*Your obsession*, she scribbles crookedly down the page.

I shut my eyes. If I wasn't obsessed with finding out what happened to my sister, what would I be? Broken? Hiding? Complacently pretending it didn't happen? Which outcome would she prefer for me?

"Peace," she says. She touches my face. She's exhausted. I kiss her forehead and help her lie down.

I lock myself in the bathroom. Cal left the floor wet, something I've talked to him about a hundred times. I drop the note on the lid of the toilet and text Leo as I lean against the sink.

Did you tell anyone what I told you?

A minute later his text bubble pops up with ??

About my sister. I don't want people to feel sorry for me.

Of course not. I would never do that to you. What's this about?

Nothing, I send back quickly. Just making sure.

Do you need a ride back to your car tomorrow?

Nope, it's all taken care of thanks ☺

# 22

**DECEMBER ARRIVES WITH** little fanfare. No one seems in the mood to celebrate. "Everyone is still in pandemic mindset," Crede says offhandedly when I mention it.

"I have a kid, I can't get out of Christmas."

He makes a face like *too bad for you*, and I laugh.

It's Thursday morning. We are huddled on the ferry, clutching gingerbread lattes, our beanies dotted with moisture. He is probably right—even a year removed, the public atmosphere is still cagey. The local Starbucks still hasn't reopened its indoor seating area. Crede pulls a pack of cigarettes out of his backpack and sets it on the empty seat next to him. His leg bounces as he waits. The woman sitting across from us gives Crede's cigarettes a dirty look before relocating to the other side if the boat.

"Do you ever take smoke breaks with Dr. Grayson?"

His eyebrow shoots up, and I feel my face grow hot.

"You obsessed with him too? Joining the gaggle of googly-eyed fans of Leo the lion?" I watch as he digs around the pockets of his backpack.

I snicker. "Leo the lion?"

"I didn't make the zodiac." He downs the last of his latte and sighs. "All the nurses do is talk about him. I know too much about that man. He doesn't smoke, by the way. What type of psychotherapist smokes cigarettes?"

"I don't know any nurses who smoke. Your lighter is inside the pack," I remind him. I hand him my empty cup so he can toss it.

"You talk shit and then you expect me to recycle your trash."

"That makes you my work husband."

He rolls his eyes, but he takes my cup anyway, dumping both in the trash can. I don't tell Crede that Dr. Grayson offered me a cigarette on my first day.

He gives me another once-over and stands up. "I hate this goddamn ferry."

He slaps his palm with the pack of cigarettes that is garishly decorated with a rotting pair of lungs. There's no smoking on the ferry, and even if he tried to sneak one outside, he'd get drenched.

"I'll be back," he says. He flips up the hood of his jacket and charges through the doors that lead to the outside deck.

I check my phone. It's a teacher workday, so Cal is spending the weekend with a friend from school.

His text tone is frantic. Where is the tiny tube of toothpaste!?

After I solve his dilemma and tell him where his duffel bag is, I text Gran. Before I left home, I set her up in her recliner with the iPad. She didn't have the mobility to type long texts, so I showed her how to use emojis to tell me things. She sends a blue heart and the pointing finger.

Love you too.

I try not to think about how frail she looked, or how thin her hair was, or how I might not hear her say *kookamatoo* ever again. My heart aches with sadness.

It's my first Thursday to Sunday shift. I was hoping that I

wouldn't have to work it with Bouncer, but I see her red jacket as we clomp down the hill. Crede is behind me, and as soon as we walk through the heavy front door, we split off. He power-walks to the dorms to secure a bunk for both of us while I check my assignment for the day. Next to my name is *back of house*, next to which someone has scribbled *dark side* with smiley face.

I can feel someone's eyes on me as I stand examining the as-signment board. Jordyn's secretary, a grandmotherly type with funky glasses, stands uncomfortably close. It's only the two of us standing here. Being elbow to elbow is quite unnecessary. I notice that she's visibly shaking. "I can't find Jordyn," she says quietly. "Her office is locked."

I try to think of her name. We are both relatively new. She started a week before me and was still in training on my first day.

*Penn!*

Behind purple-rimmed glasses, her eyes are owllike.

"Is something wrong?" I ask carefully. She bobs her head in the direction of the admissions office. Looking past her, I see a woman in an unzipped parka pacing in front of the recep-tion window.

Penn stiffens when the woman catches us watching and flips her head back to the board like she's reading. "Is she coming over here?"

I glance over her shoulder again. "She is…"

"No, no, no—" Penn whispers. I have the feeling she wants to grab me in desperation, but she doesn't. She leans in and speaks quickly. "Her name is Kyra Hoff. She says her husband works in maintenance and hasn't been in contact with her for a month."

"I didn't see her on the sea bus," I say.

"She rented a private vessel to bring her here, got here about fifteen minutes before you guys. I'd barely unlocked the office when she came through the doors. She won't leave until we produce him, and I can't find Jordyn. Her office is locked."

The woman, Kyra, closes the distance, and I can see the worry on her face. She's round-faced and red-nosed, probably around my mother's age.

"She's nuts," Penn hisses right before she reaches us.

"Do you know Adam?" she asks, looking at me. "Adam Hoff." She reaches into a bag slung across her torso and pulls out her phone. Her hair is wet like she didn't bother to pull up her hood when she walked from her boat. I watch as she scrolls through her phone, then holds it out to me. A man I don't know and have never seen smiles from behind dark sunglasses.

I shake my head. "I don't know him, but I'm new."

Her face falls, and she's already turning away to find someone else to ask. Penn wrings her hands, unsure of what to do. Civilians are not permitted to wander around the hospital.

"Give me a few minutes," I say quickly.

Kyra's wobbly gaze returns to my face, lip quivering like a child.

I don't think she's crazy; she's scared. I sigh.

"I'll see if I can find Jordyn," I tell Penn. Then I turn to Kyra. "Mrs. Hoff, can you go wait over there so I know where to find you when I come back?" I point to one of the cream chairs near the fire. To my relief, she nods. I wait until she's out of earshot. Then, turning to Penn, I say, "Call security…actually, scratch that, she's already too upset. Ask someone from maintenance to come up and we can ask them directly about Adam Hoff."

"Are you sure?" Penn takes off her glasses, polishing them on a corner of her scrub top. "She could be dangerous."

"Have you met the head of security?" I ask between my teeth. "He's a real peach…"

Her eyes narrow at my tone, but she nods.

"Did you page Jordyn?"

"Twice…"

"Page her again. I'll see if I can find her."

The admissions office window is closed with a *be back later* sign stuck to it. The hall beyond is empty. I check the bathroom, the storage room, and an exam room, but there is no sign of her. I knock on Jordyn's door and wait. Nothing. I knock again, harder, and try the knob. It's locked like Penn said.

There are noises, a groan, and what sounds like a plastic bag being crumpled. I knock again.

"I know you're in there… Jordyn?"

Everything goes quiet. I press my ear to the door. There is definitely someone in there. I pound with my fist.

When the door flies open, Jordyn is in her undies. I stare in shock, which she doesn't seem to register; her eyes are unfocused, and her skin is waxy.

"Um…" I curl and uncurl my toes in my sensible shoes, my teeth gripping the inside of my cheek. Just say it. "You need to put some clothes on."

Jordyn stares down at herself, then slams the door in my face.

"Holy shit." I lean my forehead against the door.

When she opens the door again, Jordyn is wearing dingy white scrubs, but it's an improvement over the nudity at least. She lets me in, eyeing me suspiciously.

There is a blanket and pillow without a pillowcase lying dejectedly in the corner. The room smells funky, like unwashed body and Pepsi. From what I understood, Jordyn has an apartment upstairs in the Victorian section. Why would she be sleeping in her office?

I walk to the window and crack it open. When I turn around, she's sitting behind her desk blinking slow and cow-like.

"Jordyn…" I kneel in front of her, trying to get her attention, but her eyes can't seem to focus. A sick feeling materializes in my belly. She's tripping on something. I've seen that look on my mother's face more times than I care to count.

"It's Iris," I say gently. My hands are on her knees. I shake them a little, and she seems to come to.

She holds my gaze for a second, the blue of her eyes floating in a yellow pond.

"Jordyn, are you okay?" I lower my voice. "Let me help you. Talk to me…"

"Yes." Her voice is thick. "I'm fine." She rubs a palm across her face, squinting at the brightness of the room. She's definitely not okay. I stand up, taking a step back to give her some space. She looks around as if she's surprised to be there.

"Iris?"

"That's me." I smile. "Can I get you something to drink?"

She shakes her head, leaning down among the stacks of files on the floor to reach her water bottle.

"It's a hard day for me. My brother died ten years ago today."

"I'm so sorry."

She nods. "It's just me left."

From outside the open window I hear voices…laughter. It must be outdoor time for the patients. Jordyn's head turns toward the noise.

"It just hits me some days. Hard."

I swallow the lump in my throat, nodding emphatically. She is tripping on emotion, not drugs. Personal experience taught me that sometimes the body language is the same. I feel ashamed for misinterpreting grief as addiction.

"What is it that you need, Iris?"

Concealing my feelings, I explain the situation with Kyra, emphasizing the part about her wanting to call the police.

When I finish my story, Jordyn looks unfazed. "Iris, if you knew how many disgruntled spouses pass through these doors. We can't keep track of everyone's partner. People come and go from these positions. It's a transient job…"

Something that crawls under my skin. It is easy to brush off the missing until they are yours.

I clear my throat. "I'd say she's more than disgruntled. Her husband appears to be missing—Adam Hoff—"

"If he took a job out here, he wants to be missing. My guess is that he's dodging her calls and hiding out in a bar somewhere in Seattle." She squints at me like she's in pain.

"Okay," I say slowly. "But we need to give her an answer of some kind. Maybe we can pull his time sheet and see the last day he worked…"

"Like I said, he's probably dodging her calls. Our policy is to not get involved in these types of disputes. People take this job to get away. Husbands, wives, social rejects—you name it, we've got 'em." She rolls her chair over to one of her five filing cabinets, her back to me.

"She's a little more than disgruntled," I say again. "She's hysterical. Couldn't we just do a check to see if he's here so we can tell her he's okay?"

Jordyn half turns her head to answer me when someone knocks. I turn to see Crede leaning through the door. "Jordyn, there's a woman threatening to call the police if we don't produce the man she claims is her husband."

"What's his name again?"

"Adam Hoff," I answer. They both look at me. "He…uh… she says he works in maintenance. So we could reach him on the radio…?" I feel my face contorting, my eyebrows and cheeks expanding in different directions like the emotional balloon I am.

Jordyn is nodding before I finish my sentence. "Do that. See if you can get him in here to deal with her."

"Should I get Dr. Grayson?"

She looks alarmed that I've asked.

"No, we can handle this ourselves. He has too much on his plate as-is."

"Of course." I nod. "I'll take care of it."

I stride down the hall with security on my heels. As soon as she sees me, Kyra Hoff is in my face, her features twisted with worry.

"What did they say? Do they know where Adam is?"

My mouth is dry. "We're trying to find him right now," I assure her. "Why don't you have a seat, and I'll get you some tea." Gran thinks everything can be fixed with a cup of tea.

Kyra looks at me with pure malice, her pink eyes feral.

Just as I'm about to take a step back, she bursts into tears. I put my arm around her, steering her toward the staff kitchenette.

"Can you go see if they've found anything?" I ask Crede. Surprisingly he nods, veering off in the direction of the security office. Kyra is docile when I set my Peanuts mug in front of her. She stares at the curl of steam lifting from the mug and holds it with both hands like she's trying to warm herself.

"I told him to take this job. It's my fault. There's something wrong with this place, but we needed the money—oh god! Where is he?" She dissolves into hard sobs.

I know exactly how she's feeling. My stomach tightens—a slow tourniquet. She is blaming herself already. I know the type of questions the police would ask her: Was your husband physically abusive? Were either of you cheating? Did you have an argument the last time you saw each other? What was it about? What did you fight about in general? Over and over, round and round it would go. It makes you think things you wouldn't normally think about yourself, doubt your own sanity. What I've learned—what I don't want to say—is that there are no strange places, just strange people. And sometimes, those people pollute the energy by osmosis.

"I'm sure there is a reasonable explanation—maybe his phone broke or something…" I hate the words coming out of my mouth.

"Then he could have borrowed a phone to call me, couldn't he?"

"Mrs. Hoff?" A man appears in the doorway. It's him—the

aggressive guard from my first overnight. He sees me sitting at the table and smiles.

Kyra leaps out of her chair to stand in front of him, clasping and unclasping her hands.

"Adam Hoff hasn't been to work in over a month. He was a no-call no-show."

"Adam would never not show up for work. When was the last day he clocked in?" she challenges him.

He holds an iPad in his hand—he came prepared. His fingers swipe as he pulls up the information. "November 2," he says. "A Friday…"

Her face falls. She looks glumly at Crede, who has appeared from behind. He's looking at her with a *whatchagonnadonow* look on his face.

"Did he come home that Friday night?" Crede asks.

"That's none of your business."

He looked like the cat that got the cream.

"If you call the police, they're going to ask you the same thing."

"And I'll gladly answer," she shoots back. "If you can't produce him, that is…"

"He isn't here, Mrs. Hoff. Would you like us to escort you back to your boat, and you can file your report with police on the mainland?"

Her red face and fisted hands articulate how angry she is. "I'm not going anywhere until I see him with my own eyes." She crosses her arms over her chest like that's that.

She is afraid—fear's favorite sidecar is anger. The truth is there are a hundred places her husband could be, and a hundred reasons he could be there. Jordyn is right, getting involved in a domestic issue is not our job. Still, I feel bad for her.

"I have to get back to work." I nod at everyone in the room and beeline for the exit. The last thing I see before I turn the corner is Kyra Hoff's distraught face. I want to tell her that I know how she feels.

★ ★ ★

My three-day shift ends disappointingly. I am no closer to Jude than I was before. Frustrated by my inability to move forward with my plan, I gather my things, dump my dirty linen down the chute, and head outside to catch the water taxi home. The temperature is forty degrees. All I want is to get home and cuddle with Cal, maybe watch a movie with him after dinner.

I arrive home at twenty past seven. Gran is using her walker, which I make a big deal about. She looks pretty chuffed with herself. Now that she can get around a little better, Mary-Ann only comes for a short while after school.

I'm eating my dinner when I see the pile of mail. On top is a letter addressed to me in scratchy blue pen. I glance at Cal. He has his tongue between his teeth as he builds a Lego set across the table. Inside is a single sheet of paper. It's a letter with only four lines.

Dear Iris,
Sorry for not answering your letters. I had to think on it for a while. I am doing well. I'm getting a degree in English. You can call me at the prison. Talk soon.
Chris Dupont

My hands shake. He left a phone number. A mailing address and an email address. I look at the Felix the Cat clock. It's too late to call the East Coast. It will have to wait until tomorrow. I send an email to the address he gave me and tell him I'm going to call in the morning.

I call the prison first thing in the morning. Cal is watching cartoons, and Gran is napping in her recliner. I make sure they're both situated before I take my coffee to the kitchen and dial the number he gave me. I wait, listening to the same recorded message over and over: *Please hold while inmate five-two-*

*two-six is paged.* When his voice comes on the line, he's breathless like he ran to get there.

"Iris?"

"Yeah, hey, Dupont."

I hear him blow air out of his mouth. "Wow," he says, "just wow. I never thought I'd talk to you again. Your email blew me away. Truly…I was thrilled to see it."

"I've sent you dozens of letters," I point out.

"I didn't read all of them," he says, his voice light.

Such a liar. I want to roll my eyes but I don't.

"So why do you want to talk to me now?"

Dupont clears his throat like he's about to say something important. "I'm born again."

Whoop, there it is. You can't go anywhere in prison without bumping into Jesus. Too bad they were not born again in time to save my sister. I sigh, picturing my mother's Jesus, the one who hung on the wall when Piper and I lived in yellow-yellow.

"Okay…"

"Since I've been forgiven, and as a result, I feel compelled to ask you for your forgiveness—you know what I mean? I did a lot of shitty things back in the day, got caught up with the wrong crowd and made some bad decisions. I am trying to help now. I realize how important I am to this case." I hear someone crying in the background, deep guttural sobs that drag through Dupont's words.

"Hold on…"

I can't make out what he says to the sobber, but when he comes back on the line, everything is quiet. My heart won't slow down as I wait for him to talk.

"I guess what I'm trying to say is, I'm not a bad person. I need forgiveness just like everyone else."

"Forgiveness for what, Chris?" I try to turn down the volume of my thoughts.

There's a long silence before he says, "For my part in what happened to your sister."

"What happened to her?"

"People like to talk. I heard things, you know? I should have gone to the police back then with what I knew."

"What do you know?"

"They took her to the stash house. That's where they kept the girls. You know what they do at a stash house, don't you?"

"Book a one-way ticket to hell?"

He laughs. "You were always so weird; I don't remember you being funny," he notes.

I wish he would get to the point.

"I never really thought you looked like her…"

"What?"

"Piper. I know you two are twins, but you wore different expressions on your faces. I could always tell who was who."

"Tell me what happened after they took her to the stash house," I say.

"They told me that she got away. Ran for it. They went after her, four of them, but I guess she outran them."

I feel shock followed by a surge of pride. That sounds like Piper. "Where were they taking her?"

He sniffs. "To a different stash house. They move 'em around a lot…"

"What the fuck, Dupont? You let my sister get trafficked?" Now my voice is angry.

"That's what I heard…" His voice is robotic. I close my eyes and remind myself not to say what I really want to say.

"Did you tell police this?"

"I called to give them my statement, but they never returned my call."

"So my sister got away from them, and then what? They didn't keep looking for her?"

"They looked, but she was gone. That's all I heard, man. She ran."

"So what happened to her after that?"

"I don't know, man. I'm telling you what I do know."

"Why her?" I ask. "Why not me—or some other girl? What made them choose Piper?"

"They take girls no one is going to look for. Kids in the system and shit. Twins, man, it's the jackpot, especially when you know no one will look hard for them."

"Why didn't they take me?"

"Could have been anything. They might have thought you'd fight more. Something could have went wrong with their plans. Did they give you something to eat or drink—any pills?"

"Yeah, they brought shit back from the concession stand... sodas."

"Well there you go, you can't be drinking shit strangers give you."

"What about Colby Crimball? What did he have to do with it?"

"Man, fuck Colby Crimball. His brother introduced him to those guys. Everyone thought Matt was such a clean boy, but that bitch liked to pay for pussy. He met those guys down Aurora Avenue, do you know where that is?"

"Yeah, it's where the hookers walk."

"Yup. They were pimps. Colby started hanging out with those guys even when his brother wasn't around. Colby liked to know bad people."

"Is there any chance they found Piper that night and were lying about it?"

"Maybe. I wouldn't know."

"You gonna play it like that, huh? I know you know something. Your mama knows where you are, Piper's family doesn't. I'm asking you to help me."

There's a long silence, I think he's hung up.

"I'm gonna play for me. You should start doing that too. Piper wouldn't have done this for you."

He hangs up on me before I can hang up on him.

# 23

**THIS IS ALL** so sickening. If Dupont's story is true, it confirms my theory that Piper got away and went to Jude for help. I don't understand why she chose to trust him over Gran. If she'd run to us that night instead of him, she'd be alive…but we wouldn't have Cal. It was one of those thoughts that dropped right in the middle of your grief like a tornado in a hurricane.

A large part of me thinks I'm the reason she chose Jude over us. She hated me. She wanted Gran to herself and I got in the way. She didn't necessarily have Jude to herself since he was married, but he was probably promising her things.

The following night I drive to Leo's condo. I find a spot in front of a doughnut shop, and he meets me downstairs. He looks at me in concern as we walk to the elevator hand in hand. I try not to look at him because if I do I'll break down in tears. We get off on the eighth floor. Leo leads me down a long carpeted hallway before stopping at one of the nondescript doors. Leo holds it open for me and I step inside. It's small but modern. Tastefully decorated. The living room walls are painted dark blue, a white leather sectional takes up most of the space facing an enormous TV. Two barstools sit in front of a counter that divides the kitchen from the small dining room. The only things on the counter are a Keurig machine and an empty paper towel holder. The art on the dining room wall is abstract.

"Can I get you a drink?" he asks, walking toward the kitchen. I shake my head. I'm already anxious; alcohol would only exacerbate it. He points me to the couch, and I perch on the edge closest to the kitchen. The note that was left on Gran's door is in the back pocket of my jeans. I hear him moving around the kitchen, and when he finally sits next to me, he has two bottles of water.

"So what's up? What's scared you?"

"I have to tell you something." It's the first time I've seen him frown. He searches my eyes like he's going to find the answer there. I take a steadying breath.

"I haven't been honest with you."

"Okay…" His eyebrows are furrowed.

"I wanted the job…" I tuck my hair behind my ears and lick my lips. "I don't know how to say it without sounding like an awful person…"

"I'm immune to thinking you're awful," he assures me. "No one is awful, we're just reacting."

I take a breath to steady myself. "I wanted the job because of one of your patients, Leo. I wanted to get close to one of them in particular."

He blinks in surprise. The apartment is so quiet, I can't hear any traffic from the city below.

I continue despite the look on his face. "Piper's killer is in D hall. Jude Fields killed my sister. He was her youth pastor, and I think—no, I know—he took advantage of her. Abused her. And then he killed her, just like he killed his wife and kid. The only difference is they never found Piper."

I'm too chicken to look at his expression.

"That…wow. Iris, I don't know what to say."

He clears his throat, then leans his head back against the sofa like he's thinking.

"Jude was a youth pastor. I can confirm that at least."

I'm sweating. I wipe my palms on my pants.

"The summer before Piper went missing, she was spending a lot of time at church. You know—youth group and Bible study and all that. She was really into it. She even started babysitting for the youth pastor, sleeping over at his house. Gran didn't see a problem with it because Piper said she was helping his wife. Piper played it off like they were friends."

He's watching me intently, his eyes narrowed as I speak. I go on. "It was weird because when she went missing, no one from the church called. No one came around or asked about her. I didn't care at the time, I never liked church anyway, and when I did go I sat in the main service with Gran. Gran never went back to the church because of it. She was hurt by how little they cared."

"That's very unusual," Leo says. "No one from the congregation?"

I think about it. "Gran had a few friends who reached out at the beginning because of her health issues, but no one in leadership like the main pastor or Jude believed Piper was kidnapped.

"A few years ago I was going through Gran's photo albums and I noticed a lot of the photos were missing, big gaps everywhere. It was only certain photos—like the ones at church and camp. I found the missing photos in the attic in Piper's things. It wasn't rocket science to figure out that the only common denominator in all of the photos she took was one man."

"Jude?"

"That's right," I say. "Piper took the photos that included Jude out of the album and put them in her drawer. I don't know if she did that because she was in love with him and wanted the pictures for herself, or if she was angry with him and trying to erase him from our lives. She clearly hadn't gotten rid of the photos."

"Did you tell your grandmother?"

"Yes. After I found the photos, we both looked him up online. Once I typed his name in the search engine, the internet pretty much lit up. And wouldn't you know it, he was about to be tried for capital murder: Piper's fucking youth pastor. For murdering his teen wife and baby daughter. We figured that no one from the church told us because they had a bigger fish to fry: one of their pastors was a murderer. Look, if he killed his wife and baby, what's not to say he did the same to Piper?"

Leo sets his empty water bottle on the floor. Then he runs a hand across his jaw, his expression guarded. He thinks I'm crazy.

"What's he like?" I ask. "Jude? Is he coherent…mean…passive?"

"You know I can't talk about my patients." Beneath his beard his lips are turned down. "I can't tell you that, Iris. You know that."

"Okay," I say slowly. "I'll tell you what I know, and you can tell me if I'm right."

"I need a drink." Leo goes to the kitchen and opens a cabinet. He looks inside, closes it, opens another.

"Tell me about Jude's brain—what does he have going on up there?" I ask wrapping my arms around my knees.

"He was raised in a religious home. His father called his personality a darkness and punished him by locking him in a closet for hours at a time," I say.

Leo opens the dishwasher and pulls out a coffee tumbler. He looks inside to make sure it's clean, then tilts a bottle of Tito's over the rim.

"They went to the church for help, and the pastor suggested one of those fucked-up religious boarding schools." All of that information was in the court documents.

"No." He shakes his head. "Don't give me the textbook shit. Tell me *your* thoughts."

"Okay." I shrug. "He internalized his father's views about women."

"Which were what?"

"His father thought women were whores if they had sex before marriage. Jude fetishized virginity. His victims were always underage, the first was his wife, who was only seventeen when they got married. His wife's family said that he was excessively controlling, and isolated her from her family and friends—narcissism, sociopathy. When he murdered them he was wearing his god complex on his sleeve. Piper was his second victim. What else do you want from me?" My tone is angry.

"I don't want anything from you, Iris, I like being around you. Do you like being around me, or are you just trying to get to Jude?"

My entire body stiffens, the accuracy and offense hitting at the same time.

His arm is slung across the back of the couch, grazing my neck. I lean my head back so it's resting on his warm skin. My face is already tilted up when he leans over and kisses me. The kiss is very soft and everything I need. I stand up, suddenly emboldened, and walk toward his bedroom. I am not drunk, my emotions are in check, and I want to do this. He hasn't moved from the couch. I take my clothes off, slowly so he can watch, leaving the pile of fabric where it falls. I wait for him in the doorway.

"Are you sure?" he asks. I have a moment of confusion where I think he's said *pure* instead of *sure*. My Freudian analysis of Jude is playing games with my head.

"I'm sure," I say.

Afterward we're lying in his bed, limbs tangled, when I decide to push the issue again. "Leo…" I exhale. "I know this is going to sound crazy. Maybe I am crazy—but this is the only access I'm ever going to have to the truth."

Why can't I just say it? I close my eyes. I don't want him to think that I'm using him. *But you are, you know you are.* I am attracted to him, but this wasn't in the plan. I decide to spit it out, just say it.

"I want to speak to Jude."

He accepts this news with registered shock, immediately tense and sitting up straighter. I feel shame for asking, shame for what we just did. We were both crossing a good number of moral lines.

"Absolutely not. It's one thing me telling you about him in private; without evidence, you can't just accuse him of that. This is all speculation from a grieving sister."

I recoil, feeling diminished by his words. The *speculation* part of his little speech hits hard. I don't like the parental tone he's taking with me. I bite back tears. If I were older, I wouldn't care, but I am suddenly stung by our age gap.

"Don't do that," I say. "Talk to me like that. I'm not your patient." I swing my legs over the side of the bed and sit with my back to him.

"Iris, that's not what I'm doing."

I know what he's saying makes sense, but that pisses me off more. I stare at the wall.

"Piper was kept alive for at least a year after she went missing. We know that for sure because of Cal. What we don't know is Cal's paternity."

"But his biological father could easily be one of those men. The chance that she got pregnant while—" he frowns as he looks for the word "—while they were trafficking her is high."

"I think it was Jude," I say. "He's the one who left Cal on my mother's doorstep."

"Where's your proof?"

"In cell six."

He flinches.

"All right," he says slowly. "Even if that is a possibility, I still can't let you go in there with him. He's dangerous. You understand that, right? He's been locked up for a reason. He had a bench trial. Entered a reason by insanity plea. The judge deliberated for four days before he sent him to HOTI. He's considered to be extremely dangerous, a very cunning, manipulative man."

"I know he's fucking dangerous. He killed my sister."

Leo runs a hand down his face. "What would that accomplish? He's a psychopath—he won't tell you the truth, Iris, because that's what they do—lie."

"He can't deny a blood test! If he's Cal's father, we know for sure Piper was with him after she was kidnapped by the traffickers. He has to know where she is. You could get that for me…" I've shocked him into complete silence. I swallow hard and stare at the bottle of contact solution on his dresser.

"Everything you're suggesting is unethical. I could lose my license. You could be kicked out of grad school. All of your hard work thrown away for what?"

"For my son," I say.

We don't talk as I get dressed. I do the walk of shame, refusing to cry until I'm in the car. This is on me. Instead of sticking to the plan, doing what I came to do, I knowingly entered a situationship with my boss. *Stupid, stupid.*

It's raining when I run to my car. His living room window faces the street. I know he can see me. I pause with my hand on the door handle and look up at his window.

For the next few days, I avoid him at work, volunteering to do all the jobs everyone hates so I don't have to run into him. It's miserable, and I can't stop thinking about Leo.

Someone is playing Christmas oldies in the nurses' station. I'm putting away patient files when Bouncer buzzes out of D, pushing a cart of empty meal trays toward the cafeteria. I count the trays: only four. There were five patients in D, and there was normally a tray for Leo. Why only four today? If one of those trays belonged to Jude, his DNA would be all over it. This could be my only chance, especially since Leo isn't going to help me. Four is better than none. I file the last of the folders and shut and lock the drawer. Bouncer is fighting with the cart, kicking the wheel. I grab a handful of plastic baggies from the storage room and stuff them in my pocket.

"Want me to take that to the kitchen for you?"

Bouncer frowns. "No. I can do it."

"It's no problem. I'm on my way there."

After struggling with the cart for a few more seconds, she rolls her eyes but steps away. "Fine. Whatever."

I watch her take off down A without so much as a thanks. Not that I care, I have what I want. I push the cart, and it rattles forward on a wonky wheel.

"Real drama queen, that one," Janiss comments from where she's sitting behind the care station. I hadn't seen her there. She's doing something on the computer, the glare of the screen reflecting on her glasses. I'm pushing the cart forward when I realize she isn't done.

"She thinks she's all that, but honestly, that's not even her face."

Janiss needs to gossip. I've learned that she will follow a person to finish her story. I grit my teeth, hoping to get this done with so I can be alone with the cart.

"Not her face?"

"That woman has so much filler you wouldn't recognize her without it." I make myself smile even though she's not looking at me. She leans in conspiratorially. "I'll text you photos of what she used to look like after work."

I shrug, bored, which is the wrong thing to do—she looks immediately offended.

"She injects it too. Has these fancy parties at her house for her friends…"

"Ohhh," I say mechanically. I force my eyes as large as they can go. That makes her happy.

"I know. Crazy what people do with their money."

I look at her inch-long blue nails and agree.

I have matters to take care of, and Janiss is stressing about someone's Botox. She releases me a few minutes later. I'm lucky a maintenance person hasn't come by and taken the cart from me. Pushing it forward, I turn down hall B, toward the cafeteria. Looking over my shoulder, I spot Alma and a couple of older female patients lingering in the hallway. They're not going anywhere.

My back to them, I take a straw from one tray and slip it into my pocket. From the second tray I take a soup spoon, which goes into the other pocket in my scrub pants. I start walking again, slowly, while I look for items to take from the last two trays. As I reach the doors to the cafeteria, someone calls my name. Ignoring it, I stop the cart and rattle the handle like there is something wrong. Then, walking to the front, I bend down, pretending to examine a wheel. A spork sits in reach, teetering on the edge of a tray. I snatch it up, placing it in the pocket of my hoodie as I hear feet approaching.

It's Marshal Day Monterey.

"Something wrong?"

I shake my head trying to hide my distress. "The wheel was wobbling, thought something was caught in it."

He considers me, then takes hold of the cart, pulling it backwards toward himself. It moves without a problem. I smile at Marshal, straightening up.

"Seems fine to me… I'll take it through to the kitchen for you," he offers, starting to push it away.

"Thanks, Marshal," I call after him. Looking back at me, his mouth curves into a smile. That's not a man who is incompetent to stand trial, I think, and then he's gone—having disappeared through the swinging doors of the kitchen.

My three-day ends on a higher note than it started. Leo is not on the water taxi that night, and I can't decide if I'm glad or disappointed. When I get to my car, I toss my backpack on the passenger seat and blast the heat for five minutes before warming up enough to use my hands. I call Poley on my drive home. Her phone rings twice before she picks up.

"I need a favor," I say.

"Iris?"

She knows it's me; she can see on her caller ID, but she does this every time anyway.

"Yes, it's me, Amanda. Iris."

I hear a baby crying in the background, and I feel momentarily bad for bombarding her on a Friday night. Then I remember my sister has never been found because of her. Because of what Poley and Audrain didn't do. I am still making her pay nine years later.

"What can I do for you?" The background noises disappear abruptly. I imagine she's gone into her bedroom and closed the door. Her husband—a nerdy fellow who works as a programmer for Microsoft—is probably playing with their toddler boys on the Dr. Seuss rug in the living room. I'd been to her condo three Christmas ago when she invited Gran, Cal, and me to a party. I don't know why she invited us or why we went, but we were dressed in festive outfits bought from Target. I had a panic attack standing over the gherkin tray, and she took me into her bedroom to calm me down. I hate to say we had a bonding moment, because... Poley. But we did. Or sort of. She gave me a Xanax and sat holding both of my hands until I was breathing normally again.

"What's up?" she says, not missing a beat.

I tell her about the three items tucked into my backpack,

wrapped in produce bags. She's quiet for a full minute while she thinks.

"I know a lab," she says finally. "What you're doing is illegal."

"So what?" I say. "Kidnapping is illegal, rape is illegal, murder is illegal. All three happened to my sister."

Poley doesn't have to help me, but I know she will; guilt is a powerful driving force.

"When can you get it to me?"

"Now?"

"Great."

She hangs up. Her exit is two past mine. I get off on Union and cut off a Subaru driver who throws me the finger. When I pull up to her building, she's standing on the curb with a purple blanket wrapped around her shoulders. Her hair is dark this time, cut shorter than I've ever seen it. She's wearing slippers and has one of those sleep strips on her nose that stops you from snoring. When she leans down to the passenger side window, I get a whiff of what her condo smells like. I hand her the bags.

"You gotta stop this. This is unhealthy."

"Oh yeah?" I look back at the road, where a few lonesome snowflakes are starting to fall. It hardly snows in Seattle, but when it does, everything goes to shit—the hills slicked over and vehicles skidding around like bumper cars.

"I guess if looking for my sister is unhealthy, I'll take it."

She stares at me, anime eyes disproving. "You know what I mean." She shifts her blanket, and I catch a glimpse of what's underneath. A nice-sized belly—she's pregnant.

"Congratulations," I say. "I didn't know…"

How would I? It's not like we were friends. Still, I'd known her long enough to care.

She shrugs. A guy walks out of Poley's building and gives me a look like I shouldn't be parked there. I want to give him the finger, but she'll get pissed. Poley has two slices of dark exhaustion beneath her eyes. They match her hair.

The sky is about to burst open with a zillion snowflakes. I don't have time to get into it with her. Besides, Poley has shit instincts, but she works hard. Beneath her makeup, she is perpetually exhausted.

"You're obsessed with your sister's case in a completely insane way."

I shrug. "You're obsessed with changing your hair; we all have something don't we?"

She rolls her eyes.

I liked to ride Poley's guilt. She knows she fucked up my sister's case.

"This is the last favor I'll ever ask. I swear. If this man is not Cal's father, I'll drop it. I'll move on with my life and let it go."

"I could get in trouble."

"Right," I say, making a face. She blushes; we both know she was fucking her boss when Piper went missing.

"I know you're a little bit crooked, Amanda. Just do this one thing for me…please."

"All right."

"Thank you!" I say. "You'll let me know?"

She sighs before saying, "Yeah."

She knocks twice on the roof of my car before turning away.

"Hey!" I call out the window. "Do you know what you're having?"

I watch her turn around, hand on her belly, soft white flakes landing in her hair.

"A girl," she says.

I wait until she's back inside before driving away, thinking of Cal, thinking of my sister, thinking of Poley's daughter, who for the time being is snug and safe in her belly. Poley and I had seen each other grow up in a fucked up way. Every year on Cal's birthday (which we don't know the exact day of), she's sent him a card with an Amazon gift card for forty dollars. It's been nice.

I play Lana Del Rey on my drive back for old times' sake. I am sleeping with a therapist now. That counts as seeing one, doesn't it? As I turn onto Gran's street, a text from Leo pops up.

Miss you. I'm sorry.

"Everything's fine," I say, shoving my phone in my bag and getting out of the car. "I have this under control."

This is me finishing what I've started. I'd gotten distracted, but I am back on track—things are back on track. My only regret so far happened in a moment of weakness. I should never have gone to Leo about this. Anything that happens to Jude moving forward can be tied back to me. I can't make my next move until I have confirmation of Cal's parentage.

# 24

MY SLEEP IS riddled with bad dreams and cold sweats. Sometimes when I wake up in the middle of the night, it takes a minute to remember if I'm in my bedroom at Gran's or in a HOTI bunkbed.

On the news a new kid goes missing, a little one with dark, wispy hair and dinosaur shorts; Elizabeth Holmes shows up to court pregnant; tornados ravage the Midwest. People die all the time, they disappear all the time. If you're lucky and if the story is interesting enough, a podcaster will pick up the case. Enough people interested in a case means pressure on the police by the public, and I have a special folder in my email for those inquiries.

But as soon as I found out where Jude was, I wasn't interested in doing interviews or talking about the case. I had my answers about who killed Piper. My twin is in the ground. Sometimes, when I'm holding something that belonged to her, the smell of wet dirt will creep into the room. I smell it like she's trying to tell me something.

Gran's face looks worried even when she's sleeping. Cal's looks older when he's awake. It makes me depressed.

I wake up the next morning to snow so thick the city is forced to shut down: no cars, no buses, no ferries. Everyone is trapped behind walls of snow, the emerald city painted white. Not accustomed to the snowfall, the city has too few snow-plows, and I try not to think about the people trapped on Shoal Island—none of whom would be leaving to go home today as planned. They'll be on shift until we show up to relieve them. I play in the snow with Cal during the day. We eat pea-nut butter and jelly for every meal—on crackers, on toast, on celery sticks, which is kind of gross. The neighbors bring us food—paella in a big blue bowl covered in foil from the young married couple on the corner who cook for fun, breakfast for dinner from Mary-Ann and her husband. On the second day of the snow-in, Gran's boyfriend comes over to make us fet-tuccini alfredo and Caesar salad. He puts *Andy Griffith* on the living room TV while he cooks. Cal gets into it while Gran snoozes in her chair. When dinner is ready, Gran eats a little of it but makes disgusted faces when he's not looking. She's eat-ing to be polite, but she hates bottled alfredo sauce. She thinks it tastes like deodorant.

Six days after our argument, I go back to work—we all do. The snow sits in dirty mounds all over the city. White fluff turned sooty and shit-stained. I see him get on the ferry behind me, just a flash of his unruly hair and gray jacket. It makes my chest hurt to be so close to him and so far.

On the water taxi he sits across from me and stares, so I stare back. When we get to the island, everyone who was stranded during the snow is waiting at the dock. They whoop, high-fiving us as we walk by. As soon as I walk through the doors of HOTI, I get a text from Leo asking if he can talk to me. I get a knot in my stomach. I read the text again, convinced I'm going to get fired. Not only did I sleep with my boss, I also admitted that I'd lied to get the job and told him I was trying to get to his patient for personal reasons.

At one o'clock, he meets me at D to let me in, and we walk past the six solitary rooms.

My jaw drops open when I see that Leo has set up a picnic on his desk. He beams when I ooh and ahh over the little details. He made sandwiches and brought a bottle of wine. For dessert there are oatmeal raisin cookies—which is something Gran would eat. He doesn't look amused when I tell him this.

"What's Cal like?" he asks.

"He's serious and thoughtful. He asks big questions, ones I don't feel qualified to answer. He wants to be a priest and live at the Vatican."

"Wow." Leo's head jerks, and his eyes open wide. "A priest? That's very specific. You'll be mother of a priest. How does that make you feel?"

"Not as much as it's making you feel," I tease. "I'm taking it you've never had sex with a priest's mother?"

"Listen," he says suddenly. "I've been thinking about what you said… I'm willing to run a blood test…on Jude. To see if he's Cal's father."

I leap up from where I'm sitting and throw my arms around him. "Thank you," I say into his neck. I still hadn't heard from Poley. This could speed things along for me.

I feel warm and happy, the human equivalent of a chocolate chip cookie. Making him have any type of reaction is rewarding.

"You got me. I have very religious family members, so my perception has been skewed. Does Cal enjoy Average Joe things like fishing and going to the movies?"

"He does."

"Well…I'm Average Joe." He offers me his hand as if to shake, and I bat it away, laughing.

"It's true." He grabs me around the waist and pulls me to

him. My arms automatically circle around his waist as I tilt my head up to look at him. This is all very cozy for how new things are. We play with each other's body language, and very well—this feels like we are playing house.

*Ride the wave, Iris, ride the wave…*

A week later, he takes Cal and me to a Christmas tree farm. After buying us cider and kettle corn, he marches us through the farm in muddy boots until Cal chooses his tree. Cal says a little prayer for it before he gives Leo permission to chop it down. I can see the amusement on Leo's face as he bows his head and closes his eyes. My little priest makes the sign of the cross. Then Leo positions the axe on his shoulder and poses like Gaston, showing off his muscles. Cal's response is to stand nearby and list off the types of Christmas trees as Leo wields the axe.

*Douglas fir…chop… Noble fir…chop… Balsam fir…chop…*

Gran is back from therapy and sitting in her chair when we get home. She sits in her old recliner while we decorate the tree. It's two solid hours of Christmas music and telling Cal stories about the ornaments. And by the end of it I'm exhausted. Gran looks more tired than usual. I try not to worry as I make dinner. Leo plays video games with Cal in the living room until it's Cal's bedtime; I walk him to the door, where he kisses me in full view of Gran.

When he opens the door and steps onto the cobblestone path, I feel sad. I don't want to be away from him. Any space feels like too much. We lock eyes.

"Want me to wait for you? We can drive to my place together, and I can bring you home later," he offers.

I'm giddy and still smiling when I face the living room. I have Leo on my side. Now that the DNA test will be done, I can finally relax. Gran is staring at me. I recognize the disapproval on her face. That look never ceases to make me feel like I'm a kid. Let her be angry, I think. I'll have my answers about Piper soon. I want be done with this. The trauma of losing Piper took up so much room in my life I didn't have the time or energy to think about anything else. My brain prophesized doom on the hour every hour. It was only when I was with Leo that an excited hope crept in. I walk past Gran into the kitchen, calculating the time it will take to get both of them to bed and the dishes washed before I can make it to Leo's. We both have to work tomorrow, but it will be worth it.

## 25

**ON A TUESDAY** in January, he finds me in the laundry room folding towels for the next shift. Two of the dryers are running, and we stand close to them while we talk so no one walking past can hear us. "I have something to tell you," he says close to my ear.

"Oh?"

"The results came back." He's holding a cream folder in his right hand. I try to read his face, but it's professionally blank.

"The results are in there?"

He nods. I work at the lump in my throat. "Let's go somewhere private," he says.

I nod. Okay, fine. The laundry room is opposite the clinic. He leads me through the frosted door into the waiting area. The clinic is empty; he takes me into one of the examination rooms and closes the door. Everything in the room is white. I sit on the stool meant for the doctor and swing in a circle. It's something Cal does when he's nervous. That's why I am here—Cal. If Jude is his father, I'll have my confirmation.

Leo sits on the edge of the chair meant for patients and smiles kindly at me. "You okay?"

"No."

"Are you sure you want to do this?"

"I have to," I say. "Please just tell me."

He fills his cheeks with air and blows it out. I focus on his hands when he opens the folder and pulls out a single sheet of paper.

"Okay, go," I say, closing my eyes.

Is this really how it's going to go down? Nine years of anguished waiting, and I am finally going to know one way or another in this stupid, dark room.

"It's not him, Iris."

I snatch the paper out of his hand. Turning my back to Leo, I read the results while facing the wall, my teeth already working on my thumbnail. He's not wrong. Cal is not Jude's son. I don't know which feelings to feel.

There are a hundred competing thoughts rattling my brain. I'm shocked, but more than that I'm disappointed, which is an awful thing to feel when finding out that Cal is not related to Jude.

He touches my shoulder, and I jerk away. "I can't…" I'm out of breath, dizzy. "I just need a minute…" It feels like the room is riding rusty rails; my vision sways and my throat is tightening. "Are you sure?"

"I wanted to tell you sooner, but I haven't been able to get you alone."

I nod. The wind gusts outside the window. I walk over. Parting the blinds with a finger, I look out. It's pitch-black, but I know I'm staring at the Salish Sea.

"I know you wanted this to be true."

My eyes crowd with tears. No, I didn't *want* it to be true. I didn't *want* any of this. I need closure. Gran needs closure before she dies. And most importantly, Piper's son will need closure.

Leo's face is twisted with worry.

"I'm okay," I say, "but I'd like some time alone." I offer him a weak smile.

He kisses my forehead before he leaves.

I've spent four years of my life chasing this…this…idea that I could find the answers I need. I'd convinced myself I've been on the right track. I was wrong. It hurts to be wrong, it hurts like the day I lost her. I swipe at my tears angrily. On goes life—three very unfair words.

I make my way out of the clinic, heading toward the care station. Leo is talking to Janiss; he sees me and smiles. When he looks at me with his eyes soft, I forget every bad thing that's hanging on my conscience. His is the sort of attention that makes a person feel weightless.

I wonder after his love—what would that be like? My romantic daydream is interrupted when someone calls my name.

"Iris, just the person I was looking for…" Bouncer emerges from B in a whirlwind of perfume and requests. I force a smile. She looks harried, her bun a frizzy mess.

"We have two nurses out—one of them was late to the water taxi, the other has COVID. I need you to handle art time today…can you manage alone?"

I nod.

"Good," she says. "Because you seem easily distracted."

My anger flares. She's one to talk, hanging over the doctor like a bad cold. I almost tell her so, but Leo is in earshot, and I don't want to start trouble.

My insides are still grappling with the news, and I feel particularly volatile. A patient named Glen walks by. He tries to look casual, but it's clear that he's eavesdropping on our conversation. I call on the therapy gods for help. Why get that much therapy if you're not going to use it, right?

I bite down my tart response, smiling sweetly instead. "I'll be able to handle it," I tell her. "It'll be great."

Her red lips purse together as she considers me. I notice her looking over my shoulder in Leo's direction. I wonder if he's watching us. Again, I get the recurring sense that something has happened between them. *It's not your business,* I chide myself. I decided to sleep with him; I can't fixate on who slept with him before me—even if she is a redheaded vixen with porny vibes. I make myself docile as she leads me to the art room and fills me in on what to do with them.

The art room is warm, the windows foggy. It smells like acrylic paint and cedar. The floor is splashed with the remnants of a thousand art projects. It's a messy, cozy room.

"They're painting today. We play music for them that is soothing—like classical or jazz. Make sure Esti doesn't eat the paint. She had to have her stomach pumped once from chugging Elmer's glue. And don't let Martin and the other Martin sit near each other. It always ends in a fight."

Docile Iris, sweet and pure as a flower, nods her head.

Bouncer leaves me with a couple more warnings before rushing out.

Despite the weight hanging on my heart, I pull off a great art class. I start by announcing that since I am their art teacher today, it's only appropriate that they paint irises. Most everyone thinks my proclamation is wildly funny. I even hear a little giggle out of Alma. We listen to classic rock, passing a book of flowers around. At one point, all twenty of them are tapping their feet to the music.

I get really into it too, painting my own iris, which, as one of the Martins points out, looks like a grasshopper. For a few hours today, it feels as if everything I did to be here is worth it, even if I didn't get the answers I was looking for.

There is a silver lining in the form of Leo and my work. I've spent so much energy on finding answers about Piper that I've forgotten everything about myself. That is going to change. I like helping people, so that's what I'll keep doing.

Maybe it is time to let Piper go. It hurts to think about it, but it hurts to think of her too. She'd been my helper through the years, my call-upon when making decisions—what would Piper do? Maybe it's time to ask what Iris would do.

No one wants to leave when class ends, and when a nurse comes to collect Bernie, who is wheelchair-bound, he slaps her hands away. I think about what Leo said—that I entered this line of work to help people. Today felt more rewarding than anything else I've done in the last few years. I smile to myself as I tidy up the paints. Maybe I could do this—be normal and have aspirations and goals that have nothing to do with Piper.

I see that one of my students has painted words above their iris. It takes me a minute to figure out what the letter blobs are. The brush they used is thick, and the paint is runny. Bad is coming. I step away from the canvas like it's diseased. I decide not to touch that one. I don't want any of the sentiment touching my reality.

# 26

I WAKE UP on a Saturday morning to the incessant ringing of my cell. Glancing at the window, I see it's still dark outside. It's the hospital calling.

"Hello?"

Jordyn's voice fills the line. "Iris, we need you to come in today. We're horribly understaffed."

I think of Cal sleeping in the next room; I promised him I'd take him to the aquarium today.

"I wouldn't ask unless it was absolutely necessary. Throw me a bone here, Iris."

"Okay." I toss the comforter off my legs and stand. "I have to find a babysitter."

"Do that," Jordyn says. "I've called ahead to the sea taxi. They're going to wait for you." Before I can respond, she hangs up.

I call Mary-Ann and tell her the situation while I get my things together.

"I have Bryan today," she tells me. "I can take them to the aquarium."

I'm overflowing with gratitude as I pull on my pants. Cal

won't be too disappointed. He loves hanging out with Bryan. "Thank you, Mary-Ann. You're a lifesaver."

Cal is watching TV when I come out of the room. I quickly tell him the situation while toasting him a bagel. He takes it better than I thought. When I hug him goodbye, I hold on to him so long he wriggles out of my arms.

Saturday is a mess. The patients are worked up, picking fights with each other. A fistfight breaks out between Alice and one of the other women, and when a nurse tries to split them up, she gets punched in the face. Both of them have to be put in constraints. Everyone on staff is snappy and on edge.

I feed Alice dinner, spooning corn into her mouth. She tells me she loves me for ten straight minutes, thanking me for the food. By the time her plate is empty, she's flipped the switch. She calls me a cocksucker and tells me she hopes I die. After Alice, I bounce around helping in the clinic for a few hours, and then dispensing meds to the patients from a little window. By the time I fall into my bunk, I'm too exhausted to feel anxious. I actually sleep that night.

On Sunday morning I work in the laundry room with a small crew of patients. One group is folding towels while the other folds sheets. The laundry room is the only place in HOTI that's warm; nicknamed the tropics by the patients. I fold towels alongside Agnes and Alice, whose moods are subdued. There was in incident in the staff cafeteria this morning that no one wants to talk about. I only know about it because I overheard Crede speaking to a nurse named Jackie.

"I told them he wasn't taking his meds. They gave him too much freedom."

"You two are quiet today. Where is Alma?" We've filled an entire cart with towels. Agnes shrugs.

"Did something happen this morning in the cafeteria?" Was

it my imagination or did they both stiffen? Janiss comes to find me, sporting a new set of purple nails.

"Dr. Grayson would like you to sit in today."

"Oh," I say, surprised. I finish the towel I'm folding. It wasn't on my schedule, but I'm happy to join.

Janiss looks at me out of the corner of her eye. "The whole place is going to shit, and he's having you sit in?"

"I'm sure it will just be one session," I say. "Then I'll be back out to help."

It doesn't really matter what I say to Janiss, or how I say it: she doesn't like me. She walks me through the D hall security doors, but she doesn't follow me through.

"Well, go on," she says when she sees me looking at her. "You know where it is."

Walking down D hall is eerie. The lack of windows and yellow light set me on edge.

When I walk into Leo's office, Alma is sitting in the seat across from Leo.

"Alma!"

I'm happy to see her.

She makes a clucking noise in the back of her throat and waves. Her gaze doesn't linger on me like it normally does. She turns to Leo, her face pinched.

Leo and Alma communicate through nods and noises. When he asks her a question, she shakes her head for no, and gives the thumbs-up for yes. I've seen them do this once before and I expect them to do it now, but instead Leo opens a drawer in his desk and hands Alma an iPad. I blink at the piece of technology, in surprise. The only computers I've seen are the outdated desktops in the nurses' station. Alma takes the iPad, opening the messaging app like she's used it before while Leo uses his phone.

"Alma has something urgent to talk to me about," Leo explains. "But I'd like to speak to you after if you could stick around."

"Of course," I say.

"We use the iPad to communicate sometimes, don't we?"

Alma doesn't answer. She's already typing out a message using her two pointer fingers like Gran does. I sit in the extra seat, clasping my hands. Usually I'd take notes, but I wasn't prepared to conference today. I want to ask Leo what happened and why everyone is acting cagey, but he's hardly met my eyes.

They message back and forth, with Leo occasionally looking at Alma strangely. Finally he stands up and looks at me.

"You'll wait here with Alma?" Before I can answer, he's around his desk and out the door.

"What's happening?" I ask her.

No response, Alma stares at me like a deer in the headlights, and then she looks pointedly at Leo's desk. My eyes follow hers to the discarded iPad. I stand up, my mouth dry. She sits on her hands, rocking back and forth. I walk the three steps to his desk and pick it up. Alma motions for me to hand it to her and I do, watching as she types in the code. Then she hands it back to me, the message app open.

The message from Alma to Leo reads: BAD IS HERE

I scroll up to see the messages sent before.

Marshal wasn't just making threats. He's been meeting with them in his room when everyone's asleep. I hear them talking. They're planning on using safety rafts to get to an island with a ferry stop.

I'm forming my next question when it happens—a boom so enormous the walls tremble. Our knees bend like we're surfing. Alma's eyes double in size before she crouches in the doorway.

It only lasts a second. My heart is galloping. I look at Alma, who has her hands cradling her head.

"Wh…what was that?"

She shakes her head.

"Oh my god," I say.

Alma seizes my arm and yanks it. She looks at me with pleading eyes: *Don't leave me!* I tug out of her grip. I get a horrible feeling, hopeless and panicked. Something bad has happened.

I open the door and look down the hallway, and I see it. The annex is destroyed, the care station in splinters. I try to speak and I can't. The entrances to A and B have collapsed. Everything is hazed with dust from the broken timber. Alma hasn't seen it yet, so I back up a step to block her view. For a moment I cannot believe what I'm seeing. It's like someone has hit the slow-motion button on my vision.

That's when I see the bodies. Without hesitating, I wheel around and put my arm around Alma's shoulders. "Let's wait in the doctor's office while this gets sorted out, okay?" Sorted out. I could scream from the horror of it.

I seat her in a chair and kneel in front of her. "Stay here. You're safe here. I'll be right back." She's trembling, but she nods obediently. I look at her one more time to make sure she means to stay in place before I close the door and run for the annex.

The chaos in the annex greets me like a slap in the face. Two things become apparent at once: there has been an explosion of some sort, and someone is screaming. The emergency lights are on, flashing red. I move at once, picking my way through chunks of plaster, holding my arm over my nose and mouth. What I thought was screaming is the emergency siren. I see the shape of a person through the dust and move faster. Leo is on his knees, leaning over a body. There is too much blood to see their face. When Leo stands up, I see gray sweatpants and the white ribbing of a bathrobe. I retch, vomiting into the rubble. I watch, stunned, as he checks their pulse. When he sees me, relief washes over his face. He pulls me against his chest without a word.

"What happened?" I ask.

Leo sways on his feet. I look up to see him shaking his head.

"I don't know?" The walls are black with soot. The roof is caved in down A and B hall, while C looks whole but smoky.

"A bomb," Leo says. "I was coming through the glass walkway when I heard it go off. We need to look for survivors."

I hear myself say, "I'll call for help."

I look around. I don't have my cell phone, no one does, and the landlines are buried beneath the rubble. Who do we call for help? We are on a goddamn island.

The coast guard!

I need to get my cell phone. I start toward the security door, and that's when it hits me. No one is rushing in to help. Where are the people? George?

Before I can grab the door handle Leo yells, "Iris, no!"

I look at him.

"You can't go out there. We don't know what's happening—" His face looks pale beneath the flashing red lights. He hesitates. "Alma told me that Marshal, Jude and Dalton have been planning this. They've cut the power. You need to get somewhere safe and hide."

Dalton? A D unit patient. My mind scavenges for his backstory, but I'm finding it hard to concentrate.

"What about everyone else? There are people trapped here."

"No, listen…" he says.

I do.

"There's no sound."

Aside from the alarm, there are no calls for help, no voices— nothing. That could mean one of two things: everyone is dead, or they're trapped somewhere.

"The cafeteria," I say. Leo bends over and puts his hands on his knees as he catches his breath.

"There are emergency exits. The nurses would have evacuated everyone out the back by now. We have drills. The patients know what to do." He looks less sure than me.

We hear two loud pops, and someone screams. "Gunshots," Leo says.

I have words, but I'm so scared I've forgotten how to use them. Leo shoves a hand into his pants pocket and pulls out his key card. "Where's Alma?"

"She's still in your office. The explosion didn't affect D hall."

"D used to be a bomb shelter," he says. "Take this." He holds up the key card. "The security doors for D will stay locked because of the generators. You're safe back there."

My hand shakes when I take the card.

"Promise me you'll stay there."

"I promise," I lie. He grabs my hand, squeezes it, and takes off toward the security doors.

I have the sinking feeling that it's the last time I will ever see Leo Grayson.

# 27

**THE FIRST THING** I do when I get back to Leo's office is check the landline. No dial tone. A knot forms in my belly. I snatch up the iPad and dial 911. We are in a dead zone, and Leo said they cut the power.

"Dammit!"

Alma's whimper reminds me that she's there. I look around the empty room, confused until another sniffling sound comes from beneath the desk. I find her curled up in a ball, her eyes bulging with fear.

It takes me several tries to coax her out.

"Dr. Grayson said that this part of the hospital was a bomb shelter. The power is probably run by a separate generator. That must be why the lights are still on. You told Dr. Grayson about their plan?"

She nods.

I take her hand and she shuffles closer, cocking her head sideways at me, and taps the iPad.

"You want me to look at this now?"

Opening her last message to Leo, she hands it back to me, motioning for me to scroll up. I go past everything I just read, stopping at their last therapy session two weeks ago. They talk about everything from her delusions to regular therapy thoughts. I notice the same name standing out as I scroll. Marshal. Marshal. Did he do this somehow?

I breathe in through my nose and out through my mouth. The walls of the office feel like they're closing in on me. I cannot just sit here not knowing what is going on and where everyone is. Ten minutes go by. Alma and I stand stiff as statues, watching the door. What if the same explosion happened on the other side of the hospital? People would be hurt. They'd need help. Another ten minutes go by, and I can't take it anymore.

I open Leo's office door decidedly. "We have to get out of here, Alma."

She stands, asking a thousand questions with her eyes.

"I don't know what's happening out there, but I can't sit like a duck. You can stay if you want."

She shakes her head.

"Okay," I say. "Let's go…"

I'm acutely aware of the six doors we pass on the way out. The people behind them are dangerous, but how can I just leave them here? If there is a fire they'll burn alive, trapped like animals behind the doors. *Help is coming*, I tell myself. *Help will come for them.* I push it out of my mind.

I focus on getting Alma to safety.

As soon as we leave D, the light leaves us as well. The red emergency lights have stopped flashing. The only light we have now comes from the skylights. We pluck our way through what used to be the annex. Wires hang from what's left of the ceiling like vines. When we're halfway there, Alma slips on blood and goes sprawling. She's hyperventilating as I help her up. She sees the blood on her hands and loses it. She collapses in a heap, holding her hands as far away from the rest of her as she can. She cries like a kitten, making horrible, grief-stricken noises. I drag her to her feet, away from the source of the blood. It's Bouncer. I close my eyes, but I see her on the backs of my eyelids, face up, her hands above her head. The bottom half of her body is covered in concrete. She looks like she's sleeping. I crouch down to check her pulse. Alma looks at me inquiringly, then pounds her chest with both fists when I shake my head. I know she's about to lose it. I've seen her detach and enter a catatonic state before. I hold both of her wrists gently in my hands and make eye contact. She tries to get away from me, wiry little body stiffening up with every second.

"You are alive and I am alive," I say firmly. "Do you want to stay that way? Because I certainly do." She looks me in the eyes, a rare thing for Alma, then nods. We're just starting to move again when I hear voices. I open my mouth to call for help when something hard hits my shoulder.

"Agh!" I spin around to see Alma with her finger pressed against her lips. She hit me. Before I can ask why, she tackles me with all of her ninety pounds.

She catches me off guard, and I tumble. My hand reaches to break my fall and lands on something sharp. My yelp of pain is muffled by a tiny hand. The voices are loud now. They're coming from the security door. Alma is half on top of me, and I feel her shaking.

"Whoohee yow! Look what our boy did!"

I freeze. I hear him before I see him: Marshal lets off a couple of wild yelps and kicks something across the room. There is the return of raucous laughter from maybe one…no—two men. Three of them all together. The beam of a flashlight sweeps uncomfortably close to where we are. I realize with cold shock that we are hiding.

"Anything?"

"Naw, just a bunch of dead bodies. Who do you think this is?"

I lift my head enough to watch them. Marshal uses his foot

to poke the body. Then he leans down close to its face. "Looks like a dumb bitch to me!" The two others whoop in agreement. I can't tell who they are.

"Do you think there's any others back there?"

"They would have gone out the emergency exits," Marshal replies. "Let's go hunt 'em down, boys!" They exit, taking their hyena noises with them.

*Yes. Go, go, go.* My hand is throbbing. I can feel blood pulsing from the wound. When they're out of earshot, Alma gets up, and I can finally breathe. Pushing myself up with my right hand, I cradle my left. There's something sticking out of my palm. *Don't let it be a nail*, I silently plead. Holding my hand up to the tiny bit of light still coming through the skylight, I see a piece of glass poking out of my palm. I'm too relieved to be bothered by the sting as I pull it out.

"Alma, did you know they were going to do this?"

I can't see her features, but she shakes her head. I feel like there's something more she wants me to know. "But you knew they were planning *something*?"

She nods.

"Who else other than Marshal?"

She looks toward D.

That's when it comes back to me. Dalton, the D patient Jude said was helping Marshal, he built a bomb and blew up his ex and her new lover. The explosion had to be Dalton's doing.

"That's impossible. No one has access to D patients."

Her shoulders rise and fall in a shrug.

"All right," I say. "All right, we need a plan, don't we?" I'm talking to myself. Alma stands very still, watching me.

What do I know so far? Marshal and a group of his pals somehow made a bomb and blew up the hospital. Now they are on their way outside to round everyone up. For what? They have guns. This is bad. If Leo doesn't come back, it could only mean one thing: they have him.

"I know a place to hide you." I grab her hand, slick with blood. We walk to the security door hand in hand. Taking a steadying breath, I push the door open an inch to peer out. The emergency lights are flashing; each time they blink, I see more of the destruction. There is glass under our feet. The crunch is alarmingly loud. The door on the other side is open, hanging on one hinge.

"I have to get my phone," I whisper to Alma. I hoist myself up on the counter, belly first, sliding until I reach the other side. George's chair is overturned, but there's no sign of him. There's a shelf behind where the guard sits. It's where they put the phones when we turn them in. Most of the baskets have been knocked to the floor. I pick up the first phone I see and dial 911. Nothing. No sound. When I check the screen, there's no service. I find my phone still on the shelf—the lone basket that didn't get knocked over. No service there either. I tuck it in my pocket and slide back across the counter. I jump off and hear the crunch of glass.

We pass through the doorway, her hand squeezing mine. Alma cowers against my back, trembling and warm. I put my finger against my lips as we near the staircase. We'll be completely visible to anyone downstairs. I can't hear anything except some distant shouting from outside. We keep our backs to the banister as we descend so we can see both sides of the hallway. When I hear the sound of feet, I put out a hand to stop Alma from going farther. Three women run into view. I recognize two of them as nurses, and the third is Agnes. I hold my breath as they creep forward. They haven't seen us yet. They're looking at the door. Two gunshots sound from outside: *Pop! Pop!* The three women draw together, clutching each other, and one of them screams and begins to cry. Behind me, Alma whimpers and tugs on my sweater.

"Wait here," I tell Alma for what feels like the tenth time today.

Before she can stop me, I take the stairs two at a time, keeping my eyes on the door. They see me coming and flinch away.

"It's Iris," I say. Janiss pops into view, and then they converge on me. Janiss is shaking, her eyes as large as saucers. "Those fuckers," she says, then goes silent. The other nurse—I think her name is Ruthie—speaks.

"We heard gunshots. We hid in the office but—people are dead back there. There was so much blood."

I nod, looking in the direction they came from. The administrative offices.

"Did you see Jordyn?"

The third woman shakes her head. "She was in the cafeteria the last time I saw her…"

Jackie looks scared, her silver hair is plastered flat on one side. When she turns her head, I catch a glimpse of the blood. She has blood on the front of her blouse, and another thumb-sized spot on the bridge of her nose.

"They're going for the boats," Janiss says in a low voice. "Just a couple of safety rafts, really, but they think they can make it to the mainland."

"Who was it?"

"Marshal… I heard his voice for sure. You know how he snaps his fingers when he speaks."

We nod.

"Did you call for help?"

She shook her head. "The phone lines are down and so is the Wi-Fi. By the time I realized what was happening, I made a go for it. I ran for the door, but one of them got me." She moved to touch the side of her head but thought better of it. "Got pistol-whipped by one of them. I dropped and played dead. I think they thought they killed me." She looked down the dark hallway, toward the offices.

"How many?"

She shrugged. "I saw three of them, heard maybe five when I was lying there, but I can't be sure."

"We need to get out of here," I tell them. "Hide until help comes. Alma," I call up the stairs. "Let's go…"

Alma appears a moment later, making a happy sound when she sees Agnes. They clutch each other as I start toward the dorms, motioning them to follow. I watch as Ruthie picks up a lamp, testing its weight. She's looking for a weapon.

The portico from the entry to the hallway that leads to the staff living area is deserted, and the emergency lights are flashing red. The rain is coming down hard, slapping at the glass and making it hard to hear. Jackie and I take the lead, Alma and Agnes at our center, and Ruthie following behind. "Alice is probably fine," I say reassuringly. "She probably got out with everyone else."

We reach the end of the portico and are faced with the decision to go either left or right; I choose the left, heading for the dorms and the small staff kitchen.

The doors to the dorms are shut. I don't test them; I go toward the staff kitchen with the others close behind. The door is half-open, but I don't have any light to offer the room, so I stand for a minute letting my eyes adjust to the dark. From behind us—coming from the portico—I hear men's voices: whooping, laughing, then the shattering of glass.

"Oh my god, they're coming…" Ruthie pushes Alma and Agnes farther into the kitchen, closing the door behind her. We are plunged into complete darkness. I hold a hand out in front of me as I step forward.

"Grab my shoulder," I say to Jackie, "Alma, grab hers." I feel them shuffling behind me. The kitchen is dark but I move to the pantry, flinging open the first door and pushing on the back shelf like I've seen Benni do. It swings inward, revealing the hidden pantry. Alma is making mewling sounds in the back of her throat. "Hush, now," I hear Jackie say. "We're all with you. Don't be afraid."

"Step as far as you can, until you're touching the shelves," I tell them. I hear them moving to obey to me. The men must've gone right toward the cafeteria, because their voices sound farther away.

When we're all in, I pull the swinging shelf closed behind us. Lifting an arm around Alma's shoulders, I pull her against me, and she quiets down. We wait, our breath mingling together in the small space, my heart beating so fast it hurts. Outside the staff kitchen I hear two distinct male voices. It's completely dark, but I close my eyes anyway like it'll make me hear better. At first I think they're arguing, but then I hear the barking of orders: "Go! Get in there!" And then—"Sit against the wall." We all jump when we hear the gunshot.

Without warning, Alma wails, her hands clawing at my chest. "Shut up," Ruthie says. "They're going to hear us." I strain to hear what's happening outside. Footsteps. Then—

"I heard something. There's someone in here."

"I checked already." The voice is high, tinny…

Their shoes clonk around the room, checking the corners. The beam of a flashlight shines through a crack in the cabinetry. I'm certain they're going to find us. We are collectively breathing too loudly. Someone is in the pantry. I hold my breath. "Hey, look at this…"

They stand crowded in the doorway of the pantry.

"Fuck, all they give us is cheap-ass granola bars." I hear something slide off a shelf directly in front of my face. "Don't mind if I do." They take whatever it is and leave.

"What happened back there?" Ruthie whispers. I can't see her, but I can hear the tremble in her voice.

I whisper, with a hand on Alma's arm to keep her settled. "I was shadowing Grayson's conference with Alma. He left in the middle of it. Then the explosion happened."

Voices start up again outside, and I press my lips together, my breath jagged and scared. Ruthie tenses up beside me. They walk past the pantry, but no one comes in this time. I try to reach my phone, but we're crammed so tight it's hard to move. I ask Jackie to get it out.

She slips it into my hand. "None of us have service," she whispers. She's not lying—I don't have a single bar.

It's 4:30 p.m. In winter the sun sets at four, so it must be completely dark outside. There's a stack of text messages that came through before we lost service. Three from Cal, one from Mary-Ann, and a very long paragraph from Poley. I don't read any of them for fear someone will see the light. I type a quick message to Poley and hit Send. On the slim chance that service comes back, the network will send it out.

"What are we going to do?" Ruthie whispers.

"I don't know," I say. Now that my adrenaline's gone, my hand aches. Agnes opens a box of Zebra Cakes and passes them around. I don't have an appetite, but the sugar will help. I eat both cakes and feel slightly better. There are bottles of water on the lowest shelf. It's not until I'm gulping it down that I realize how thirsty I am. When I check my phone again, it's five o'clock. I can't hear the men anymore, only us rustling around in the closet. If we can make it out of the staff kitchen and into the hallway, we can run for the emergency exit. The gun, I remind myself.

"I'm going to go check if it's clear," I whisper.

But before I can Ruthie says, "Oh my god, I smell smoke."

# 28

**WE STEP INTO** the waiting darkness. Jackie is line leader since she knows the building the best. We follow, each with a hand on the shoulder in front of us. The smell of smoke grows stronger once we're in the hallway.

"It's coming from the dorms!"

Ruthie is right. We shuffle in the opposite direction, toward the emergency exit.

I'm behind Jackie, Alma is next, then Agnes. Ruthie volunteered to be in the back.

"Did you recognize any of the voices?" Jackie asks quietly.

"Just one. Marshal Day Monterey."

"Shit."

"Yeah."

"Guys?" Ruthie calls from the back. I look toward her and see flames. Ruthie starts coughing. "We have to go faster," I tell Jackie. But faster can't outrun the smoke. It catches up to us in seconds. My lungs ache for oxygen.

Through my own coughing spasm, I manage to yell, "Crawl!"

We have to let go of each other to crawl. I feel the wound on my palm reopen. The pain isn't as bad as the one in my lungs. I can't see the others, but I can hear them.

Jackie reaches the door first. She stands to open it. Fresh air. I get to my feet and stumble out, falling back to my knees, and I roll onto my back gasping. Jackie is bent over, vomiting in the grass. I watch the door for the others. Alma comes next, and then I see Ruthie.

Seconds tick by with no Agnes. Stumbling to my feet, I make to go back inside to get her. Ruthie stands in my way, still coughing while holding out her hand to stop me.

"You…can't…" she gasps. "She's gone." I don't believe her. The fire is chewing its way down the hallway. I can hear it eating the lodge. Jackie, who has regained her wits, grabs a handful of my scrubs and yanks me back.

"You're going to get yourself killed!"

I watch helplessly, a scream of denial building in my chest. We hear the snapping of beams followed by a crash as part of the roof caves in. We huddle together and watch in disbelief.

"Where is everyone?" Ruthie asks weakly.

"Hiding," I say. We all look toward the woods.

"I'm scared," Ruthie says. Alma takes her hand.

"We need to move," I say. "If they come back…"

Jackie takes the lead again, turning away from the woods. With no moon to give us even a glimmer of light, we are forced to move slowly. The dark feels bottomless.

"Here… I think it's here." Jackie's voice is strained. "Reach out with your left hands and you'll feel it."

I reach with my throbbing hand and feel cold metal.

"It's the mower shed." I hear the grate of metal as she yanks open the door. We pile in, our legs brushing up against the machines. It's below thirty degrees, and none of us have jackets.

"Check your phone for service." Jackie's voice is hoarse. I nod though no one can see me. The screen gives us enough light to make out four lawnmowers. "Let's get behind them." We slide in the gap between the wall of the shed and the mowers.

"No service," I whisper. Ruthie starts crying.

I check my phone, hoping for the impossible. My message to Poley did not send.

The message is trapped on the island with the rest of us. I stare at the unsent text, frustrated. My fingers are stiff from the cold.

Jackie pulls the tarp from one of the mowers and wraps it around Ruthie and Alma. She tells them to huddle together to keep warm before going to look for another. I scroll up to read the last text Poley sent me, the long one. I don't understand what I'm reading.

Jackie comes back with a box of garbage bags, and she drops a handful next to me. I scroll past the medical terminology, the sinking feeling returning to my stomach. I'd forgotten about the favor—the plastic baggies I passed her from my car window. I already had my answer. At the bottom she typed, *It's a match! It's him!*

Jackie is wrapping herself in garbage bags, making her own jacket. She snaps her fingers in my face. "Hypothermia," she says.

She wants me to put them on, but I can't. I scroll up again. That can't be right. All three items she sent to the lab have the same DNA on them. Bouncer collected the trays. I took something from each one. Poley tried to call me. I hadn't been able to call her back. But here it is right in front of my face in her text—her last-ditch effort to tell me. Jude is Cal's father.

I stand up. But... Leo had shown me results too. No, he handed me a single sheet of paper. I barely glanced at it because I trusted him when he said the results were negative. Why would he lie?

"I have to get the patients out of D," I hear myself say. "When the fire reaches them, they'll be trapped."

Ruthie looks at me like I've lost my mind.

"You can't go back in there. Someone has probably let them out—just let it go, or you're going to get yourself killed."

Alma whimpers.

I don't let them stop me this time. I'm through the mowers and out the door, no longer cold but hot—so hot. The fire is huge, I look at it as I run. It has reached the Victorian side, the white roof starting to cinder. With my legs pumping wildly, I run past the pink walls. Timber cracks to my right. Jordyn's office will burn next. Has she gotten out in time? I push it out of my thoughts. It's too late to do anything about it.

My legs are moving on their own. The ground is steep and getting steeper. I reach a handrail and suddenly I'm being battered by the wind. Concrete stairs lead up, up, up. There is a sign bolted in the ground. I use the flashlight on my phone to read it. *DANGER. Do not enter. High winds.*

The tree cover that was to my left a moment ago is gone. I'm cliffside. I can hear the waves beating against rock. My legs feel like Jell-O as I grab the handrail, keeping the light pointed on the side of the building. The stairs plateau. I can't keep going—a portion of chain-link fence cuts off my path. I can't go any farther. I want to scream. I went the wrong way. I sweep my precious beam of light around one last time before I begin my descent. The fire is burning toward me now, but slower. The rain is helping. I keep the light pointed down, watching my feet. Every few seconds I glance up to check my progress. It's then that I see that the railing is no longer supported by the side of the building. A space opens up barely three feet wide. I point my light through space and see a door.

I peer down, unsure of how to get to it. I'd have to lower myself through the space and drop into the courtyard. Once I jumped down, there'd be no way for me to get back up. I only take a minute to consider. This is not what Piper would do! I tuck my phone into my pocket. I get on my stomach and lower myself through the space backwards so I can land feet-down. I have to wriggle through the space. My scrubs pull up and my stomach scrapes against rough concrete. I'm holding on to the edge of a stair. For one horrifying second, I think the space is too small and I'm going to get stuck, but then my torso is through, my belly exposed to the cold. All I have to do is let go. One…two…three…

# 29

I LAND HARD on my butt. The pain takes a second or two to reach me, and when it does, it's powerfully sharp. I cry out and roll to my side, knees up to my chest. My eyes water but I force them open. No time. Gingerly, I test my limbs for breaks. The worst thing that could happen did not.

I stumble to my feet, whole. When I reach for my phone, I already know what I'll find. Smashed to smithereens. It hurts to walk. I hobble the three steps it takes to get to the door. How bleak would it be to die in this horrible cliffside cage? That's exactly what will happen if the door is locked. I grip the knob with little to no faith.

Three gunshots pop in succession—pow, pow, pow. The knob turns. I cry out in relief and fling it wide open. It's a machine room. I can feel the ground vibrating beneath my shoes. No phone means I'll have to navigate it in the dark. I close my eyes, picture Cal's sweet face, and step inside.

The machine that lives inside the dark takes up most of room. I keep away from it, pressing my back against the opposite wall. I walk sideways using the wall as my guide. I don't know how far I've gone when I reach the corner. I face the new wall, running my hands up and down to feel for a door. It's there. The knob is the same as the one outside. It turns. I'm in yet another hallway, this one lit by emergency lights. I know this place. I can't smell smoke and I remember Leo's words: D was once an army bunker. A bomb shelter. It doesn't take long to find the way out. I have to use Leo's key card to open the metal security door. When I step through, I am in a closet. Fabric brushes my face, and I catch a whiff of cologne as I shove my way past the coats. I'm in Leo's office.

Holy shit. Everything is the same as when Alma and I left it. I can't tell if Leo has been back. He keeps a Taser in the top drawer of his desk. Worry ebbs in the back of my mind. Leo, where is he? His Taser is where it's supposed to be. There's a first aid kit next to the Taser. I ignore it, grabbing the flashlight instead. I can't smell smoke outside of his office either, but it's only a matter of time. I am tired, but not—wired is what I am.

I stand in front of *the* door—Jude's door. I'm terrified, not just of him, but of myself. Of what I came here to do. I lift Leo's card and swipe. A green light appears on the reader, followed by a loud click. I give the door one hard shove. It swings open, and I very cautiously step inside, shining the thin beam of light.

"Jude…" My voice is loud in the small space. The room is empty. The mattress on the bed is bare. The shelves are bare. There isn't a door on the bathroom; I can see into it from where I stand. Leo said they had a small outdoor space. I see that too. Empty. I back out of the room. Five more doors. I open them one by one until I reach the end. *Empty, empty, empty.* I don't understand.

I scream, pound the wall with my fists. *You're going to die for nothing*, I think. I'm not nearly as frightened as I thought I'd be. *I'll be with Piper*, I think calmly. I wheel around like I'm drunk. No way out. The fire is on the other side of the security door. I think of all the people lying dead in the annex. Their families will never be able to bury their bodies. How sad, I think. They'll be as sad as me. I slide down the closest wall until I'm sitting.

I have not cried yet. Ruthie cried, Alma cried, Jackie cried. I take my turn, sobbing into my knees. Another granddaughter gone, Cal's mother gone. I know what their grief will feel like, and I don't want it for them.

I have to try…for them. One…two…three. I haul myself to my feet. I use Leo's card for the last time, dropping it as soon as the door opens. Smoke. Holding an arm over my nose, I plunge forward.

In a split second, I decide to try to get through the collapsed A hall. I claw at chunks of drywall, moving through the roof tiles and timber, kicking and ripping until I can't feel my fingers. I have no sense of self, just raw survival. I'm somehow on the other side. The exit sign is the most beautiful thing I've ever seen in my life. Air, air, air. It's easier this time. I make it outside and fall on my knees.

"What have we got here?"

I wake up to that awful voice. It's still dark, still wet. HOTI is still burning. I couldn't have been out long. It takes effort to sit up.

"Hurts to open my eyes," I mumble.

"Give her something to drink," Marshal barks at one of the men. Something is put in my hand, bottled water. I drink most of the bottle, then use the rest of the water to pour on my eyes.

When I open them, I see three men standing in a circle around me. I gaze past Marshal to the other two.

"Am I seeing what I'm seeing, or do I need to wash my eyes out again?"

He crouches down in front of me, and I scoot away from him.

"You're a smart girl, teacher's pet." I keep my mouth shut. "You ain't much," he scoffs, standing.

"George?" I address him directly. He won't make eye contact.

"His name is Arthur Barton. He don't say much." Marshal spits a wad of something into the grass. "Room number three down D hall. They weren't gonna ever let you out, right, Artie?" He hooks his fingers in the waistband of his jeans, bouncing on the balls of his feet. "Isn't that right, boys?"

The third man, whose face I've yet to see, pokes me in the back with the barrel of a shotgun. "Get up."

I do, but slowly. Everything hurts.

I feel another jab between the shoulder blades, harder this time. I spin around to look at him.

The security guard who gave me shit for taking a walk on my first overnight. I stare dumbfounded. He's wearing the same filthy beanie, the same evil grin he wore when he tried to intimidate me.

"You."

He blinks at me with bloodshot eyes, bored and amused at the same time. He's wearing a camo vest, the type hunters wear, and a knife belt with all sorts of gadgets attached.

"Boo," he says.

I cock my head and give him the silent fuck-you smirk.

"That's Ellis." Marshal walks over to the fire and throws a log on it. "Before he came to Shoal he was a soldier, isn't that right, Ellis?"

Ellis, not quite smiling, looks me over. "That's right. A soldier." Something about the way he says it makes my stomach roll. Ellis Conrad Jr. has lived at HOTI for three decades after stalking and then attempting to kill a presidential candidate. A jury found him not guilty by reason of insanity.

I look around the circle: Marshal Day Monterey… Arthur Barton, Ellis Conrad Jr. The only ones missing from the D hall reunion are Dalton and Jude.

Marshal lets out a low whistle as he looks at his watch. "It's time, folks."

Ellis nudges me in the back with the gun.

"Move," he orders. I walk behind Marshal, and Ellis flanks me. Arthur, who is my strongest hope, stays in back looking like he's having less fun than the others. On paper, Arthur is the least accomplished criminal of the bunch. I knew very little about him except that he was on antipsychotics, and if he refused them he became violent. I only knew that because I read his medical chart when Janiss told me to file it.

The tree line is—fifteen, maybe twenty yards away. I could make a run for it, but there are too many of them, and they know the island better than me. They'd hunt me and enjoy it. *And Marshal will roast your eyeballs like marshmallows over the campfire.*

"Where are you taking me?"

"You'll see when you get there. Now shut up." I feel the butt of the gun again.

I look back at him. "You're just having the time of your life, aren't you?"

We've reached the tree line. They're moving me away from HOTI. We walk for ten minutes before I see a fire through the trees, this one meant for warmth, not destruction. And then to my surprise we arrive at a campsite, and by the looks of it, it's been here for a while.

I count six tents—big ones, too. A funny collection of chairs circles the fire: a computer chair, a beanbag, two ancient dining room chairs, and one soggy love seat. There's a kitchen area if you can call it that. A gas stove and stacks of canned food sit under a tarp stretched between two tree trunks.

"Well, look at you Boy Scouts," I say. "Cozy, cozy."

Marshal throws a log on the fire. "Don't let that bitch mouth get you in trouble, girl. Don't forget who has the gun."

Oh, I won't forget. I've seen the footage of him walking through the produce aisle, pausing to aim and shoot.

"Put her in the close tent," he tells George. Marshal is jittery.

He pulls a flask from his back pocket and unscrews the cap. I watch his scrawny neck as he tilts his head back.

George lets me walk into the tent myself. I imagine the other two would have pushed me. I look at him urgently, and he looks away. "The fuck, Arthur? Why are you doing this?"

Using his real name gets me eye contact. He lingers like he is about to say something. I want to ask how long they've been doing this. I can't wrap my mind around it. I don't believe Marshal did this on his own.

I lower my voice. "Arthur. You're not like them. I can tell. You look mean but you're not mean, right?"

"I have to tie your hands." His voice is soft…and he has a lisp. He looks embarrassed. I hold out my wrists for him. He looks at me out of the corner of his eye, then slowly takes my wrists like he's afraid he'll break them.

"Did you live in D?"

He focuses on his knot, but I catch the quick bob of his chin. Things are pulling together in my head. I'd read about Arthur Barton. I read about all of them. Arthur killed his mother. I watched an interview his distraught father gave to the press. He said that Arthur and his mother had a loving relationship. She was a mother who cried herself to sleep out of concern for her son.

After the attack, he called 911. He was found in the house when police arrived, cradling her bludgeoned head.

"You didn't like being in that room, did you?"

He shook his head. "They said, 'You live out here and be the security guard…'"

Despite looking upset, he's quick on his feet. He backs out of the tent and zips me in. There's a sleeping bag rolled in the back corner, but with my hands tied, I can't unroll it. I sit cross-legged in the center of the tent, urgently alert and deeply tired.

They start drinking ten minutes later. They're celebrating,

dancing around the fire like the Lost Boys. I hear someone else join them. "I locked them in. Should be good for tonight."

*Who is lucky number four?*

Whoever he is, he barks at Marshal to "shut the fuck up," and Marshal listens.

Here is the boss. The alpha dog. The brain? *The bomb maker!* I think suddenly. They're afraid of him. I know who he is. He didn't just kill his ex and her new boyfriend, he was in some skinhead cult. They wanted to blow people up. They bought explosives from an undercover cop. The other four guys got twenty years each. Dalton, who was only sixteen when it all went down, got sent to juvie. Instead of getting better, he got worse. He had a taste for violence.

After getting into a fight and killing some kid in juvie, he was tried for murder. His lawyer came in strong. He was a product of systemic abuse. The boys who raised him were serving twenty years, because they deserved it. Dalton, he said, needed rehabilitation. The jury agreed, and he moved into HOTI. He'd pretty much been here most of his life.

Dalton tells them he's keeping watch. They get in their tents and zip up.

A sheet of green vinyl separates me from one of the most violent men in Washington state. A genius, violent man who spent his teens building bombs.

I'm not afraid. I don't feel anything at all, other than a little cold. For some reason I find this insanely funny. All I am is cold. The laughter fills me with air like a balloon. I can't stop. I can see Dalton's shape through the tent. A hulking man. The top half of his body rotates to look at the tent. I wish I could see his face. I…sound…scary—which makes me laugh harder. I don't sound human. I haven't been human since Piper left me. The laughter cuts off in my throat. I lie on my side, propping my head on the sleeping bag.

George—or Arthur—sat behind the guard window for

months. I saw him every week. I'd never questioned or wondered why it was always and only him. No, I was wrong, there had been another guard once, a mean one. I never saw him again. Was he a patient too? I'd been too busy with my own problems. My God, what else have I missed?

I drift in and out of a light sleep, jolting awake anytime one of them laughs.

I'm running. Gunshots echo behind me. I'm falling face-first off a cliff. I bolt upright. A dream. I am still in the nightmare. Another one of those loud pops. Someone is shooting a gun in the air.

"Cut it out," Dalton barks.

They grow quieter as the hours tick by. I know from listening to them that Dalton is taking the first shift. The cut on my hand throbs like it's infected. It probably doesn't matter because the ropes on my wrists are so tight, I'll need both arms amputated. Restless and emboldened by my small nap, I kick at the side of the tent.

"Hey! Hey hello, I have to take a piss."

It's a stranger's face I see when the zipper opens. A human meerkat in a concert tee stares at me from behind thick glasses. He looks like a geek on steroids.

"Hello, Dalton."

I clock the surprise on his face, and then he looks embarrassed. He doesn't try to touch me like the others did. He stands back, the gun hanging limply at his side.

"Come out." I do as I'm told. He's even shorter than Marshal but a lot smarter. He calculates me, tilting his head to the side like he's trying to work out my wires.

Such a fucking geek. He gestures to the woods with his gun hand.

Dalton stops at a giant rock and looks at me.

I show him my wrists. "I can't with these on." He unties my hands. I walk around the rock.

"I'll shoot you if you do anything stupid."

Yanking down my pants, I almost groan in relief.

"You guys have a pretty great setup back here. My gran would make herself right at home. She loves to camp."

I chat through the longest pee of my life. When I come out from behind the rock I clear my throat.

"A little looser this time, please."

I'm surprised by both the agility and gentleness with which he ties the knots. His face is unreadable. I'm allowed to sit on one of the chairs. Arthur puts a bowl in my hands. I stare at the beans and globs of gray meat and thank him. I drink it, eyeing him over the rim of the bowl. He's sweating like a pig in cellophane, glancing every few minutes at a spot in the trees. I chew without tasting, grateful for the warm-up.

When I'm done, Dalton collects my bowl and offers me a bottle of water.

"I can't open it," I say. "Can you please…"

He won't look at me as he screws off the lid; he studies the fire instead, putting the open bottle between my tied hands.

"Who taught you how to cook?"

He stares at me before wiping his face on the crook of his arm. "My grandma."

"Mine did too," I say. "All it takes is one good gran to save a kid. In my case, two, because it was me and my twin sister. Where is everyone?" I speak to Dalton, since he's the boss. He's bent over his bowl with the same dead expression on his face.

"Some of them are in the old chapel. Some of them are dead." He goes back to eating.

I didn't know there was an old chapel. Maybe that's why Jackie led us in the opposite direction. She might have known the chapel would be a hotspot. I wonder if they got caught or were still hiding in the shed.

"I've come to collect the little flower." Marshal is wearing a filthy undershirt and jeans. He winks at me. Dalton nods, not lifting his head from the bowl.

"Off we go," Marshal sings. He grabs my upper arm, digging his fingers into my flesh. I don't flinch. He looks disappointed. He doesn't speak as he drags me through the trees until we reach a small clearing. It's a pretty place to die.

He shoves me left, and I see an RV. He manhandles me up the stairs, reaching around me to turn the handle, purposefully brushing my breast with his arm in the process. I jump away from his touch, but he's right behind me, laughing when I have nowhere to go. The RV smells stale like mold and piss. He pushes me through the tiny kitchen area, past the cracked leather seats, to a yellowing wood panel door. My jaw muscles shiver, clanging my teeth together. Marshal has me face him so he can untie my wrists. "You have ten minutes to take a shower," he says. "A minute over and I'll come in there and drag you out myself." I'm pushed inside a tiny bathroom: sink, toilet, shower.

I'm locked in. I rattle the handle and shove at the panel with my shoulder.

"I fuckin' warned you!" Marshal pounds on the other side of the door with his fist. The space I'm in is impossibly small. I am trapped. I cry, silent streaming tears that are heavy, and they drip like rain to the cracked linoleum floor. I turn on the water, biting the insides of my cheeks as I think. A hand towel is folded on the counter like someone left it for me. What looks like a beige button-down and a pair of sweatpants are folded underneath it.

I think of the Polaroid photos of Piper, half-naked and sexually posed. I'll kill them, strip their skin from their bones and—what? They are stronger, they are many.

I open every drawer, look under the little sink, in the closet… There are things: a bar of unwrapped blue soap, a half roll of toilet paper, a waterlogged book with the cover torn off, and some goopy stuff that looks like spilled bodywash. Someone resides here. The water is lukewarm. I hold my cut hand under the stream, crying out when the water hits it.

I don't know how many minutes I've used, and I don't want Marshal to make good on his threat. I get into the shower still wearing my underwear, the flimsy cotton the only protection I have. I never stop shivering, not even when I quickly dry off with the hand towel and pull on the clothes left for me. In the mirror a bloodless face stares back at me. The shirt is miles too big. I stare at FFOH above my breast pocket. It takes me a few seconds to see it: HOFF. I groan, clenching the material in my fist. Kyra Hoff's face is burned into my memory; I am wearing her missing husband's shirt.

When Marshal finds me dressed and ready, he is surly. He snaps his fingers three times before prodding me out of the RV and through the woods. I can hear the crash of the waves, and as the wind surges, the trees creak and moan around us like they're about to give.

We walk a trail until we reach a scarred old barn. Not a barn—I see the crooked steeple and the cross. As we get closer, a flash of lightning illuminates the building, and I see the roots of a fallen tree. What's left of the front of the chapel is so dilapidated it shivers in the wind. Surely he wasn't taking me to the sodden church rubble. I look back at Marshal, whose footfalls have slowed. He spits and points to the left of the building with his flashlight. I squint through the rain and see a path through the trees. My shoes sink into fresh mulch as we walk, the smell of cedar burning in my nostrils. I can only see as far as Marshal allows with his beam of light, but it's clear someone laid this mulch recently. I lose count of the beer cans—crushed, crumpled, and dented, they mar the mulch with the frequency of a city highway. I could take my chances and run, but he'd catch me pretty fast, and then what? *They're not going to kill you yet, they just let you shower.* The thought is so silly—is so asinine, I laugh out loud. If Marshal hears, he doesn't say anything.

On either side of the path, blackberry bushes weave walls between the woods and us. We walk for a few more minutes before he calls for me to stop. I turn around, blank-faced as a mannequin. I will not be shot in the back. Instead of pointing the gun, he's pointing the flashlight—not at me, past me.

"There," he says flatly. My eyes follow the direction of the beam to a space between the trees. A small gazebo sits nestled in the brush; it looks to be in relatively good shape compared to the chapel, but just as frightening. Broken bottles and beer cans litter the base of a tree, a clear hangout spot.

I spin around to confront Marshal, fists clenched, ready to fight. I will not go in there with him. Running toward or away from the gazebo makes me a shooting target, but I could crawl into the blackberry bushes, slip through the branches easier than he could. Let's see who could wriggle through thorns faster.

"What do you mean? What's there?" I look between him and the gazebo. The seconds tick by achingly slow; I am all too aware of my ragged breathing and the throbbing ache in my hand.

Instead of answering me, he turns his back and walks away—quickly, like he's running from something.

He is leaving me here? My choices are to go where he told me to go, or head back the way I came—where Marshal is surely waiting for me with the gun. An impossible choice; I've been set up to fail. A noise, a voice... There is someone in the gazebo; I hear them walking around, the *clomp clomp clomp* of boots. There is a trap in every direction, ill intent meant to degrade and denigrate women. I hate them, I hate that my sister felt what I am feeling now—helpless and trapped, her fate sealed by the lowest form of coward.

"Iris."

My name stops me short.

I walk up the two stairs, ready to jump over the wood rail-ings and disappear into the sea of thorns. How fast would the bullets find me?

When I face Leo, he is empty-handed, his cleanly shaven face resigned.

"Iris Walsh," he repeats my name. I don't move, I'm afraid to move. An alarm is sounding in my head, and Piper's face appears where only I can see it.

There are only the woods, the rain, the darkness, and us. Thunder cracks above us and we both jump. Neither of us says anything, and my stomach plummets through the floor. I feel the crawl of his gaze and it sends my heart skittering. He doesn't look like himself. He's wearing a flannel shirt, much like the khaki one I'm wearing, and blue jeans. I eye his fresh buzz and close my eyes. I know his face—from then...from now.

"No..." The pain and grief crash over me. "Jude," I say.

He closes his eyes, swaying on the spot like I've uttered the most delicious thing he's ever heard.

My heart feels like it's about to explode. I press a hand against my chest and squint at him through the tears. I know what he's going to say next. Guilty people always say it.

"Let me explain..."

I was mistaken about Dalton. Here is the real alpha. Here is the man who organized the coup. I shake my head. Leo is Jude. How? *How?!*

"What the fuck?" I scream. I launch myself at him, shoving him in the chest with my bound hands. He stumbles backward, a look of surprise on his face, but recovers quickly. He grabs my hands, holding on to them while I try to pull away. I think he's going to hit me, but he unties the rope from my wrists instead.

He drops the rope and looks at me. "Are you going to keep hitting me or can we talk about this?"

Terror seeps into every chamber of my heart. I thought I was the only player in this game.

"Where's Piper, Jude?" I was staring at him angrily while he stared back, expressionless. He goes on like he hasn't heard me.

"At first I was curious. I mean, what were the chances that Piper's twin sister would fall right into my lap?"

The sheer shock and pain of the moment are so overwhelming I am winded.

"Sounds like we were looking for each other," I say dryly.

He laughs.

"I have two critiques: you show your cards too soon, and despite everything that's happened to you, you're still too trusting." He wags a finger at me. "But you didn't just fall, did you? No, you knew I was here and you came."

I see a photograph in my mind, of a group of teenagers posing in front of a church, their youth pastor grinning, wearing an orange shirt and ugly orange Adidases like he was trying too hard to be cool. That man's physique… I see him now. As Dr. Grayson, he has never made that facial expression; I remember it from another place and time—a small gap between his front teeth, thinking he'd be better-looking if he didn't smile. The orange Adidases—how Piper went on and on about how great they were. I'd glared out the backseat window, hating the color, hating the man, hating the church scene as a whole.

I want to vomit. I hold on to the side of the gazebo, grating between denial and realization as splinters bite into my palm. It feels as if I've fallen to a floor of ice. Finally, a sob tears out of my mouth, and I double over like I've been punched. Jude's voice is so familiar and so strange at the same time. He's slipping back into Jude, his old pastoral voice creeping down my spine like ice. My God, how had I not seen it?

"You son of a bitch," I say. Rain slants through the gazebo

at an angle, blowing against my back. I spin in a circle; I don't
know what to do with my body. I feel like I'm going to explode.

"I deserve that," he says. "I lied to you."

"You fucking murdered my sister!"

"Easy, tiger," he warns. I'm spoiling things for him. If I
want to survive, I need him to believe this is going the way
he wants it to go.

Gran didn't raise a moron.

"You're judging my shock. That's not very Dr. Grayson of
you…"

He laughs at my teasing tone; he thinks we're okay. He's that
easy or I'm that good.

"How did you do this? For real. I'm so confused."

"Well, it took a while. And I had a while."

"Where is Dr. Grayson?"

He backs down the stairs until he's standing beyond the roof
of the gazebo and directly in the rain, blocking off any path of
escape. He closes his eyes, tilting his face to the sky and lifting
his hands as if he's in the throes of worship. He fooled everyone…every time. I guess we did have something in common.
Except I'd been too lovestruck to see the truth…just like Piper.

"Dr. Grayson helped me…" He sounds so genuine. "I owe
him everything. We were a lot alike, same parents, same
trauma…"

I find myself nodding.

"We got to know each other, like friends. None of that
shrink shit. He treated me like a son."

Another one of his delusions. I swallow.

"Is he dead?"

"What do you think, Iris?"

My heart lugs and strains and somehow carries on, but a
cold sliver of fear enters my bloodstream. He comes back up
the stairs and leans on the side.

"For how long?"

"How long has he been dead?" He looks at the broken ceiling of the gazebo while he calculates. "A year."

"Oh my god." It slips out.

"You're wondering how you didn't see it," he says. "Our desires affect how we see things. And I had a little help from my friends." He uses his middle finger to pull his lower eyelid down until the pink interior is exposed. I watch as he uses his pointer finger and thumb to pinch out a contact, which he produces for me on the tip of his finger.

"Heterochromia," I say. "I remember Piper talking about it. She thought it was really cool."

Outside the rain has slowed to a light drizzle. I wish I could see even a few feet past the gazebo. I have no doubt Marshal is within shouting distance, and where are the others?

"You never came to church, and when you were there, you definitely were not looking at my eyes." His flirty tone makes me want to vomit.

"Ha! True." I make a *you caught me* face. "I came some Sundays and sat in the service with Gran. It was one of the few times I had her to myself."

"You have her all to yourself all the time now." He smiles a broad, harmless grin. I don't answer, only look down at my feet.

"Tell me how you did this. You can't drop all of this on me and not explain." I fix him with my most glittery gaze, like I'm really impressed.

"Before Bouncer came to…what do they call it—?" he snaps his fingers while he thinks. "HOTI?"

I nod.

"Right, before Bouncer came to HOTI, she worked for a plastic surgeon."

"How did that help you?" I frown.

"I broke my nose on my cell wall, fucked it up so bad they were forced to send me to a surgeon. She blackmailed her old boss to volunteer his time. I got a new nose, just like Dr. Grayson's."

Just like that.

Was he right? Had I seen what I wanted to see? Leo Grayson and Jude were the same height; Jude's jaw was softer than Leo Grayson's, but he'd hidden it behind a beard. He'd been a different weight back then, a dad body, plus some.

"I studied him. Spent every day with him. He was an egomaniac. All I needed to do to gain his trust was play the good student. In his mind, he was fixing me."

"It wasn't just Grayson, though. You got an entire hospital to believe you."

He shrugs.

"I killed the ones who got in the way. I didn't always have to do the killing—someone was always willing to do it for me. If they didn't want to work with me, I replaced them."

Arthur took the security job, Ellis took watch outside, and Dalton built his bombs in D hall while Jude ran the hospital.

"And I happen to be very good at making people see things my way. You don't know what spending seventeen hours a day in those rooms does to a man. You have all the time in the world to think…hatch a plan. We could talk to each other when we were outside in our individual gardens. *Garden* is a generous word, Iris. They're like grassed apartment patios. All in our own chain-link cage."

Tears spill down my cheeks, and I rub them away with the back of my hand.

"A cage?" I am shaking, the words stuttering from my mouth. "Like the one you put Piper in?"

"Come on, you and I both know it wasn't like that. Piper wanted to be with me. She loved me more than she loved you. That's what makes you upset, isn't it?"

He's enjoying this.

Red explodes behind my eyes. I can barely catch my breath.

"Who helped you?"

"Do you want the full list? In order of importance?"

He laughs a foreign laugh. In all the time I've known him, he's never made a noise that terrible. The back of my neck tingles.

"Grayson was an old prick. He wanted to fuck Bouncer, so he had her sit in on our conferences. He impressed her pretty good, but I'd say I impressed her more." He winks at me.

I see her lifeless face in my mind, red hair redder with blood. He'd made her feel like he was in love with her to get her to do what he wanted. Kept her under control with that too. I look at him in shock. Like me.

"I went on the prison diet. Lost a hundred pounds in my first year here. Grayson and I were the same height. With Bouncer's help, I managed to change my face significantly." I hadn't recognized him, but I wasn't sure I'd ever really looked at him either; my gaze had been elsewhere.

"It's incredible what filler can do...hair dye..." He juts out his chin, running a palm over his jaw like a cartoon villain. He runs his thumbs over his eyebrows. "These are tattooed—no, what do they call it. Microbladed. Some people noticed." He shrugs. "I made a big deal about losing weight and working out. I gave them a better version of Leo Grayson."

"You wanted her to die. You planned it."

"She was in the wrong place at the wrong time. Like you were that day at the movie theater..."

"You actually believe that. You studied Leo Grayson, but did you ever study yourself?"

He laughs. "You're smart as a whip, Iris—smarter than your sister."

"Fuck you," I say. My voice is clinical, lifeless. "Tell me about Piper."

His expression changes. "That's in the past..."

"Bullshit!" I say. "How dare you say that?"

He flinches. "It was an accident."

"What kind of accident?"

He's starting to get pissed. The muscles in his jaw are tight.

"She showed up at my house one night at three o'clock in the morning, pounding on my back door. My wife was out of town, so I let her in. We'd already started our relationship by then."

Relationship. Is that what he thought it was?

"She was hysterical. She said men were chasing her. I calmed her down. She spent the night, but the next morning she wouldn't leave. She was scared they'd find her. I got scared my wife would come back, so I told her I'd take her to my cabin. It's a couple hours away. I used it for hunting. My wife never went out there because there was no indoor plumbing."

He pauses to gauge my expression. I show him my numb, dumb face.

"She seemed to like it there. I asked her if she wanted to go home. She didn't. She was ashamed of what those men did to her."

It feels as if I've swallowed a mouthful of gravel. I clasp my hands in front of me to keep them from shaking.

"You did the same thing to her," I say. "The exact same thing as those pigs."

He holds his hands in front of him as if he's holding a basketball. "No. You of all people should understand the bond I had with Piper. You feel it too. We loved each other. We were going to be together…"

"Don't make me fucking throw up. She was fifteen years old. You were a man! A man who got a *kid* pregnant!"

"Yes. With Cal."

"Don't you fucking say his name!"

"You should be thanking me. You wouldn't have Cal without me."

I want to claw his eyes out. He is not worthy to speak Cal's name. I release my clasped hands to point a warning finger at him and shake my head. "You leave him out of this."

He holds up both hands, acquiescing.

"It was you who left the note on my door."

"No, Ellis left the letter on your door."

Jude doesn't seem to notice my distress; he mistakes the look on my face for curiosity.

"When you have a good team, you don't even have to delegate. They do what needs to be done. Ellis is on my team—our team. I'm not trying to lie to you, Iris. When I said I have feelings for you—that was a hundred percent the truth. You have to believe me." He reaches for me, but I take a step back. For a minute he looks confused, like he can't imagine why. Then he smiles like he knows me, like he can read me.

"Do you have a gun?" I ask.

"Don't do that, Iris, look at me. Please."

"Do you?"

He nods.

I have stopped listening. It was Piper I was seeing: her collection of smiles, her unwashed hair, the way she spat out the apple skin instead of peeling it beforehand. She liked exotic birds, the color blue, and the idea of being a surfer, even though she couldn't swim. She wore the same puka shell necklace every day for a year, and when it finally broke, she had a tan line around her neck. She was deathly afraid of slugs and snails—anything slimy, though spiders didn't bother her at all.

"We both know you can't feel anything, Jude. That's why you take from those of us who do."

I see anger flash across his face. Then it's gone, carefully folded away. I can't tell if what I've said has bothered him, or if he's pissed that the situation isn't going his way. The entire time I was trying to get to Jude he was right there, in my life and in my body.

"I did lie to you, Iris, and I'm sorry about that. I didn't expect the feelings. Did you?" He runs his hands through his hair, smoothing it back. "I wanted to get to know you authentically as yourself, not as a shadow of your sister." Anger boils and spits in my chest. I want to get as far away from him as I can.

"Please, just tell me where Piper is." Lightning flashes. My voice is hoarse. I don't want his lies or excuses; people are dead. "Where is Piper? You owe Cal his mother…"

He wasn't expecting that. He looks annoyed.

"I'm leaving. I have a boat. I want you and Cal to come with me."

"You…" My voice falters. "You murdered your wife and baby… Where is Piper, what did you do with her?"

"We can be together," he says. "Piper brought us Cal, and now we can be the family you've always wanted. I hurt my wife, that's true, but I didn't murder my son. He died in his crib. I believe it was SIDS. What happened with Mary is separate from that. I promise you…"

"You buried them both in the fucking church cemetery in someone else's grave…"

I look for shame in his eyes, or maybe even remorse, but there's only a matter-of-fact man with his moral mask down in front of me. I've imagined this moment of confrontation a hundred thousand times, but I could not have conceived it would be with my lover.

"Where is my sister?"

"If you come with me, I'll take you to her."

I can't tell if he's lying. I don't say anything.

"I put her somewhere nice. You'll like it."

My breath is ragged. I don't know how long I can hold on to my sanity. I clench my fists and stare at the rusted gazebo ceiling. I'm starting to feel dizzy. My hand.

"I'm not going anywhere with you, Jude," I explain calmly. "You are a rapist, a pedophile, and a murderer."

I have to give it to him, he looks genuinely crestfallen.

"I was afraid you'd say that."

I finally meet the real Jude, the one I've been looking for. He grabs me by the hair closest to my scalp and pulls me up to his face. I refuse to look afraid.

I'm pressed against his body; I feel his heat. It's revolting. He doesn't bother with my hands because he has me by the hair. I'm up on my tiptoes, not even a close match in strength. I reach into my pants pocket and shove the Taser into his belly. And then he's screaming. He falls backward, his body flexed like a dead spider. I'm not done. Before he leaves, I want to take something from him. I Tase him again. I know I'm running out of time. Any minute his buddies are going to break into this clearing and shoot me dead. I've been dancing around this goddamn gazebo for fifteen minutes trying to figure out how to pick up the jagged shard of beer bottle glass from between the floor planks.

The louder I scream, the harder he closes his eyes. Now that he's on his back, I walk around his body until I'm standing above his head. I hold the glass to his eye right as he opens it.

"Where is she?"

He tries to move his head away from the glass, but there's nowhere to go.

"She's in the cemetery behind the church. The angel."

I speak quickly. "You preached a sermon once. An eye for an eye."

I push the glass into his eye and stand.

As I run, his screams get farther away. I can see what's left of HOTI through the trees. The rubble looks like an old hag lying in the ashes. I hear the noise as I stumble out of the trees and onto the lawn. A helicopter. I fall to my knees and just sit there as it lands. People in red jackets are cresting the top of the hill. The coast guard. Out of the helicopter jumps Poley. She runs toward me, the wind from the blades whipping a dark ponytail. I've never been happier to see anyone in my life. She drops to her knees and wraps her arms around me.

"You're not pregnant." I have to yell to be heard.

"I named her Piper," Poley shouts.

I start crying.

Everyone is converging on us, medical professionals, police, the coast guard. They run for me like a herd.

"They're locked in a chapel about two hundred yards that way," I tell Poley. "There are four armed men that I know of. They have a camp in the woods on the east side of the island."

She breaks away from me to talk to a group of men in bulletproof vests. I'm swept away after that.

I don't remember anything that happened, not the helicopter ride to the hospital, or the four days I spent lying in the hospital bed. I was roped on painkillers, pretty beat up. Turns out squeezing yourself through impossibly tight spaces can fracture your ribs. I have nerve damage in my hand from the glass—but I have hands, which I'm grateful for.

I remember the first time I saw Cal after everything happened. The way we raced for each other, meeting in the middle. I remember sitting on the ground right where we collided and holding him for ten solid minutes. And I remember Gran, weak as she was—squeezing me tight, tight. She would never say what I did was right, but she wouldn't say it was wrong either.

On that day, they found Jude hiding in the RV, the glass still poking out of his eye. When they took him into custody, Poley said he showed no emotion. I wonder if that's the true him, or if any part of what he gave me was real. He wouldn't confess to killing Piper. But he'd already told me where to look for her. On a rainy day in March, Piper's remains were exhumed from someone else's grave. True to his word, the tombstone was in the shape of an angel. There was a lot of police work to be done with her body before they would let us have her back. The autopsy showed that Jude strangled her. I couldn't stop thinking about that part; Cal's life had been in his hands the day he killed Piper. Jude had enough human in him to spare his son of the same fate as his three other victims.

He stares at me with his remaining eye—the eye I ruined with a shard of glass sat behind a patch that Jude often reached up to touch. He could have brought Piper back to us. It would have been a long road, but one I would have gladly taken for my sister.

Sometimes when I'm alone, I think about Leo. I pretend he's separate from Jude—it's sick, and I always feel guilty after. I can't understand how someone could pretend on the level he pretended. It disgusts me more than it hurts me. That's how I've survived.

Of the two hundred patients and staff that were on the island that day, one hundred eight survived. There was a private memorial service for them on the island. The immediate family put wreaths into the water from a boat while the rest of us watched from shore.

Before Jordyn ran HOTI, she lived in B hall as a patient. Her promotion came when Jude killed Dr. Grayson and he needed help with his charade. Jordyn got free rein of the hospital, an apartment in the Victorian section, and control—a rare commodity for patients. In exchange all she had to do was show up and keep her mouth shut. Which she did until Dalton's bomb detonated. I asked Poley to find out if she had any family, but as it turns out, Jordyn was telling the truth. I paid for her wreath myself, and handed it to the captain, who promised to put it in the water for me.

When police searched Jude's cabin, they found Piper's diary. A notebook stuffed under the mattress. We finally had the answers to what happened the day she went missing.

When Poley brought the man who posed as RJ in for questioning, he turned on Angel for a plea deal.

The beginning of Piper's nightmare started after they drove away from the movie theater. At 3:45, the man I knew to be RJ bound her wrists in the back seat of the car while Angel maneuvered the Ford down the planned route. They both worked for a sex trafficking ring, and it wasn't their first job. RJ pushed Piper into the trunk through the lowered back seat. Eager to head home, he got rid of her bag like he was told, and drove the Pontiac onto the 4:20 ferry. He was on his way home for dinner, though as he recalled in his statement, he hadn't been able to eat. Angel William Fennery was on trial for his portion of my sister's kidnapping.

Piper was taken to the stash house, where they took the Polaroids that Poley showed me that day. She was moved often and they kept her drugged. The night she got away from the traffickers, they were driving her to a house in Sultan. She recognized the area as being near the church, saw the train coming, and in one very brave moment, she opened the car door while they were driving and jumped out. They were near a field. She'd always been a fast runner, but that night she ran like her life depended on it. She had a plan. It came minutes later, the eerie whistle and the *clack clack clack* of the wheels traveling over points. By then the car had spun to a stop, and four men inside of it were pursuing her across the field. But Piper had a head start; Piper was racing the train, not them. She didn't care if the train killed her. At least it wouldn't be them. If she was going to die, Piper wanted them to die too. Bracing herself, ignoring the pain in her muscles, she pushed them harder and harder. The train, hauling cargo from Portland to British Columbia, was moving at a speed of forty-nine miles per hour as it passed through. She never looked back. Piper went flying over the tracks, landing on her side. She missed being hit by seconds. When she looked back, she was alone, her kidnappers trapped on the other side of the train. She knew they'd come after her, so she ran.

Piper ran faster than she ever had, but not in the direction her kidnappers anticipated. She ran next to the train until it passed her. Instead of running for the woods, she doubled back across the field. There was nothing in that direction but miles of farmland, and then some distance away was Freeland, the tiny town at the end of suburbia. There was no Starbucks, or chain grocery store, or even a Walmart within twenty miles, but she knew the area well. She knew where Pastor Jude lived with his wife and baby. She knew he'd help her because they were seeing each other. But he hadn't. Piper wrote about their relationship and her pregnancy with optimism. She thought he was going to leave his wife and be with her. Jude told her he'd take care of everything. She wrote letters to Cal, and some to me too. She drew pictures and wrote poems and imagined what her baby would look like. The entries got darker after Cal was born. She became distrustful of Jude and tried to run away. Her last entry was her planning her escape. And then there were no more entries. We think he killed her when he caught her.

I am what's left of us—one side of the yin-yang. The one left to tell her story. I don't know how I'm going to explain to Cal what happened to his mother. I'm dreading the day he asks. He is my boy, my joy, my peace. He is a tiny piece of Piper that I get to keep safe. I am happy. I don't expect I'll ever feel whole again, but for Cal's sake, I pretend to be.

In the end, that's what we're all doing anyway.

★ ★ ★ ★ ★

# ACKNOWLEDGMENTS

Susan Swinwood, I liked you from the moment I met you. You have very good taste in shoes. I have so appreciated your grace and good vibes. Sara Rodgers, my editor, you have been so patient and professional. Thank you so much!

Thank you to my amazingly talented female team at Harper-Collins. Oh, how I love you! Justine Sha, my publicity manager, you're really cool and you're exceptionally good at your job. Lindsey Reeder, the kindest, brightest light, you make publishing feel warm and cozy—it's a gift, lady. Diane Lavoie, Ambur Hostyn, Amy Jones, Margaret Marbury O'Neill—you ladies are rock stars. Thank you. Can't wait to hang out. Heather Connor, hey, girl, hey! I'm so grateful. Ana Luxton, so excited to have you back! Your presence is soul balm.

I am obsessed with my agent, Jane Dystel, who is the queen of everything. Thank you, Lady Jane. Traci Finlay, I could not have written this book without you. Gratitude for twenty years of friendship, editing and sarcasm.

Cait, you can check my reflexes anytime. I love you. 74 sister. Jamesrey18, thanks for the writing inspiration and for always believing I was crazy enough to do this.

Thank you to the Knautz family for the unconditional love and endless support, especially Luke, Cash and Sophia, who so graciously share The Serena. I love you guys!

Midas, I went on a search for something true, I was almost there when I found you. Thanks for walking the rest of the way with me. You turned my life to gold. Jolene, Jolene, Jolene, Jolene—my favorite tiny warrior, can't wait for your book!

Avett, my little method actor, your antics have inspired me all year. Scarlet, I'm stronger to have you on my side. Thank you for encouraging me this year and for being so sweet to your mama—so proud of you. Ryder, you're the greatest son a parent could ask for, practically perfect like Mary Poppins. Speaking of Mary Poppins—Mom, I love you. I am this because of you. You're the queen of my heart.

Joshua, the biggest fan of my life, I am so in love with you. Thank you for the beautiful life and constant support.

PLNs—we ride at dawn… You ready?